D0298568

KLARA AND THE SUN

KAZUO ISHIGURO

KLARA AND THE SUN

faber

First published in 2021
by Faber & Faber Limited
Bloomsbury House
74–77 Great Russell Street
London WC1B 3DA

Typeset by Faber & Faber Limited
Printed and bound by CPI Group (UK) Ltd, Croydon, CR0 4YY

The right of Kazuo Ishiguro to be identified as author of this work
has been asserted in accordance with Section 77 of the Copyright,
Designs and Patents Act 1988

A CIP record for this book
is available from the British Library

HARDBACK ISBN 978–0–571–36487–9
INDEPENDENT BOOKSHOPS ISBN 978–0–571–36620–0
WATERSTONES ISBN 978–0–571–36621–7

2 4 6 8 10 9 7 5 3 1

In memory of my mother
Shizuko Ishiguro
(1926–2019)

PART ONE

When we were new, Rosa and I were mid-store, on the magazines table side, and could see through more than half of the window. So we were able to watch the outside – the office workers hurrying by, the taxis, the runners, the tourists, Beggar Man and his dog, the lower part of the RPO Building. Once we were more settled, Manager allowed us to walk up to the front until we were right behind the window display, and then we could see how tall the RPO Building was. And if we were there at just the right time, we would see the Sun on his journey, crossing between the building tops from our side over to the RPO Building side.

When I was lucky enough to see him like that, I'd lean my face forward to take in as much of his nourishment as I could, and if Rosa was with me, I'd tell her to do the same. After a minute or two, we'd have to return to our positions, and when we were new, we used to worry that because we often couldn't see the Sun from mid-store, we'd grow weaker and weaker. Boy AF Rex, who was alongside us then, told us there was nothing to worry about, that the Sun had ways of reaching us wherever we were. He pointed to the floorboards and said, 'That's the Sun's pattern right there. If you're worried, you can just touch it and get strong again.'

There were no customers when he said this, and Manager was busy arranging something up on the Red Shelves, and I didn't want to disturb her by asking permission. So I gave Rosa a glance, and when she looked back blankly, I took two steps

1

forward, crouched down and reached out both hands to the Sun's pattern on the floor. But as soon as my fingers touched it, the pattern faded, and though I tried all I could – I patted the spot where it had been, and when that didn't work, rubbed my hands over the floorboards – it wouldn't come back. When I stood up again Boy AF Rex said:

'Klara, that was greedy. You girl AFs are always so greedy.'

Even though I was new then, it occurred to me straight away it might not have been my fault; that the Sun had withdrawn his pattern by chance just when I'd been touching it. But Boy AF Rex's face remained serious.

'You took all the nourishment for yourself, Klara. Look, it's gone almost dark.'

Sure enough the light inside the store had become very gloomy. Even outside on the sidewalk, the Tow-Away Zone sign on the lamp post looked gray and faint.

'I'm sorry,' I said to Rex, then turning to Rosa: 'I'm sorry. I didn't mean to take it all myself.'

'Because of you,' Boy AF Rex said, 'I'm going to become weak by evening.'

'You're making a joke,' I said to him. 'I know you are.'

'I'm not making a joke. I could get sick right now. And what about those AFs rear-store? There's already something not right with them. They're bound to get worse now. You were greedy, Klara.'

'I don't believe you,' I said, but I was no longer so sure. I looked at Rosa, but her expression was still blank.

'I'm feeling sick already,' Boy AF Rex said. And he sagged forward.

'But you just said yourself. The Sun always has ways to reach us. You're making a joke, I know you are.'

2

I managed in the end to convince myself Boy AF Rex was teasing me. But what I sensed that day was that I had, without meaning to, made Rex bring up something uncomfortable, something most AFs in the store preferred not to talk about. Then not long afterwards that thing happened to Boy AF Rex, which made me think that even if he had been joking that day, a part of him had been serious too.

It was a bright morning, and Rex was no longer beside us because Manager had moved him to the front alcove. Manager always said that every position was carefully conceived, and that we were as likely to be chosen when standing at one as at another. Even so, we all knew the gaze of a customer entering the store would fall first on the front alcove, and Rex was naturally pleased to get his turn there. We watched him from mid-store, standing with his chin raised, the Sun's pattern all over him, and Rosa leaned over to me once to say, 'Oh, he does look wonderful! He's bound to find a home soon!'

On Rex's third day in the front alcove, a girl came in with her mother. I wasn't so good then at telling ages, but I remember estimating thirteen and a half for the girl, and I think now that was correct. The mother was an office worker, and from her shoes and suit we could tell she was high-ranking. The girl went straight to Rex and stood in front of him, while the mother came wandering our way, glanced at us, then went on towards the rear, where two AFs were sitting on the Glass Table, swinging their legs freely as Manager had told them to do. At one point the mother called, but the girl ignored her and went on staring up at Rex's face. Then the child reached out and ran a hand down Rex's arm. Rex said nothing, of course, just smiled down at her and remained still, exactly as we'd been told to do when a customer showed special interest.

3

'Look!' Rosa whispered. 'She's going to choose him! She loves him. He's so lucky!' I nudged Rosa sharply to silence her, because we could easily be heard.

Now it was the girl who called to the mother, and then soon they were both standing in front of Boy AF Rex, looking him up and down, the girl sometimes reaching forward and touching him. The two conferred in soft voices, and I heard the girl say at one point, 'But he's perfect, Mom. He's beautiful.' Then a moment later, the child said, 'Oh, but Mom, come on.'

Manager by this time had brought herself quietly behind them. Eventually the mother turned to Manager and asked:

'Which model is this one?'

'He's a B2,' Manager said. 'Third series. For the right child, Rex will make a perfect companion. In particular, I feel he'll encourage a conscientious and studious attitude in a young person.'

'Well this young lady here could certainly do with that.'

'Oh, Mother, he's perfect.'

Then the mother said: 'B2, third series. The ones with the solar absorption problems, right?'

She said it just like that, in front of Rex, her smile still on her face. Rex kept smiling too, but the child looked baffled and glanced from Rex to her mother.

'It's true,' Manager said, 'that the third series had a few minor issues at the start. But those reports were greatly exaggerated. In environments with normal levels of light, there's no problem whatsoever.'

'I've heard solar malabsorption can lead to further problems,' the mother said. 'Even behavioral ones.'

'With respect, ma'am, series three models have brought immense happiness to many children. Unless you live in Alaska or down a mineshaft, you don't need to worry.'

The mother went on looking at Rex. Then finally she shook her head. 'I'm sorry, Caroline. I can see why you like him. But he's not for us. We'll find one for you that's perfect.'

Rex went on smiling until after the customers had left, and even after that, showed no sign of being sad. But that's when I remembered about him making that joke, and I was sure then that those questions about the Sun, about how much of his nourishment we could have, had been in Rex's mind for some time.

Today, of course, I realize Rex wouldn't have been the only one. But officially, it wasn't an issue at all – every one of us had specifications that guaranteed we couldn't be affected by factors such as our positioning within a room. Even so, an AF would feel himself growing lethargic after a few hours away from the Sun, and start to worry there was something wrong with him – that he had some fault unique to him and that if it became known, he'd never find a home.

That was one reason why we always thought so much about being in the window. Each of us had been promised our turn, and each of us longed for it to come. That was partly to do with what Manager called the 'special honor' of representing the store to the outside. Also, of course, whatever Manager said, we all knew we were more likely to be chosen while in the window. But the big thing, silently understood by us all, was the Sun and his nourishment. Rosa did once bring it up with me, in a whisper, a little while before our turn came around.

'Klara, do you think once we're in the window, we'll receive so much goodness we'll never get short again?'

I was still quite new then, so didn't know how to answer, even though the same question had been in my mind.

Then our turn finally came, and Rosa and I stepped into the window one morning, making sure not to knock over any of the display the way the pair before us had done the previous week. The store, of course, had yet to open, and I thought the grid would be fully down. But once we'd seated ourselves on the Striped Sofa, I saw there was a narrow gap running along the bottom of the grid – Manager must have raised it a little when checking everything was ready for us – and the Sun's light was making a bright rectangle that came up onto the platform and finished in a straight line just in front of us. We only needed to stretch our feet a little to place them within its warmth. I knew then that whatever the answer to Rosa's question, we were about to get all the nourishment we would need for some time to come. And once Manager touched the switch and the grid climbed up all the way, we became covered in dazzling light.

I should confess here that for me, there'd always been another reason for wanting to be in the window which had nothing to do with the Sun's nourishment or being chosen. Unlike most AFs, unlike Rosa, I'd always longed to see more of the outside – and to see it in all its detail. So once the grid went up, the realization that there was now only the glass between me and the sidewalk, that I was free to see, close up and whole, so many things I'd seen before only as corners and edges, made me so excited that for a moment I nearly forgot about the Sun and his kindness to us.

I could see for the first time that the RPO Building was in fact made of separate bricks, and that it wasn't white, as I'd always thought, but a pale yellow. I could now see too that it was even taller than I'd imagined – twenty-two stories – and that each repeating window was underlined by its own special ledge. I saw how the Sun had drawn a diagonal line right across the face of the RPO Building, so that on one side of it there was a triangle that looked almost white, while on the other was one that looked very dark, even though I now knew it was all the pale yellow color. And not only could I see every window right up to the rooftop, I could sometimes see the people inside, standing, sitting, moving around. Then down on the street, I could see the passers-by, their different kinds of shoes, paper cups, shoulder bags, little dogs, and if I wanted, I could follow with my eyes any one of them all the way past the pedestrian crossing and beyond the second Tow-Away Zone sign, to where two overhaul men were standing beside a drain and pointing. I could see right inside the taxis as they slowed to let the crowd go over the crossing – a driver's hand tapping on his steering wheel, a cap worn by a passenger.

The day went on, the Sun kept us warm, and I could see Rosa was very happy. But I noticed too that she hardly looked at anything, fixing her eyes constantly on the first Tow-Away Zone sign just in front of us. Only when I pointed out something to her would she turn her head, but then she'd lose interest and go back to looking at the sidewalk outside and the sign.

Rosa only looked elsewhere for any length of time when a passer-by paused in front of the window. In those circumstances, we both did as Manager had taught us: we put on 'neutral' smiles and fixed our gazes across the street, on a spot midway up the RPO Building. It was very tempting to look more closely at a passer-by who came up, but Manager had explained that it was highly vulgar to make eye contact at such a moment. Only when a passer-by specifically signaled to us, or spoke to us through the glass, were we to respond, but never before.

Some of the people who paused turned out not to be interested in us at all. They'd just wanted to take off their sports shoe and do something to it, or to press their oblongs. Some though came right up to the glass and gazed in. Many of these would be children, of around the age for which we were most suitable, and they seemed happy to see us. A child would come up excitedly, alone or with their adult, then point, laugh, pull a strange face, tap the glass, wave.

Once in a while – and I soon got better at watching those at the window while appearing to gaze at the RPO Building – a child would come to stare at us, and there would be a sadness there, or sometimes an anger, as though we'd done something wrong. A child like this could easily change the next moment and begin laughing or waving like the rest of them, but after our second day in the window, I learned quickly to tell the difference.

I tried to talk to Rosa about this, the third or fourth time a child like that had come, but she smiled and said: 'Klara, you worry too much. I'm sure that child was perfectly happy. How could she not be on a day like this? The whole city's so happy today.'

But I brought it up with Manager, at the end of our third day. She had been praising us, saying we'd been 'beautiful and dignified' in the window. The lights in the store had been dimmed by then, and we were rear-store, leaning against the wall, some of us browsing through the interesting magazines before our sleep. Rosa was next to me, and I could see from her shoulders that she was already half asleep. So when Manager asked if I'd enjoyed the day, I took the chance to tell her about the sad children who'd come to the window.

'Klara, you're quite remarkable,' Manager said, keeping her voice soft so as not to disturb Rosa and the others. 'You notice and absorb so much.' She shook her head as though in wonder. Then she said: 'What you must understand is that we're a very special store. There are many children out there who would love to be able to choose you, choose Rosa, any one of you here.

But it's not possible for them. You're beyond their reach. That's why they come to the window, to dream about having you. But then they get sad.'

'Manager, a child like that. Would a child like that have an AF at home?'

'Perhaps not. Certainly not one like you. So if sometimes a child looks at you in an odd way, with bitterness or sadness, says something unpleasant through the glass, don't think anything of it. Just remember. A child like that is most likely frustrated.'

'A child like that, with no AF, would surely be lonely.'

'Yes, that too,' Manager said quietly. 'Lonely. Yes.'

She lowered her eyes and was quiet, so I waited. Then suddenly she smiled and, reaching out, removed gently from my grasp the interesting magazine I'd been observing.

'Goodnight, Klara. Be as wonderful tomorrow as you were today. And don't forget. You and Rosa are representing us to the whole street.'

■

It was almost midway through our fourth morning in the window when I saw the taxi slowing down, its driver leaning right out so the other taxis would let him come across the traffic lanes to the curb in front of our store. Josie's eyes were on me as she got out onto the sidewalk. She was pale and thin, and as she came towards us, I could see her walk wasn't like that of other passers-by. She wasn't slow exactly, but she seemed to take stock after each step to make sure she was still safe and wouldn't fall. I estimated her age as fourteen and a half.

Once she was close enough so all the pedestrians were passing behind her, she stopped and smiled at me.

'Hi,' she said through the glass. 'Hey, can you hear me?'

Rosa kept staring ahead at the RPO Building as she was supposed to do. But now I'd been addressed, I was able to look directly at the child, return her smile and nod encouragingly.

'Really?' Josie said – though of course I didn't yet know that was her name. 'I can hardly hear *me* myself. You can really hear me?'

I nodded again, and she shook her head as if very impressed.

'Wow.' She glanced over her shoulder – even this movement she made with caution – to the taxi from which she'd just emerged. Its door was as she'd left it, hanging open across the sidewalk, and there were two figures still in the back seat, talking and pointing to something beyond the pedestrian crossing. Josie seemed pleased her adults weren't about to get out, and took one more step forward till her face was almost touching the window.

'I saw you yesterday,' she said.

I recalled our previous day, but finding no memory of Josie, looked at her with surprise.

'Oh, don't feel bad or anything, there's no way you'd have seen me. I was like in a taxi, going by, not even that slow. But I saw you in your window, and that's why I got Mom to stop today right here.' She glanced back, again with that carefulness. 'Wow. She's *still* talking with Mrs Jeffries. Expensive way to talk, right? That taxi meter just keeps turning over.'

I could then see how, when she laughed, her face filled with kindness. But strangely, it was at that same moment I first wondered if Josie might be one of those lonely children Manager and I had talked about.

She glanced over to Rosa – who was still gazing dutifully at the RPO Building – then said: 'Your friend's really cute.' Even as she said this, Josie's eyes were already back on me. She went on looking at me quietly for several seconds, and I became worried her adults would get out before she could say anything more. But she then said:

'Know what? Your friend will make a perfect friend for someone out there. But yesterday, we were driving by and I saw *you*, and I thought that's her, the AF I've been looking for!' She laughed again. 'Sorry. Maybe that sounds disrespectful.' She turned once more to the taxi, but the figures in the back showed no signs of getting out. 'Are you French?' she asked. 'You look kind of French.'

I smiled and shook my head.

'There were these two French girls,' Josie said, 'came to our last meeting. Both had their hair that way, neat and short like you. Looked cute.' She regarded me silently for another moment, and I thought I saw another small sign of sadness, but I was still quite new then and couldn't be sure. Then she brightened, saying:

'Hey, don't you guys get hot sitting there like that? Do you need a drink or something?'

I shook my head and raised my hands, palms up, to indicate the loveliness of the Sun's nourishment falling over us.

'Oh yeah. Wasn't thinking. You love being in the sunshine, right?'

She turned again, this time to look up at the building tops. At that moment the Sun was in the gap of sky, and Josie screwed up her eyes immediately and turned back to me.

'Don't know how you do that. I mean keep looking that way without being dazzled. I can't do it even for a second.'

She put a hand to her forehead then turned away once more, this time looking not at the Sun, but to somewhere near the top of the RPO Building. After five seconds, she turned back to me again.

'I guess for you guys, where you are, the Sun must go down behind that big building, right? That must mean you never get to see where he *really* goes down. That building must always get in the way.' She looked over quickly to check the adults were still inside the taxi, then went on: 'Where we live, there's nothing in the way. From up in my room you can see exactly where the Sun goes down. The exact place he goes to at night.'

I must have looked surprised. And at the edge of my vision I could see that Rosa, forgetting herself, was now staring at Josie in astonishment.

'Can't see where he comes up in the morning though,' Josie said. 'The hills and the trees get in the way of that. Kind of like here, I guess. Things always in the way. But the evening's something else. Over that side, where my room looks out, it's just wide and empty. If you came and lived with us, you'd see.'

One adult, then another, climbed from the taxi out onto the sidewalk. Josie had not seen them, but perhaps she'd heard something for she began to talk more quickly.

'Cross my heart. You can see the exact place he goes down.'

The adults were women, both dressed in high-rank office clothes. The taller one I guessed to be the mother Josie had mentioned because she kept watching Josie even as she exchanged cheek kisses with her companion. Then the companion was gone, mixing with the other passers-by, and the Mother turned fully our way. And for just one second, her piercing stare was no longer on Josie's back, but on me, and I immediately looked away, up at the RPO Building. But Josie was speaking again through the glass, her voice lowered but still audible.

'Have to go now. But I'll come back soon. We'll talk more.'

Then she said, in a near-whisper which I could only just hear, 'You won't go away, right?'

I shook my head and smiled.

'That's good. Okay. So now it's goodbye. But only for now.'

The Mother by this time was standing right behind Josie. She was black-haired and thin, though not as thin as Josie, or some of the runners. Now she was closer and I could see her face better, I raised my estimate of her age to forty-five. As I've said, I wasn't so accurate with ages then, but this was to prove more or less correct. From a distance, I'd first thought her a younger woman, but when she was closer I could see the deep etches around her mouth, and also a kind of angry exhaustion in her eyes. I noticed too that when the Mother reached out to Josie from behind, the outstretched arm hesitated in the air, almost retracting, before coming forward to rest on her daughter's shoulder.

They entered the flow of passers-by, going in the direction of the second Tow-Away Zone sign, Josie with her cautious walk, her mother's arm around her as they went. Once, before they left my view, Josie looked back, and even though she had to disturb the rhythm of their walk, gave me one last wave.

■

It was later that same afternoon, Rosa said: 'Klara, isn't it funny? I always thought we'd see so many AFs out there once we got in the window. All the ones who'd found homes already. But there aren't so many. I wonder where they are.'

This was one of the great things about Rosa. She could fail to notice so much, and even when I pointed something out to her, she'd still not see what was special or interesting about it. Yet every now and then she'd make an observation like this one. As soon as she said what she did, I realized that I too had expected to see many more AFs from the window, walking happily with their children, even going about their business by themselves, and that even if I hadn't acknowledged it to myself, I too had been surprised and a little disappointed.

'You're right,' I said, looking from right to left. 'Just now, among all these passers-by, there isn't a single AF.'

'Isn't that one over there? Going past the Fire Escapes Building?'

We both looked carefully, then shook our heads at the same time.

Though she'd been the one to bring up this question about the AFs outside, it was typical that she soon lost all interest in it. By the time I finally spotted a teenage boy and his AF walking past the juice stand on the RPO Building side, she barely looked their way.

But I went on thinking about what Rosa had said, and whenever an AF did go by, I made sure to watch closely. And before long, I noticed a curious thing: there were always more AFs to be seen on the RPO Building side than on ours. And often, if an AF did happen to be coming towards us on our side, walking with a child past the second Tow-Away Zone sign, they would then use the crossing and not come past our store. When AFs did go by us they almost always acted oddly, speeding up their walk and keeping their faces turned away. I wondered then if perhaps we – the whole store – were an embarrassment to them. I wondered if Rosa and I, once we'd found our homes, would feel an awkwardness to be reminded that we hadn't always lived with our children, but in a store. However much I tried, though, I couldn't imagine either Rosa or me ever feeling that way about the store, about Manager and the other AFs.

Then as I continued to watch the outside, another possibility came to me: that the AFs weren't embarrassed, but were afraid. They were afraid because we were new models, and they feared that before long their children would decide it was time to have them thrown away, to be replaced by AFs like us. That was why they shuffled by so awkwardly, refusing to look our way. And that was why so few AFs could be seen from our window. For all we knew, the next street – the one *behind* the RPO Building – was crowded with them. For all we knew, the AFs outside did all they could to take any route other than one that would bring them past our store, because the last thing they wanted was for their children to see us and come to the window.

I shared none of these thoughts with Rosa. Instead, whenever we spotted an AF out there I made a point of wondering aloud if they were happy with their child and with their home, and this always pleased and excited Rosa. She took it up as a kind of game, pointing and saying: 'Look, over there! Do you see, Klara? That boy just loves his AF! Oh, look at the way they're laughing together!'

And sure enough, there were plenty of pairs that looked happy with each other. But Rosa missed so many signals. She would often exclaim delightedly at a pair going by, and I would look and realize that even though a girl was smiling at her AF, she was in fact angry with him, and was perhaps at that very moment thinking cruel thoughts about him. I noticed such things all the time, but said nothing and let Rosa go on believing what she did.

Once, on the morning of our fifth day in the window, I saw two taxis, over on the RPO Building side, moving slowly and so close together someone new might have supposed they were a single vehicle – a kind of double taxi. Then the one in front

15

became slightly faster and a gap appeared, and I saw through that gap, on the far sidewalk, a girl of fourteen, wearing a cartoon shirt, walking in the direction of the crossing. She was without adults or an AF but seemed confident and a little impatient, and because she was walking at the same speed as the taxis, I was able to keep watching her through the gap for some time. Then the gap between the taxis grew wider still, and I saw she was with an AF after all – a boy AF – who was walking three paces behind. And I could see, even in that small instant, that he hadn't lagged behind by chance; that this was how the girl had decided they would always walk – she in front and he a few steps behind. The boy AF had accepted this, even though other passers-by would see and conclude he wasn't loved by the girl. And I could see the weariness in the boy AF's walk, and wondered what it might be like to have found a home and yet to know that your child didn't want you. Until I saw this pair it hadn't occurred to me an AF could be with a child who despised him and wanted him gone, and that they could nevertheless carry on together. Then the front taxi slowed because of the crossing, and the one behind drew up and I couldn't see them any more. I kept watching to see if they would come over at the crossing, but they weren't in the crossing crowd, and I could no longer see the other side because of all the other taxis.

■

I wouldn't have wanted anyone other than Rosa beside me in the window during those days, but our time there did bring out the differences in our attitudes. It wasn't really that I was more eager to learn about the outside than Rosa: she was, in her own way, excited and observant, and as anxious as I was to prepare herself to be as kind and helpful an AF as possible. But the more I watched, the more I wanted to learn, and unlike Rosa, I became puzzled, then increasingly fascinated by the more mysterious emotions passers-by would display in front of us. I realized that if I didn't understand at least some of these mysterious things, then when the time came, I'd never be able to help my child as well as I should. So I began to seek out – on the sidewalks, inside the passing taxis, amidst the crowds waiting at the crossing – the sort of behavior about which I needed to learn.

At first I wanted Rosa to do as I was, but soon saw this was pointless. Once, on our third window day, when the Sun had already gone behind the RPO Building, two taxis stopped on our side, the drivers got out and began to fight each other. This wasn't the first time we'd witnessed a fight: when we were still quite new, we'd gathered at the window to see as best we could three policemen fighting with Beggar Man and his dog in front of the blank doorway. But that hadn't been an angry fight, and Manager had later explained how the policemen had been worried about Beggar Man because he'd become drunk and they'd only been trying to help him. But the two taxi drivers weren't like the policemen. They fought as though the most important thing was to damage each other as much as possible. Their faces were twisted into horrible shapes, so that someone new might not even have realized they were people at all, and all the time they were punching each other, they shouted out cruel words. The passers-by were at first so shocked they stood back, but then some office workers and a runner stopped them from fighting any more. And though one had blood on his face, they each got back into their taxis, and everything went back to the way it was before. I even noticed, a moment later, the two taxis – the ones whose drivers had just been fighting – waiting patiently, one in front of the other, in the same traffic lane for the lights to change.

But when I tried to talk with Rosa about what we'd seen, she looked puzzled and said: 'A fight? I didn't see it, Klara.'

'Rosa, it's not possible you didn't notice. It happened in front of us just now. Those two drivers.'

'Oh. You mean the taxi men! I didn't realize you meant them, Klara. Oh, I did see them, of course I did. But I don't think they were fighting.'

'Rosa, of course they were fighting.'

'Oh no, they were pretending. Just playing.'

'Rosa, they were fighting.'

'Don't be silly, Klara! You think such strange thoughts. They were just playing. And they enjoyed themselves, and so did the passers-by.'

In the end I just said, 'You may be right, Rosa,' and I don't think she gave the incident any more thought.

But I couldn't forget the taxi drivers so easily. I'd follow a particular person down the sidewalk with my gaze, wondering if he too could grow as angry as they had done. Or I would try to imagine what a passer-by would look like with his or her face distorted in rage. Most of all – and this Rosa would never have understood – I tried to feel in my own mind the anger the drivers had experienced. I tried to imagine me and Rosa getting so angry with each other we would start to fight like that, actually trying to damage each other's bodies. The idea seemed ridiculous, but I'd seen the taxi drivers, so I tried to find the beginnings of such a feeling in my mind. It was useless, though, and I'd always end up laughing at my own thoughts.

Still, there were other things we saw from the window – other kinds of emotions I didn't at first understand – of which I did eventually find some versions in myself, even if they were perhaps like the shadows made across the floor by the ceiling lamps after the grid went down. There was, for instance, what happened with the Coffee Cup Lady.

It was two days after I'd first met Josie. The morning had been full of rain, and passers-by were walking with narrow eyes, under umbrellas and dripping hats. The RPO Building hadn't changed much in the downpour, though many of its windows had become lit as if it were already evening. The Fire Escapes Building next to it had a large wet patch down the left side of its front, as though some juice had leaked from a corner of its roof. But then suddenly the Sun pushed through, shining onto the soaked street and the tops of the taxis, and the passers-by all came out in large numbers when they saw this, and it was in the rush that followed that I spotted the small man in the raincoat. He was on the RPO Building side, and I estimated seventy-one years old. He was waving and calling, coming so near the edge of the sidewalk I was worried he'd step out in front of the moving taxis. Manager happened to be in the window with us just at that moment – she'd been adjusting the sign in front of our sofa – and she spotted the waving man at the same time I did. He had on a brown raincoat and its belt was dangling down one side, almost touching his ankle, but he didn't seem to notice, and kept waving and calling over to our side. A crowd of passers-by had formed right outside our store, not to look at us, but because, for a moment, the sidewalk had become so busy no one had been able to move. Then something changed, the crowd grew thinner, and I saw standing before us a small woman, her back to us, looking across the four lanes of moving taxis to the waving man. I couldn't see her face, but I estimated sixty-seven years old from her shape and posture. I named her in my mind the Coffee Cup Lady because from the back, and in her thick wool coat, she seemed small and wide and round-shouldered like the ceramic coffee cups resting upside down on the Red Shelves. Although the man kept waving and calling, and she'd clearly seen him, she didn't wave or call back. She kept completely still, even when a pair of runners came towards her, parted on either side, then joined up again, their sports shoes making small splashes down the sidewalk.

Then at last she moved. She went towards the crossing – as the man had been signaling for her to do – taking slow steps at first, then hurrying. She had to stop again, to wait like everyone else at the lights, and the man stopped waving, but he was watching her so anxiously, I again thought he might step out in front of the taxis. But he calmed himself and walked towards his end of the crossing to wait for her. And as the taxis stopped, and the Coffee Cup Lady began to cross with the rest, I saw the man raise a fist to one of his eyes, in the way I'd seen some children do in the store when they got upset. Then the Coffee Cup Lady reached the RPO Building side, and she and the man were holding each other so tightly they were like one large person, and the Sun, noticing, was pouring his nourishment on them. I still couldn't see the Coffee Cup Lady's face, but the man had his eyes tightly shut, and I wasn't sure if he was very happy or very upset.

'Those people seem so pleased to see each other,' Manager said. And I realized she'd been watching them as closely as I had.

'Yes, they seem so happy,' I said. 'But it's strange because they also seem upset.'

'Oh, Klara,' Manager said quietly. 'You never miss a thing, do you?'

Then Manager was silent for a long time, holding her sign in her hand and staring across the street, even after the pair had gone out of sight. Finally she said:

'Perhaps they hadn't met for a long time. A long, long time. Perhaps when they last held each other like that, they were still young.'

'Do you mean, Manager, that they lost each other?'

She was quiet for another moment. 'Yes,' she said, eventually. 'That must be it. They lost each other. And perhaps just now, just by chance, they found each other again.'

Manager's voice wasn't like her usual one, and though her eyes were on the outside, I thought she was now looking at nothing in particular. I even started to wonder what passers-by would think to see Manager herself in the window with us for so long.

Then she turned from the window and came past us, and as she did so she touched my shoulder.

'Sometimes,' she said, 'at special moments like that, people feel a pain alongside their happiness. I'm glad you watch everything so carefully, Klara.'

Then Manager was gone, and Rosa said, 'How strange. What could she have meant?'

'Never mind, Rosa,' I said to her. 'She was just talking about the outside.'

Rosa began to discuss something else then, but I went on thinking about the Coffee Cup Lady and her Raincoat Man, and about what Manager had said. And I tried to imagine how I would feel if Rosa and I, a long time from now, long after we'd found our different homes, saw each other again by chance on a street. Would I then feel, as Manager had put it, pain alongside my happiness?

■

One morning at the start of our second week in the window, I was talking to Rosa about something on the RPO Building side, then broke off when I realized Josie was standing on the sidewalk in front of us. Her mother was beside her. There was no taxi behind them this time, though it was possible they'd got out of one and it had driven off, all without my noticing, because there'd been a crowd of tourists between our window and the spot where they were standing. But now the passers-by were moving smoothly again, and Josie was beaming happily at me. Her face – I thought this again – seemed to overflow with kindness when she smiled. But she couldn't yet come to the window because the Mother was leaning down talking to her, a hand on her shoulder. The Mother was wearing a coat – a thin, dark, high-ranking one – which moved with the wind around her body, so that for a moment she reminded me of the dark birds that perched on the high traffic signals even as the winds blew fiercely. Both Josie and the Mother went on looking straight at me while they talked, and I could see Josie was impatient to come to me, but still the Mother wouldn't release her and went on talking. I knew I should keep looking at the RPO Building, in just the way Rosa was doing, but I couldn't help stealing glances at them, I was so concerned they'd vanish into the crowd.

At last the Mother straightened, and though she went on staring at me, altering the tilt of her head whenever a passer-by blocked her view, she took her hand away and Josie came forward with her careful walk. I thought it encouraging the Mother should allow Josie to come by herself, yet the Mother's gaze, which never softened or wavered, and the very way she was standing there, arms crossed over her front, fingers clutching at the material of her coat, made me realize there were many

22

signals I hadn't yet learned to understand. Then Josie was there before me on the other side of the glass.

'Hey! How you been?'

I smiled, nodded and held up a raised thumb – a gesture I'd often observed inside the interesting magazines.

'Sorry I couldn't come back sooner,' she said. 'I guess it's been . . . how long?'

I held up three fingers, then added a half finger from the other hand.

'Too long,' she said. 'I'm sorry. Miss me?'

I nodded, putting on a sad face, though I was careful to show I wasn't serious, and that I hadn't been upset.

'I missed you too. I really thought I'd get back before this. You probably thought I'd cleared right out. Really sorry.' Then her smile weakened as she said: 'I suppose a lot of other kids have been here to see you.'

I shook my head, but Josie looked unconvinced. She glanced back to the Mother, not for reassurance, but rather to check she hadn't come any closer. Then, lowering her voice, Josie said:

'Mom looks weird, I know, watching like that. It's because I told her you're the one I wanted. I said it had to be you, so now she's sizing you up. Sorry.' I thought I saw, as I'd done the time before, a flash of sadness. 'You will come, right? If Mom says it's okay and everything?'

I nodded encouragingly. But the uncertainty remained on her face.

'Because I don't want you coming against your will. That wouldn't be fair. I really want you to come, but if you said, Josie, I don't want to, then I'd say to Mom, okay, we can't have her, no way. But you do want to come, right?'

23

Again I nodded, and this time Josie appeared to be reassured.

'That's so good.' The smile returned to her face. 'You'll love it, I'll make sure you do.' She looked back, this time in triumph, calling: 'Mom? See, she says she wants to come!'

The Mother gave a small nod, but otherwise didn't respond. She was still staring at me, her fingers pinching at the coat material. When Josie turned back to me, her face had clouded again.

'Listen,' she said, but for the next few seconds remained silent. Then she said, 'It's so great you want to come. But I want things straight between us from the start, so I'm going to say this. Don't worry, Mom can't hear. Look, I think you'll like our house. I think you'll like my room, and that's where you'll be, not in some cupboard or anything. And we'll do all these great things together all the time I'm growing up. Only thing is, sometimes, well . . .' She glanced back quickly again, then lowering her voice further, said: 'Maybe it's because some days I'm not so well. I don't know. But there might be something going on. I'm not sure what it is. I don't even know if it's something bad. But things sometimes get, well, unusual. Don't get me wrong, most times you wouldn't feel it. But I wanted to be straight with you. Because you know how lousy it feels, people telling you how perfect things will be and they're not being straight. That's why I'm telling you now. Please say you still want to come. You'll love my room, I know you will. And you'll see where the Sun goes down, like I told you the last time. You still want to come, right?'

I nodded to her through the glass, as seriously as I knew how. I wanted also to tell her that if there was anything difficult, anything frightening, to be faced in her house, we would do so together. But I didn't know how to convey such a complex message through the glass without words, and so I clasped my hands together and held them up, shaking them slightly, in a

24

gesture I'd seen a taxi driver give from inside his moving taxi to someone who'd waved from the sidewalk, even though he'd had to take both hands off his steering wheel. Whatever Josie understood from it, it seemed to make her happy.

'Thank you,' she said. 'Don't get me wrong. It may not be anything bad. It may only be me thinking things . . .'

Just then the Mother called and started to move towards us, but there were tourists in her way, and Josie had time to say quickly: 'I'll be back really soon. Promise. Tomorrow if I can. Bye just for now.'

■

Josie didn't return the following day, or the day after that. Then in the middle of our second week, our turn in the window came to an end.

Throughout our time, Manager had been warm and encouraging. Each morning, as we'd prepared ourselves on the Striped Sofa and waited for the grid to rise, she'd said something like, 'You were both wonderful yesterday. See if you can do just as well today.' And at the end of each day, she'd smiled and told us, 'Well done, both of you. I'm so proud.' So it never occurred to me we were doing anything wrong, and when the grid came down on our last day, I was expecting Manager to praise us again. I was surprised, then, when after locking the grid, she simply walked away, not waiting for us. Rosa gave me a puzzled look, and for a moment we remained on the Striped Sofa. But with the grid down, we were in near-darkness, and so after a while we rose and came down off the platform.

We were then facing the store, and I could see all the way to the Glass Table at the back, but the space had become partitioned into ten boxes, so that I no longer had a single unified picture of the view before me. The front alcove was in the box furthest to my right, as might be expected; and yet the magazines table, which was nearest the front alcove, had become divided between various boxes, so that one section of the table could even be seen in the box furthest to my left. By now the lights had been dimmed, and I spotted the other AFs in the backgrounds of several boxes, lining the walls mid-store, preparing for their sleep. But my attention was drawn to the three center boxes, at that moment containing aspects of Manager in the act of turning towards us. In one box she was visible only from her waist to the upper part of her neck, while the box immediately beside it was almost entirely taken up by her eyes. The eye closest to us was much larger than the other, but both were filled with kindness and sadness. And yet a third box showed a part of her jaw and most of her mouth, and I detected there anger and frustration. Then she had turned fully and was coming towards us, and the store became once more a single picture.

'Thank you, both of you,' she said, and reaching out, touched us gently in turn. 'Thank you so much.'

Even so, I sensed something had changed – that we had somehow disappointed her.

■

We began after that our second period mid-store. Rosa and I were still often together, but Manager would now change our positions around, and I might spend a day standing beside Boy AF Rex or Girl AF Kiku. Most days, though, I'd still be able to see a section of the window, and so go on learning about the outside. When the Cootings Machine appeared, for instance,

I was on the magazines table side, just in front of the middle alcove, and had almost as good a view as if I'd still been in the window.

It had been obvious for days that the Cootings Machine was going to be something out of the ordinary. First, the overhaul men arrived to prepare for it, marking out a special section of the street with wooden barriers. The taxi drivers didn't like this at all, and made a lot of noise with their horns. Then the overhaul men began to drill and break up the ground, even parts of the sidewalk, which frightened the two AFs in the window. Once, when the noise became really awful, Rosa put her hands to her ears and kept them there, even though there were customers in the store. Manager apologized to every customer who came in, even though the noise had nothing to do with us. Once, a customer began talking about Pollution, and pointing to the overhaul men outside, said how dangerous Pollution was for everyone. So when the Cootings Machine first arrived, I thought it might be a machine to fight Pollution, but Boy AF Rex said no, it was something specially designed to make more of it. I told him I didn't believe him, and he said, 'All right, Klara, you just wait and see.'

It turned out of course that he was right. The Cootings Machine – I named it that in my mind because it had 'Cootings' in big letters across its side – began with a high-pitched whine, not nearly as bad as the drills had been, and no worse than Manager's vacuum cleaner. But there were three short funnels protruding from its roof, and smoke began to come up out of them. At first the smoke came in little white puffs, then grew darker, till it no longer rose as separate clouds but as one thick continuous one.

When I next looked, the street outside had become partitioned into several vertical panels – from my position I could see three of them quite clearly without leaning forward. The amount of dark smoke appeared to vary from panel to panel, so that it was almost as if contrasting shades of gray were being displayed for selection. But even where the smoke was at its most dense, I could still pick out many details. In one panel, for instance, there was a section of the overhaul men's wooden barrier, and seemingly now attached to it, the front part of a taxi. In the neighboring panel, diagonally cutting off its top corner, was a metal bar which I recognized as belonging to one of the high traffic signals. Indeed, looking more closely, I could decipher the dark edge of a bird's outline perched upon it. At one point I saw a runner pass from one panel into the next, and as he crossed, his figure altered both in terms of size and trajectory. Then the Pollution became so bad that, even from the magazines table side, I could no longer see the gap of sky, and the window itself, which the glass men cleaned so proudly for Manager, became covered with dirty dots.

I felt so sorry for the two boy AFs who'd waited so long for their turn in the window. They went on sitting there with good postures, but at one stage I saw one of them raise an arm across his face as though the Pollution might come in through the glass. Manager then stepped up onto the platform to whisper reassuring things to him, and when she eventually came back down, and started rearranging the bracelets inside the Glass Display Trolley, I could see she too was upset. I thought she might even go outside and talk to the overhaul men, but then she noticed us, and she smiled and said:

'Everyone, please listen. This is unfortunate, but nothing to worry about. We'll bear it for a few days, then it will be over.'

But the next day, and the day after, the Cootings Machine carried on and on, and daytime became almost like night. At one point I looked for the Sun's patterns on our floor, alcoves and walls, but they were no longer there. The Sun, I knew, was trying his utmost, and towards the end of the second bad afternoon, even though the smoke was worse than ever, his patterns appeared again, though only faintly. I became worried and asked Manager if we'd still get all our nourishment, and she laughed and said, 'That horrible thing has come here several times before and no one in the store ever suffered from it. So just put it out of your mind, Klara.'

Even so, after four continuous days of Pollution, I could feel myself weakening. I tried not to show it, especially when customers were in the store. But perhaps because of the Cootings Machine, there were now long stretches with no customers at all, and I sometimes allowed my posture to sag so that Boy AF Rex had to touch my arm to make me stand straight again.

Then one morning the grid went up and not only the Cootings Machine but its whole special section had vanished. The Pollution too was gone, the gap of sky had returned and was a brilliant blue, and the Sun poured his nourishment into the store. The taxis were once more moving smoothly, their drivers happy. Even the runners went by with smiles. All the time the Cootings Machine had been there, I'd worried that Josie might have been trying to come back to the store, and had been prevented by the Pollution. But now it was over, and there was such a rise in spirits both inside and outside the store, I felt if there was any day for Josie to come back, it would have to be this one. By mid-afternoon, though, I came to realize how unreasonable an idea this was. I stopped looking for Josie out in the street, and concentrated instead on learning more about the outside.

■

Two days after the Cootings Machine went away, the girl with the short spiky hair came into the store. I estimated twelve and a half years old. She was dressed that morning like a runner, in a bright green tank top, and her too-thin arms were showing all the way up to the shoulders. She came in with her father, who was in a casual office suit, quite high-ranking, and neither said much at first as they browsed. I could tell immediately the girl was interested in me, even though she only glanced my way quickly before returning front-store. After a minute, though, she came back and pretended to be absorbed by the bracelets in the Glass Display Trolley just in front of where I was standing. Then, glancing around to check that neither her father nor Manager was watching, she put her weight experimentally against the trolley, making it move forward an inch or two on its castors. As she did this, she looked at me with a small smile, as if the moving of the trolley was a special secret between us. She pulled the trolley back to its original position, grinned at me again, and called out, 'Daddy?' When the father didn't reply – he was absorbed by the two AFs sitting on the Glass Table at the back – the girl gave me a last look, then went over to join him. They began a conversation in low whispers, continually glancing my way, so there could be no doubt they were discussing me. Manager, noticing, rose from her desk and came to stand near me, her hands clasped in front of her.

Eventually, after a lot more whispering, the girl came back, striding past Manager, till she was directly facing me. She touched each of my elbows in turn, then took my left hand within her right one, and held me like that, her eyes looking into my face. Her expression was quite stern, but the hand holding mine squeezed gently, and I understood this was intended as another little secret between us. But I didn't smile at her. I kept

30

my expression blank, throwing my gaze over the girl's spiky head to the Red Shelves on the wall opposite, and in particular, at the row of ceramic coffee cups displayed upside down along the third tier. The girl squeezed my hand twice more, the second time less gently, but I didn't lower my gaze to her or smile.

The father, meanwhile, had come nearer, treading softly so as not to disturb what might be a special moment. Manager too had moved closer and was standing just behind the father. I noted all this, but kept my eyes fixed on the Red Shelves and the ceramic coffee cups, and kept my hand, inside hers, slack so that had she let go, mine would have flopped down at my side.

I became increasingly aware of Manager's gaze on me. Then I heard her say:

'Klara is excellent. She's one of our finest. But the young lady might be interested to look at the new B3 models that just came in.'

'B3s?' The father sounded excited. 'You have those already?'

'We enjoy an exclusive relationship with our suppliers. They're only just in, and not yet calibrated. But I'd be happy to show them to you.'

The spiky-haired girl squeezed my hand again. 'But Daddy, I want this one. She's just right.'

'But they have the new B3s in, honey. Don't you want just to look at those? No one you know has one.'

There was a long wait, then the girl released my hand. I let my arm fall and continued to look at the Red Shelves.

'So what's the big deal about these new B3s anyway?' the girl said, moving off towards her father.

I hadn't been thinking about Rosa while the girl had been holding my hand, but I now became aware of her, standing to my left, watching me with amazement. I wanted to make her

31

look away, but decided to keep gazing at the Red Shelves until the girl, her father and Manager were all safely rear-store. I could hear the father laughing at something Manager had said, then when I finally glanced their way, Manager was opening the Staff Only Door at the very rear of the store.

'You'll have to excuse me,' she was saying. 'It's a little untidy in here.'

And the father said, 'We're privileged to be allowed back here. Right, honey?'

They went in, the door closed behind them, and I couldn't hear their words any more, though at one point I heard the spiky-haired girl's laugh.

The rest of the morning remained busy. Even while Manager was completing the delivery forms with the father for their new B3, more customers came in. So it wasn't until the afternoon, when there was finally a lull, that Manager came over to me.

'I was surprised at you this morning, Klara,' she said. 'You of all people.'

'I'm sorry, Manager.'

'What came over you? It was so unlike you.'

'I'm very sorry, Manager. I didn't mean to cause embarrassment. I just thought, for that particular child, I perhaps wouldn't be the best choice.'

Manager went on looking at me. 'Perhaps you were correct,' she said in the end. 'I believe that girl will be happy with the B3 boy. Even so, Klara, I was very surprised.'

'I'm very sorry, Manager.'

'I supported you this time. But I won't do it again. It's for the customer to choose the AF, never the other way round.'

'I understand, Manager.' Then I said quietly: 'Thank you, Manager, for what you did today.'

'That's all right, Klara. But remember. I shan't do it again.'

She began to move away, but then turned and came back.

'It can't be, can it, Klara? That you believe you've made an arrangement?'

I thought Manager was about to reprimand me, the way she'd reprimanded two boy AFs once for laughing at Beggar Man from the window. But Manager placed a hand on my shoulder and said, in a quieter voice than before:

'Let me tell you something, Klara. Children make promises all the time. They come to the window, they promise all kinds of things. They promise to come back, they ask you not to let anyone else take you away. It happens all the time. But more often than not, the child never comes back. Or worse, the child comes back and ignores the poor AF who's waited, and instead chooses another. It's just the way children are. You've been watching and learning so much, Klara. Well, here's another lesson for you. Do you understand?'

'Yes, Manager.'

'Good. So let's have no more of this.' She touched my arm, then turned away.

■

The new B3s – three boy AFs – were soon calibrated and took up their positions. Two went straight into the window, with a big new sign, and the other was given the front alcove. A fourth B3, of course, had already been bought by the spiky-haired girl and shipped without any of us meeting him.

Rosa and I remained mid-store, though we were moved to the Red Shelves side once the new B3s arrived. After our turn in the window had finished, Rosa had taken to repeating something

Manager had said to us: that every position in the store was a good one, and that we were as likely to be chosen mid-store as in the window or the front alcove. Well, in Rosa's case, this turned out to be true.

There was nothing about the way the day started to suggest such a huge thing was about to happen. There was nothing different about the taxis or the passers-by, or in the way the grid had gone up, or the way Manager had greeted us. Yet by that evening, Rosa had been bought, and she'd vanished behind the Staff Only Door to prepare for shipping. I suppose I'd always thought that before either of us left the store, there would be plenty of time to talk everything over. But it happened very quickly. I barely took in anything useful about the boy and his mother who came in and chose her. And as soon as they'd left, and Manager had confirmed she'd been bought, Rosa became so excited it was impossible for us to have a serious talk. I wanted to go over the many things she'd have to remember in order to be a good AF; to remind her of all the things Manager had taught us, and to explain to her everything I'd learned about the outside. But she just kept rushing from one topic to the next. Would the boy's room have a high ceiling? What color car would the family have? Would she get to see the ocean? Would she be asked to pack a picnic into a basket? I tried to remind her about the Sun's nourishment, how important that was, and I wondered aloud if her room would be easy for the Sun to look into, but Rosa wasn't interested. Then before we knew it, it was time for Rosa to go away into the back room, and I saw her smiling over her shoulder at me one last time before she disappeared behind the door.

■

In the days after Rosa left, I remained mid-store. The two B3s in the window had been bought, one day apart, and Boy AF Rex also found a home around that time. Soon, three more B3s arrived – boy AFs again – and Manager positioned them almost directly across from me, over on the magazines table side, alongside the two boy AFs from the older series. The Glass Display Trolley was between me and this group, so I didn't converse with them much. But I had plenty of time to observe them, and I saw how welcoming the older boy AFs were being, giving the new B3s all kinds of useful advice. So I supposed they were getting on well. But then I began to notice something odd. During the course of a morning, say, the three B3s would move, little by little, away from the two older AFs. Sometimes they would take tiny steps to the side. Or a B3 would become interested in something through the window, walk over to look, then return to a spot slightly different from the one Manager had chosen for him. After four days, there could be no more doubt: the three new B3s were deliberately moving themselves away from the older AFs so that when customers came in, the B3s would look like a separate group on their own. I didn't wish to believe this at first – that AFs, in particular AFs handpicked by Manager, could behave in this way. I felt sorry for the older boy AFs, but then realized they hadn't noticed anything. Nor did they notice, as I soon did, how the B3s exchanged sly looks and signals whenever one of the older boy AFs took the trouble to explain something to them. The new B3s, it was said, had all sorts of improvements. But how could they be good AFs for their children if their minds could invent ideas like these? If Rosa had been with me, I would have discussed what I'd seen with her, but of course she'd gone by then.

■

One afternoon, when the Sun was looking in all the way to the back of the store, Manager came to where I was and said:

'Klara, I've decided to give you another turn in the window. You'll be by yourself this time, but I know you won't mind that. You're always so interested in the outside.'

I was so surprised I looked at her and said nothing.

'Dear Klara,' Manager said. 'And it was always Rosa I was concerned about. You're not worried, are you? You mustn't worry. I'll make sure you find a home.'

'I'm not worrying, Manager,' I said. I almost said something about Josie, but stopped myself in time, remembering our conversation after the spiky-haired girl had come to the store.

'From tomorrow then,' Manager said. 'Just six days. I'm giving you a special price too. Remember, Klara, you'll be representing the store again. So do your best.'

My second time in the window felt different from the first, and not just because Rosa wasn't with me. The street outside was as lively as before, but I found I had to make more effort to be excited by what I saw. Sometimes a taxi would slow, a passer-by would stoop down to talk to the driver, and I would try to guess if they were friends or enemies. At other times I'd watch the small figures going across the windows of the RPO Building and try to understand what their movements meant, and to imagine what each person had been doing just before they'd appeared in their rectangle, and what they might do afterwards.

The most important thing I observed during my second time was what happened to Beggar Man and his dog. It was on the fourth day – on an afternoon so gray some taxis had on their small lights – that I noticed Beggar Man wasn't at his usual place greeting passers-by from the blank doorway between the RPO and Fire Escapes buildings. I didn't think much about it at first because Beggar Man often wandered away, sometimes for long periods. But then once I looked over to the opposite side and realized he was there after all, and so was his dog, and that I hadn't seen them because they were lying on the ground. They'd pushed themselves right against the blank doorway to keep out of the way of the passers-by, so that from our side you could have mistaken them for the bags the city workers sometimes left behind. But now I kept looking at them through the gaps in the passers-by, and I saw that Beggar Man never moved, and neither did the dog in his arms. Sometimes a passer-by would notice and pause, but then start walking again. Eventually the Sun was almost behind the RPO Building, and Beggar Man and the dog were exactly as they had been all day, and it was obvious they had died, even though the passers-by didn't know it. I felt sadness then, despite it being a good thing they'd died together, holding each other and trying to help one another. I wished someone would notice, so they could be taken somewhere better, and quieter, and I thought about saying something to Manager. But when it was time for me to step down from the window for the night, she looked so tired and serious I decided to say nothing.

The next morning the grid went up and it was a most splendid day. The Sun was pouring his nourishment onto the street and into the buildings, and when I looked over to the spot where Beggar Man and the dog had died, I saw they weren't dead at all – that a special kind of nourishment from the Sun had saved them. Beggar Man wasn't yet on his feet, but he was smiling and sitting up, his back against the blank doorway, one leg stretched out, the other bent so he could rest his arm on its knee. And with his free hand, he was fondling the neck of the dog, who had also come back to life and was looking from side to side at the people going by. They were both hungrily absorbing the Sun's special nourishment and becoming stronger by the minute, and I saw that before long, perhaps even by that afternoon, Beggar Man would be on his feet again, cheerfully exchanging remarks as always from the blank doorway.

Then soon my six days were finished, and Manager told me I'd been a credit to the store. Above-average numbers, she said, had come in while I'd been in the window, and I was happy when I heard this. I thanked her for giving me a second turn, and she smiled and said she was sure I wouldn't now have to wait long.

■

Ten days later, I was moved to the rear alcove. Manager, knowing how much I liked to have a view of the outside, assured me it would only be for a few days, then I'd be able to return mid-store again. In any case, she said, the rear alcove was a very good position, and sure enough, I found I didn't mind it at all. I'd always liked the two AFs who were now sitting on the Glass Table against the back wall, and I was close enough to them to have extended conversations, calling across to them, provided there were no customers. The rear alcove, however, was beyond the arch, so not only was there no view of the outside, it was hard to see even the front part of the store. If I wished to see customers as they first came in, I had to lean all the way forward to peer round the side of the arch, and even then – even if I took a few steps – the view would still be interrupted by the silver vases on the magazines table, and the B3s standing mid-store.

On the other hand, perhaps because we were further from the street – or because of the way the ceiling sloped down at the rear of the store – I could hear sounds more clearly. That was why I knew, just from her footsteps, long before she started to speak, that Josie had come into the store.

'Why did they have to have all that perfume? I almost gagged.'

'Soap, Josie,' the Mother's voice said. 'Not perfume. Handcut soap and very fine it was too.'

'Well, that wasn't the store. It was this one. I told you, Mom.' I heard her careful steps move along the floor. Then she said, 'This is definitely the right store. But she's not here any more.'

I took three small steps forward till I could see, between the silver vases and the B3s, the Mother staring at something out of my vision. I could see her face only from one side, but I thought she appeared even more tired than that time I'd seen her on the sidewalk, looking like one of the high-perched birds in the wind. I guessed that she was watching Josie – and that Josie was looking at the new girl B3 in the front alcove.

For a long time nothing happened. Then the Mother said, 'What do you think, Josie?'

Josie didn't reply, and I heard Manager's footsteps move across the floor. I could now feel that special stillness in the store when every AF is listening, wondering if a sale is about to be made.

'Sung Yi is a B3, of course,' Manager said. 'One of the most perfect I've yet seen.'

I could now see Manager's shoulder, but I still couldn't see Josie. Then I heard Josie's voice say:

'You're really fantastic, Sung Yi. So please don't take this the wrong way. It's just that . . .' She trailed off, I heard again her careful steps, then for the first time I could see her. Josie was casting her gaze all around the store.

The Mother said: 'I've heard these new B3s are very good with cognition and recall. But that they can sometimes be less empathetic.'

Manager made a sound that was a sigh and also a laugh. 'At the very beginning, perhaps, one or two B3s were known to be a little headstrong. But I can absolutely assure you, Sung Yi here will present no such issues.'

'Would you mind,' the Mother said to Manager, 'if I address Sung Yi directly? I have some questions I'd like to put to her.'

'But Mom,' Josie broke in – and now she was again out of my vision – 'what's the point? Sung Yi's great, I know. But she's not who I want.'

'We can't keep searching forever, Josie.'

'But it was this store, I'm telling you, Mom. She was here. I guess we're too late, that's all.'

It was unfortunate Josie should have come in just when I was rear-store. Even so, I was sure she would in time come to my part of the store and see me, and that was one reason why I remained where I was, not making a sound. But perhaps there was a further reason. For a fear had entered my mind almost at the same moment I'd felt joy on realizing who had come into the store – a fear to do with what Manager had said to me that day, about how children often made promises, then didn't return, or if they did, ignored the AF to whom they'd made the promise and chose another. Perhaps that was why I went on waiting there quietly.

Then Manager's voice came again, and there was something new in it.

'Excuse me, miss. Do I understand you were looking for a particular AF? One you'd seen here before?'

'Yes, ma'am. You had her in your window a while back. She was really cute, and really smart. Looked almost French? Short hair, quite dark, and all her clothes were like dark too and she had the kindest eyes and she was so smart.'

'I think I might know who you mean,' Manager said. 'If you'd follow me, miss, we'll find out.'

Only then did I move to where they would see me. I'd been out of the Sun's patterns all morning, but now I stepped into two bright intersecting rectangles just as Manager, and Josie following, came up to the arch. When Josie saw me her face filled with joy and she quickened her stride.

'You're still here!'

She had become even thinner. She kept coming with her uncertain stride, and I thought she was about to embrace me, but she stopped at the last moment and looked up into my face.

'Oh boy! I really thought you'd gone!'

'Why would I be gone?' I said quietly. 'We made a promise.'

'Yeah,' Josie said. 'Yeah, I guess we did. I guess I was the one who screwed up. I mean taking so long.'

As I smiled at her, she called over her shoulder: 'Mom! This is her! The one I've been looking for!'

The Mother came slowly towards the arch, then stopped. And for a moment, all three were looking at me: Josie at the front, beaming happily; Manager, just behind her, also smiling, but with a caution in her look which I took as an important signal from her; and then the Mother, her eyes narrowed like people on the sidewalk when they're trying to see if a taxi is free or already taken. And when I saw her and the way she was looking at me, the fear – the one that had all but vanished when Josie had cried, 'You're still here!' – came back into my mind.

'I didn't mean to take so long,' Josie was saying. 'But I got a

41

little sick. I'm fine again though.' Then she called back: 'Mom? Can we buy her right away? Before someone else comes in and takes her?'

There was silence, then the Mother said quietly, 'This one isn't a B3, I take it.'

'Klara is a B2,' Manager said. 'From the fourth series, which some say has never been surpassed.'

'But not a B3.'

'The B3 innovations are truly marvelous. But some customers feel, for a certain sort of child, a top-range B2 can still be the most happy match.'

'I see.'

'Mom. Klara's the one I want. I don't want any other.'

'One moment, Josie.' Then she asked Manager: 'Every Artificial Friend is unique, right?'

'That's correct, ma'am. And particularly so at this level.'

'So what makes this one unique? This . . . Klara?'

'Klara has so many unique qualities, we could be here all morning. But if I had to emphasize just one, well, it would have to be her appetite for observing and learning. Her ability to absorb and blend everything she sees around her is quite amazing. As a result, she now has the most sophisticated understanding of any AF in this store, B3s not excepted.'

'Is that so.'

The Mother was once again looking at me with narrowed eyes. She then took three more steps towards me.

'You mind if I ask her a few questions?'

'Please go ahead.'

'Mom, please . . .'

'Excuse me, Josie. Just stand over there a moment while I talk to Klara.'

42

Then it was the Mother and me, and though I tried to keep a smile on my face, it was not easy, and I might even have let the fear show.

'Klara,' the Mother said. 'I want you not to look towards Josie. Now tell me, without looking. What color are her eyes?'

'They're gray, ma'am.'

'Good. Josie, I want you to keep absolutely silent. Now, Klara. My daughter's voice. You heard her speak just now. How would you say her voice was pitched?'

'Her conversational voice has a range between A-flat above middle C to C octave.'

'Is that so?' There was another silence, then the Mother said: 'Last question. Klara. What did you notice about the way my daughter walks?'

'There's perhaps a weakness in her left hip. Also her right shoulder has potential to give pain, so Josie walks in a way that will protect it from sudden motion or unnecessary impact.'

The Mother considered this. Then she said, 'Well, Klara. Since you appear to know so much about it. Will you please reproduce for me Josie's walk? Will you do that for me? Right now? My daughter's walk?'

Behind the Mother's shoulder, I saw Manager's lips part, as though about to speak. But she said nothing. Instead, meeting my gaze, she gave me the smallest of nods.

So I started to walk. I realized that, as well as the Mother – and of course Josie – the whole store was now watching and listening. I stepped beneath the arch, onto the Sun's patterns spread across the floor. Then I went in the direction of the B3s standing mid-store, and the Glass Display Trolley. I did all I could to reproduce Josie's walk just as I'd seen it, that first time after she'd got out of the taxi, when Rosa and I were in

43

the window, then four days later, when she'd come towards the window after the Mother had removed her hand from her shoulder, then finally as I'd seen her a moment ago, hurrying to me with relieved happiness in her eyes.

When I reached the Glass Display Trolley I started to go around it, taking care not to lose the character of Josie's walk even as I tried not to brush against the boy B3 standing beside the trolley.

But as I was about to start on the return lap, I glanced up and caught sight of the Mother, and something in what I saw made me stop. She was still watching me carefully, but it was as if her gaze was now focused straight through me, as if I was the glass in the window and she was trying to see something a long way behind it. I remained there beside the Glass Display Trolley, one foot poised, heel off the floor, and there was a strange stillness in the store. Then Manager said:

'As you see, Klara has extraordinary observational ability. I've never known one like her.'

'Mom.' This time Josie's voice was hushed. 'Mom. Please.'

'Very well. We'll take her.'

Josie came hurrying to me. She put her arms around me and held me. When I gazed over the child's head, I saw Manager smiling happily, and the Mother, her face drawn and serious, looking down to search in her shoulder bag.

PART TWO

The kitchen was especially difficult to navigate because so many of its elements would change their relationships to one another moment by moment. I now appreciated how in the store – surely out of consideration for us – Manager had carefully kept all the items, even smaller ones like the bracelets or the silver earrings box, in their correct places. Throughout Josie's house, however, and in the kitchen in particular, Melania Housekeeper would constantly move items around, obliging me to start afresh in my learning. One morning, for instance, Melania Housekeeper altered the position of her food blender four times within as many minutes. But once I'd established the importance of the Island, things became much easier.

The Island was in the center of the kitchen, and perhaps to emphasize its fixed-down nature, had pale brown tiles that mimicked the bricks of a building. Sunk into its middle was a shiny basin, and there were three highstools along the longest edge where residents could sit. In those early days, when Josie was still quite strong, she often sat at the Island to do her tutorial work, or just to relax with her pencil and sketchpad. I found it hard at first to sit on the Island's highstools because my feet couldn't touch the floor, and if I tried to swing them, they would become obstructed by a rod that crossed the highstool frame. But then I copied Josie's method of placing elbows firmly down on the Island's surface, and from then on felt more secure – though there always remained the possibility that Melania Housekeeper would appear suddenly behind me, reach for the taps and make water come out with great force. The first time this happened, I was so startled I nearly lost balance, but Josie beside me barely moved, and I soon learned there was nothing to fear from a few specks of moisture.

The kitchen was an excellent room for the Sun to look into. There were large windows facing a wide sky and an outdoors almost permanently empty of traffic and passers-by. Standing at the large windows, it was possible to see the road rising over the hill past faraway trees. The kitchen often filled with the Sun's best nourishment, and in addition to the large windows, there was a skylight on the high ceiling which could be revealed or concealed with a remote. I at first worried about the way Melania Housekeeper often made the blind come over the skylight just as the Sun was sending in his nourishment. But then I saw how easily Josie could grow too warm, and learned to use the remote myself if the Sun's pattern over her became too intense.

I found strange for a while not only the lack of traffic and passers-by, but also the absence of other AFs. Of course, I hadn't expected other AFs to be in the house, and I was in many ways pleased to be the only one, since I could focus my attention solely on Josie. But I realized how much I'd grown used to making observations and estimates in relation to those of other AFs around me, and here too was another adjustment I had to make. In those early days, at stray moments, I'd often look out at the highway going over the hill – or at the view across the fields from the bedroom rear window – and search with my gaze for the figure of a distant AF, before remembering how unlikely a prospect that was, so far away from the city and other buildings.

During my very first days in the house, I foolishly thought Melania Housekeeper might be a person rather like Manager, and this led to a few misunderstandings. For instance, I'd thought it might be her duty to introduce me to the various aspects of my new life, and understandably, Melania Housekeeper had found my frequent presence in her vicinity both puzzling and irritating. When at last she turned angrily around to me and shouted, 'Quit follow me AF get lost!' I was surprised, but soon came to appreciate that her role in the house was quite unlike Manager's, and that I'd been at fault.

Even allowing for such misunderstandings on my part, it remains hard not to believe Melania Housekeeper was opposed from the start to my presence. Although I behaved towards her with consistent politeness, and especially in the first days, tried to do small things to please her, she never returned my smiles, or spoke to me other than to issue an instruction or reprimand. Today, as I gather together these memories, it seems obvious that her hostility had to do with her larger fears concerning what might be happening around Josie. But at the time there was no easy way for me to account for her coldness. She seemed often to wish to shorten the time I spent with Josie – which of course ran counter to my duty – and, initially, she even attempted to prevent me coming into the kitchen for the Mother's quick coffee and Josie's breakfast. It was only after Josie insisted strongly – the Mother finally ruling in my favor – that I was permitted to be in the kitchen for these pivotal moments each morning. Even then, Melania Housekeeper tried to insist that I remain standing by the refrigerator while Josie and the Mother sat at the Island, and I was allowed to join them only after more protests from Josie.

The Mother's quick coffee was, as I say, an important moment every morning, and it was one of my tasks to wake Josie up in good time for it. Often, despite my repeated efforts, Josie wouldn't rise until the very last moment, and would then start shouting from inside her en suite bathroom, 'Hurry up, Klara! We'll be late!' even though I was already outside on the landing, waiting anxiously.

We would find the Mother sitting at the Island, staring at her oblong as she drank her coffee, Melania Housekeeper hovering nearby ready to refill her cup. There was often not much time for Josie and the Mother to converse, but I soon learned how important it was, nonetheless, for Josie to be able to sit with the Mother during the quick coffee. Once, when her illness had disturbed much of her night, I allowed Josie to fall back asleep after I'd woken her, thinking it best she rest a little more. When she woke up, she shouted angry words at me, and for all her being weak, hurried to get downstairs in time. But as she was emerging from her en suite, we heard the Mother's car down on the loose stones below, and we hurried to the front window in time to see her car moving away towards the hill. Josie didn't shout at me again, but once we were down in the kitchen, she didn't smile while she ate her breakfast. I understood then that if she failed to join the Mother for the quick coffee, there was the danger of loneliness creeping into her day, no matter what other events filled it.

Occasionally there were mornings when the Mother didn't have to hurry; when though she was in her high-rank clothes, and her bag was against the refrigerator, she would drink her coffee slowly, even getting off the highstool and walking around with the cup and saucer in her hands. Sometimes she would stand before the large windows, the Sun's morning pattern over her, and say something like:

'You know, Josie, I get the impression you've given up on your color pencils. I love those black-and-whites you're doing. But I do miss the color pictures.'

'I decided, Mom, my color pictures were a major embarrassment.'

'An embarrassment? Oh, come on!'

'Mom. Me drawing in color is like you playing that cello. In fact, worse.'

When Josie said this, the Mother's face broke into a smile. The Mother didn't smile often, but when she did, her smile was surprisingly like Josie's: her whole face seemed to overflow with kindness, and the same creases that usually created such a tense expression would refold into ones of humor and gentleness.

'I have to admit. My cello-playing, even at its glorious best, sounded like Dracula's grandmother. But your use of color is more like, well, a pond on a summer's evening. Something like that. You do beautiful things with color, Josie. Things no one else even thought about.'

'Mom. People's children's pictures always look that way to them. Something to do with the evolutionary process.'

'You know what? I think this all has to do with when you took that very good flyer you made into that meeting that time. The meeting before last. And that Richards girl said something a little ironic. I've told you before, I know, but here it is again. That young lady was jealous of your talent. That's why she said what she did.'

'Okay. If you really mean that, Mom, I might even go back to the color. And maybe in return, you could take up your cello again.'

'Oh no. That's all behind me now. Unless someone's desperate for a soundtrack for their homemade zombie picture.'

But there were other mornings when the Mother would remain unsmiling and tense, even if the quick coffee didn't have

51

to be hurried. If Josie was talking about her oblong tutors, doing her best to be humorous about them, the Mother would listen with a serious expression, then interrupt to say:

'We could switch. If you don't like the guy, we can always switch.'

'No, Mom, please. I'm just talking, okay? In fact, this guy's so much better than the last one. He's funny too.'

'That's good.' The Mother would nod, her face still serious. 'The way you're always willing to give people a decent chance. That's a good trait.'

In those days, when Josie's health was quite good, she still liked to eat her evening meal after the Mother had come in from her work. This meant we would often go up to Josie's bedroom to wait for the Mother's return – and to watch the Sun go to his resting place.

Just as Josie had promised, the bedroom rear window had a clear view across the fields all the way to the horizon, allowing us to watch the Sun sinking into the ground at the end of his day. Although Josie always talked about 'the field', it was in fact three fields adjoining one another, and anyone looking carefully could see the posts marking their boundaries. The grass was tall in all three fields, and when the wind blew, it would move as if invisible passers-by were hurrying through it.

The sky from the bedroom rear window was far larger than the gap of sky at the store – and capable of surprising variations. Sometimes it was the color of the lemons in the fruit bowl, then could turn to the gray of the slate chopping boards. When Josie wasn't well, it could turn the color of her vomit or her pale feces, or even develop streaks of blood. Sometimes the sky would become divided into a series of squares, each one a different shade of purple to its neighbor.

There was a soft cream couch beside the bedroom rear window which I named in my mind 'the Button Couch'. Although it faced inwards into the room, Josie and I liked to kneel on it, our arms against its cushioned back, and gaze out at the sky and the fields. Josie appreciated how much I enjoyed the last part of the Sun's journey, and we tried to watch it from the Button Couch whenever possible. There was a time, when the Mother had come back earlier than usual, and she and Josie were talking on the highstools of the Island – and to give privacy, I'd gone to stand beside the refrigerator. The Mother that evening was in an energetic mood, speaking rapidly, recounting humorous things about the people in her office, pausing every now and then to laugh, sometimes in long bursts that made her almost lose breath. In the middle of this talk, when the Mother seemed about to break into more laughter, Josie interrupted to say:

'Mom, that's just great. But do you mind if Klara and I go up to my room for a minute? Klara just loves to watch the sunset and if we don't go now we'll miss it.'

When she said this I glanced round and saw the kitchen had become filled with the Sun's evening light. The Mother was staring at Josie, and I thought she was about to become angry. But then her face softened into her kind smile, and she said: 'Of course, honey. You go ahead. Go watch your sunset. Then we'll get supper.'

Apart from the fields and the sky, there was something else we could see from the bedroom rear window that drew my curiosity: a dark box-like shape at the end of the furthest field. It didn't move as the grass shifted around it, and when the Sun came so low it was almost touching the grass, the dark shape remained in front of his glow. It was on the evening Josie risked the Mother's anger on my behalf that I pointed it out to her.

When I did so, she raised herself higher on the Button Couch and moved her hands to her eyes to shade them.

'Oh, you must mean Mr McBain's barn.'

'A barn?'

'It's maybe not really a barn because it's open on two sides. More a shelter, I guess. Mr McBain keeps stuff in there. I went there once with Rick.'

'I wonder why the Sun would go for his rest to a place like that.'

'Yeah,' Josie said. 'You'd think the Sun would need a palace, minimum. Maybe Mr McBain's done a big upgrade since I was last there.'

'I wonder when it was Josie went there.'

'Oh, a long time ago now. Rick and I were still quite little. Before I got sick.'

'Was there anything unusual nearby? A gateway? Or perhaps steps going down into the earth?'

'Uh uh. Nothing like that. Just the barn. And we were glad of it too because we were little and we'd got really tired walking all that way. Mind you, it was nowhere near sunset. If there's an entrance to a palace, it might be hidden. Maybe the doors open just before the Sun gets there? I saw a movie like that once, where all these bad guys had their HQ inside a volcano, and what you thought was a lava lake on top slid open just before they came down in helicopters. Maybe the Sun's palace works the same way. Anyway, me and Rick, we weren't looking for it. We'd gone out there for the hell of it, then we got hot and wanted some shade. So we sat inside Mr McBain's barn for a time then came back.' She touched my arm gently. 'Wish we'd seen more, but we didn't.'

The Sun had become just a short line glowing through the grass.

'There he goes,' Josie said. 'Hope he gets a good sleep.'

'I wonder who this boy was. This Rick.'

'Rick? Only my best friend.'

'Oh, I see.'

'Hey, Klara, did I just say something wrong?'

'No. But . . . it's now my duty to be Josie's best friend.'

'You're my AF. That's different. But Rick, well, we're going to spend our lives together.'

The Sun was now barely a pink mark in the grass.

'There's nothing Rick won't do for me,' she said. 'But he worries too much. Always worrying things will get in our way.'

'What kind of things?'

'Oh, you know. The whole love and romance stuff to figure out. And I guess there's the other thing too.'

'Other thing?'

'But he's worrying over nothing. Because with me and Rick it got decided a long time ago. It's not going to change.'

'Where is this Rick now? Does he live nearby?'

'Lives next door. I'll introduce you. Can't wait for you two to meet!'

∎

I met Rick the following week, on the day I first saw Josie's house from the outside.

Josie and I had been having many friendly arguments about how one part of the house connected to another. She wouldn't accept, for instance, that the vacuum cleaner closet was directly beneath the large bathroom. Then one morning, after another such friendly argument, Josie said:

'Klara, you're driving me crazy with this. As soon as I'm

done with Professor Helm, I'm taking you outside. We're going to check all this out from out there.'

I became excited at this prospect. But first Josie had her tutorial, and I watched her spread her papers over the surface of the Island and turn on her oblong.

To give privacy, I sat with an empty highstool separating us. I could soon tell the lesson wasn't going smoothly: the tutor's voice escaping from Josie's headset seemed frequently to reprimand her, and she kept scribbling meaninglessly on her worksheets, sometimes pushing them dangerously close to the sink. At one point I noticed she'd become very distracted by something outside the large windows and was no longer listening to her professor. A little later, she said angrily to the screen, 'Okay, I've done it. I really have. Why won't you believe me? Yes, exactly the way you said!'

The lesson went on longer than usual, but at last came to an end with Josie saying quietly, 'Okay, Professor Helm. Thank you. Yes. I'll be sure to. Goodbye. Thank you for today's lesson.'

She turned off the oblong with a sigh and removed her headset. Then seeing me, she immediately brightened.

'I haven't forgotten, Klara. We're going outside, right? Just let me get my sanity back. That Professor Helm, wow, am I glad I don't have to look at him any more! Lives somewhere hot, you can tell. I could see him perspiring.' She got off the highstool and stretched out her arms. 'Mom says we have to let Melania know any time we go outside. Will you go and tell her while I put a coat on?'

I could see Josie was also feeling excitement, though in her case I guessed it had to do with whatever she'd seen through the large windows during her lesson. In any case, I went to the Open Plan to find Melania Housekeeper.

The Open Plan was the largest room in the house. It had two sofas and several soft rectangles on which residents could sit; also cushions, lamps, plants and a corner desk. When I opened the sliding doors that day, its furniture was a series of interlocking grids, the figure of Melania Housekeeper almost indistinguishable amidst their complex pattern. But I was able to spot her, sitting upright on the edge of a soft rectangle, busily doing something on her oblong. She looked up at me with unfriendly eyes, but when I told her Josie wanted to go outside, she tossed aside her oblong and marched out past me.

I found Josie in the hall, putting on her brown padded jacket, a favorite of hers she sometimes also wore indoors when she was less well.

'Hey, Klara. I can't believe you've been in this house all this time and never been out.'

'No, I've never been outside.'

Josie looked at me for a second, then said, 'You mean you've never been *outside*? Not just outside here, but outside anywhere?'

'That's correct. I was in the store. Then I came here.'

'Wow. Then this is going to be so great for you! There's nothing to be afraid of, right? No wild animals or anything. So come on, let's go.'

As Melania Housekeeper opened the front door, I felt new air – and the Sun's nourishment – entering the hall. Josie smiled at me, her face full of kindness, but then Melania Housekeeper came between us, and before I was fully aware, had taken Josie's arm, tucking it under her own. Josie too was surprised by this, but didn't protest, and I appreciated that Melania Housekeeper had concluded I might not be able to protect Josie reliably while outdoors due to my unfamiliarity. So the two of them went out together, and I followed.

We walked onto the loose stones area, which I supposed had been kept deliberately rough for the car. The wind was mild and pleasant, and I wondered how it was the tall trees up on the hill were even then bending and waving under its push. But I soon had to concentrate on my feet, because the loose stones area contained many dips, perhaps created by the car's wheels.

The view before me was familiar from the bedroom front window. I continued to follow Josie and Melania Housekeeper onto the road, which was smooth and hard like a floor, and we walked on it for some time, even when cut grass appeared to either side. I wished to look back at the house – to see it as a passer-by would, and to confirm my estimates – but Josie and Melania Housekeeper kept walking, their arms still linked, and I didn't dare to pause.

After a while I no longer had to attend to my feet so carefully, and looked up to see a grass mound rising to our left – and the figure of a boy moving about near its summit. I estimated he was fifteen, though I couldn't be sure since his figure was a silhouette against the pale sky. Josie moved towards the mound, and Melania Housekeeper said something I might have heard had we been indoors, but outside the sound behaved differently. In any case, I could see there was now a disagreement. I heard Josie say:

'But I want Klara to meet him.'

There were further words I didn't hear, then Melania Housekeeper said, 'All right but only short,' and freed Josie's arm.

'Come on, Klara,' Josie said, turning to me. 'Let's go up and see Rick.'

As we climbed the side of the green mound, Josie's breath became short and she clung tightly to me. This meant I was only able to look back briefly, but I became aware that behind us was not just Josie's house, but a second house standing further back in the fields – a neighbor house that wasn't visible from any of Josie's windows. I was eager to study the appearance of both houses, but had to concentrate on ensuring Josie came to no harm. At the top of the hill, she stopped to recover her breath, but the boy didn't greet us or even look our way. He had in his hands a circular device, and was looking at the sky between the two houses where a group of birds was flying in formation, and I quickly realized these were machine birds. He kept his gaze on them and when he touched his control, the birds responded by changing their pattern.

'Wow, they're beautiful,' Josie said, though still short of breath. 'Are they new?'

Rick kept his gaze fixed on the birds, but said:

'Those two on the end are new. You can tell they don't really match.'

The birds swooped till they were hovering directly above us.

'Yeah, but real birds don't all look the same either,' Josie said.

'I suppose. At least I've got the whole team taking the same commands now. Okay, Josie, watch this.'

The machine birds began to come down, landing one by one on the grass in front of us. But two remained in the air, and Rick, frowning, pressed his remote again.

'God. Still not right.'

'But they look great, Ricky.'

Josie was standing surprisingly close to Rick, not actually touching him, but with hands raised just behind his back and left shoulder.

'What those two need is a complete recalibration.'

'Don't worry, you'll get it right. Hey, Ricky, you're remembering about Tuesday, right?'

'I'm remembering it. But look, Josie, I didn't say I was coming.'

'Oh come on! You agreed!'

'Like hell I agreed. Anyway, I don't think your guests will be so pleased.'

'I'm hosting, so I can invite who I like. And Mom will be great about it. Come on, Rick, we've been through this enough. If we're serious about the plan, we need to do stuff like this together. You've got to be able to handle it just as well as me. And why should I have to face that crowd alone?'

'You won't be alone. You've got your AF now.'

The last two birds had come down. He touched his remote and they all went into sleep mode on the grass.

'Oh God, I haven't even introduced you! Rick, this is Klara.'

Rick went on concentrating on his remote and didn't look my way. 'You said you'd never get an AF,' he said.

'That was a while ago.'

'You said you'd never get one.'

'Well, I changed my mind, okay? Anyway, Klara's not *any* AF. Hey, Klara, say something to Rick.'

'You said you'd never get one.'

'Come on, Rick! We don't do everything we said when we were small. Why shouldn't I have an AF?'

She had by now both hands on Rick's left shoulder, resting her weight there as if trying to make him less tall and the two of them the same height. But Rick seemed not to mind her nearness – in fact he seemed to think it normal – and the idea occurred to me that perhaps, in his own way, this boy was as important to Josie as was the Mother; and that his aims and mine might in some ways be almost parallel, and that I should observe him carefully to understand how he belonged within the pattern of Josie's life.

'It's very nice to meet Rick,' I said. 'I wonder if he lives in that neighbor house. It's strange, but I hadn't noticed such a house before.'

'Yeah,' he said, still not looking directly at me. 'That's where I live. My mum and me.'

We then all turned to the view of the houses, and for the first time, I was really able to look at the exterior of Josie's house. It was slightly smaller, and its roof's edges a little sharper, but otherwise much as I'd estimated from the inside. The walls had been constructed from carefully overlapping boards which had all been painted a near-white. The house itself was three separate boxes that connected into a single complex shape. Rick's house was smaller, and not just because it was further away. It too had been built from wooden planks, but its structure was more simple – a single box, taller than it was wide, standing in the grass.

'I think Rick and Josie must have grown up side by side,' I said to Rick. 'Just like your houses.'

He shrugged. 'Yeah. Side by side.'

'I think Rick's accent is English.'

'Just a little perhaps.'

'I'm happy Josie has such a good friend. I hope my presence will never come in the way of such a good friendship.'

'Hope not. But a lot of things come in the way of friendships.'

'Okay enough now!' Melania Housekeeper's voice shouted from the foot of the mound.

'Coming!' Josie yelled back. Then she said to Rick: 'Look, Ricky, I'm not going to enjoy this meeting any more than you. I need you there. You have to come.'

Rick was concentrating again on his remote, and the birds rose together into the air. Josie watched them, both her hands still on his shoulder, so that the two of them formed a single shape against the sky.

'Okay hurry up!' Melania Housekeeper shouted. 'Wind too strong! You want die up there or what?'

'Okay, coming!' Then Josie said quietly to Rick: 'Tuesday lunchtime, okay?'

'Okay.'

'Good boy, Ricky. You've promised now. And Klara's a witness.'

Taking her hands from his shoulder, she stepped away. Then grasping my arm, she began to lead us down off the mound.

We descended a different slope from the one we'd climbed, which I saw would bring us down just in front of Josie's house. Its gradient was steeper, and down below, Melania Housekeeper began to protest, then giving up, hurried around the mound to meet us. As we came down through the cut grass, I glanced back and saw Rick's figure, once more a silhouette against the sky. He wasn't looking our way, but up at his birds hovering in the grayness.

After we returned to the house, and Josie had put away her padded jacket, Melania Housekeeper made her a yogurt drink, and the two of us sat together at the Island while she sipped it through a straw.

'Can't believe that's the first time you've been outside,' she said. 'So what did you think?'

'I liked it very much. The wind, the acoustics, everything was so interesting.' Then I added: 'And of course it was wonderful to meet Rick.'

Josie was pinching her straw close to where it emerged from her drink.

'I guess he didn't make such a great impression. He gets awkward sometimes. But he's a special person. When I get sick and

I try to think of good things, I think about all the stuff we're going to do together. He's definitely coming to that meeting.'

■

That evening, as they often did during their supper, they turned down all the lights except those falling directly on the Island itself. I was present, as Josie liked me to be, but wishing to give privacy, stood in the shadows, my face turned to the refrigerator. For several minutes I listened to Josie and the Mother making light-hearted remarks as they ate. Then, still maintaining her light manner, Josie asked:

'Mom, if my grades are so good, do I really have to host this interaction meeting?'

'Sure you do, honey. It's not enough just being clever. You have to get along with others.'

'I know how to get along with others, Mom. Just not with this crowd.'

'This crowd happens to be your peer group. And when you get to college, you'll have to deal with all kinds. By the time *I* got to college, I'd had years of being alongside other kids each and every day. But for you and your generation, it's going to be pretty tough unless you put in some work now. The kids who don't do well in college are always the ones who didn't attend enough meetings.'

'College is a long way off, Mom.'

'Not so long as you think.' Then the Mother said more gently, 'Come on, honey. You can introduce Klara to your friends. They'd be excited to meet her.'

'They're not my friends, Mom. And if I have to host this meeting, I want Rick there.'

For a moment there was silence behind me. Then the Mother said: 'Okay. We can certainly do that.'

'But you think it's a bad idea, right?'

'No. Not at all. Rick is a very good person. And he's our neighbor.'

'So he's coming, right?'

'Only if he wants to come. It has to be his choice.'

'So you think the other kids will be rude to him?'

There was another wait before the Mother said: 'I don't see why they would be. If someone does behave inappropriately, that'll only show how far behind they are.'

'So no reason Rick can't come.'

'The only reason, Josie, is if he doesn't want to.'

Later on in the bedroom, when it was just the two of us, and Josie was lying in bed ready to go to sleep, she said quietly:

'I hope Rick does come to this awful party.'

Despite the lateness, I was pleased she'd brought up the interaction meeting, because I was uncertain about many aspects of it.

'Yes, I hope so too,' I said. 'Will the other young people bring their AFs?'

'Uh uh. Not the done thing. But the AF who lives in the house usually attends. Especially if they're new like you. They'll all want to inspect you.'

'So Josie would wish me to be present.'

'Sure I want you to be present. It might not be so great for you though. These meetings stink and that's the truth.'

■

On the morning of the interaction meeting, Josie was filled with anxiety. She returned to the bedroom after breakfast to try on different clothes, and even when we could hear her guests arriving, and Melania Housekeeper had called up a third time, she continued brushing her hair. Finally, with many voices audible downstairs, I said to her, 'Perhaps it's time for us to join Josie's guests.'

Only then did she drop the hairbrush onto the dressing table and rise to her feet. 'You're right. Time to face the music.'

Coming down the staircase, I saw the hall was filled with strangers talking in humorous voices. These were the accompanying adults – all of them female. Younger voices were coming from the Open Plan but the sliding doors had been pulled together, so Josie's guests weren't yet visible to us.

Josie, on the stairs in front of me, stopped with four steps to go. She might even have turned back if one of the adults hadn't called out, 'Hi, Josie! How you doing?'

Josie raised a hand, and then the Mother, moving through the adults in the hall, gestured towards the Open Plan. 'Go on in,' she called. 'Your friends are waiting for you.'

I thought the Mother was about to say something further to reinforce this, but other adults had gathered around her, talking and smiling, and she was obliged to turn away from us. Josie did seem to find new courage then, and she went down the remaining steps into the crowd. I followed, expecting her to go towards the Open Plan, but instead she went through the adults towards the front door, which was open and bringing in fresh air. Josie kept moving as though she had a clear purpose, and a passer-by might have thought she was engaged on some important errand on behalf of her guests. In any case, no one impeded her, and as I followed, I heard many voices around me. Someone was saying, 'Professor Kwan may be wonderful at teaching our children mathematical physics. That doesn't give him the right to be uncivil to us,' and another voice said, 'Europe. The best housekeepers still come from Europe.' More voices greeted Josie as she passed, and then we were at the front door, touched by the outside air.

Josie looked out, her foot on the threshold, and shouted into the outdoors: 'Come on! What are you doing?' Then she grasped the doorframe and leaned out at an angle. 'Hurry up! Everyone's already here!'

Rick appeared in the doorway, and Josie, taking his arm, drew him into the hall.

He was dressed as he'd been on the grass mound, in normal jeans and sweater, but the adults seemed immediately to notice him. Their voices didn't actually stop, but the volume fell. Then the Mother came through the crowd.

'Rick, hello! Welcome! Come on in.' She placed a hand behind him, ushering him towards the guest adults. 'Everyone, this is Rick. Our good friend and neighbor. Some of you already know him.'

'How are you, Rick?' a woman nearby said. 'Great you could make it.'

Then the adults began to greet Rick all at once, calling out kind things, but I noticed a strange caution in their voices. The Mother, speaking above them, asked:

'So Rick. Is your mother keeping well? It's been a while since she came over.'

'She's fine, thank you, Mrs Arthur.'

As Rick spoke, the room became quiet. A tall woman behind me asked: 'Did I hear you lived nearby, Rick?'

Rick's gaze moved across the faces to locate the speaker's.

'Yes, ma'am. In fact, ours is the only house you can see if you step outside.' Then he did a small laugh and added: 'Aside from this one, I mean.'

Everyone laughed loudly at his addition, and Josie, beside him, smiled nervously as if she'd made the remark herself. Another voice said:

'A lot of clean air out here. Good place to grow up, I bet.'

'It's just fine, thank you,' Rick said. 'That is until you need a fast pizza delivery.'

Everyone laughed even more loudly, and this time Josie joined in, beaming happily.

'Go ahead, Josie,' the Mother said. 'Take Rick in. You should be hosting all your other guests too. Go on in now.'

The adults stood back, and Josie, still holding Rick's arm, led him towards the Open Plan. Neither of them looked at me, so I was unsure if I should follow. And then they were gone, the adults once more filling the hall, and I was left standing near the front door. A new voice nearby said:

'Nice boy. Lives next door did he say? I couldn't hear.'

'Rick's a neighbor, yes,' the Mother said. 'He's been friends with Josie forever.'

'That's wonderful.'

Then a large woman whose shape resembled the food blending machine said: 'Seems so bright too. Such a shame a boy like that should have missed out.'

'I wouldn't even have known,' another voice said. 'He presents himself so well. Is that a British accent he has?'

'What's important,' the food blending woman said, 'is that this next generation learn how to be comfortable with every sort of person. That's what Peter always says.' Then as other voices murmured in agreement, she asked the Mother: 'Did his folks just . . . decide not to go ahead? Lose their nerve?'

The Mother's kind smile vanished and everyone who'd heard seemed to stop talking. The food blending woman

67

herself froze in horror. Then she reached out a hand towards the Mother.

'Oh, Chrissie. What did I say? I didn't mean . . .'

'It's okay,' the Mother said. 'Please forget it.'

'Oh, Chrissie, I'm so sorry. I'm so stupid sometimes. I only meant . . .'

'It's our worst fear,' a firmer voice nearby said. 'Every one of us here.'

'It's okay,' the Mother said. 'Let's leave it.'

'Chrissie,' the food blending woman said, 'I only meant a nice boy like that . . .'

'Some of us were lucky, some of us weren't.' A black-skinned woman, saying this, stepped forward and touched the Mother's shoulder kindly.

'But Josie's fine now, isn't she?' another voice asked. 'She looks so much better.'

'She has good days and bad,' the Mother said.

'She's looking so much better.'

The food blending woman said: 'She's going to be just fine, I know it. You were so courageous, after all you'd been through. Josie will be really grateful to you one day.'

'Pam, come on.' The black-skinned woman reached forward and began to lead the food blending woman away. But the Mother, looking at the food blending woman, said quietly:

'Do you suppose Sal would want to thank me?'

At this, the food blending woman burst into tears. 'Look, I'm sorry, I'm sorry. I'm so stupid, I just open my mouth and . . .' She sobbed, then continued loudly: 'And now you all know it, know for certain I'm the world's greatest fool! It was just that nice boy, it seems so unfair . . . Chrissie, I'm so sorry.'

'Look, really, please forget it.' The Mother, now making

more effort, reached forward and held the food blending woman in a light hug. The food blending woman immediately returned the hug, and went on crying, her chin on the Mother's shoulder.

There was an awkward quiet, then the black-skinned woman said in a cheerful voice: 'Well, they seem to be managing okay in there. No sounds yet of an all-out brawl.'

Everyone laughed loudly, and then the Mother said in a new voice:

'Hey, what are we doing still out here? Let's go in the kitchen, please, everyone. Melania's been preparing more of those wonderful pastries from her homeland.'

A voice said in a pretend whisper: 'I believe we're still out here . . . so we can eavesdrop!'

This brought another big laugh, and the Mother was smiling once more.

'If they need us,' she said, 'we'll hear about it. Please, go on through.'

As the adults started to move into the kitchen, I could hear more clearly the voices from the Open Plan, but couldn't make out any words. An adult passed near me saying: 'Our Jenny got quite upset after that last meeting. We spent the whole weekend explaining to her how she'd misinterpreted everything.'

'Klara. You're still here.'

The Mother was standing before me.

'Yes.'

'Why aren't you in there? With Josie?'

'But . . . she didn't take me in.'

'Go on. She needs you with her. And the other kids want to meet you.'

'Yes, of course. Then excuse me.'

69

The Sun, noticing there were so many children in the one place, was pouring in his nourishment through the wide windows of the Open Plan. Its network of sofas, soft rectangles, low tables, plant pots, photograph books, had taken me a long time to master, yet now it had been so transformed it might have been a new room. There were young people everywhere and their bags, jackets, oblongs were all over the floor and surfaces. What was more, the room's space had become divided into twenty-four boxes – arranged in two tiers – all the way to the rear wall. Because of this partitioning, it was hard to gain an overall view of what was before me, but I gradually made sense of things. Josie was near the middle of the room talking with three guest girls. Their heads were almost touching, and because of how they were standing, the upper parts of their faces, including all their eyes, had been placed in a box on the higher tier, while all their mouths and chins had been squeezed into a lower box. The majority of the children were on their feet, some moving between boxes. Over at the rear wall, three boys were seated on the modular sofa, and even though they were sitting apart, their heads had been placed together inside a single box, while the outstretched leg of the boy nearest the window extended not only across the neighboring box, but right into the one beyond. There was an unpleasant tint on the three boxes containing the boys on the sofa – a sickly yellow – and an anxiety passed through my mind. Then other people moved across my view of them, and I began to attend instead to the voices around me.

Although someone had said as I'd come in, 'Oh, here's the new AF, she's cute!' almost all the voices I now heard were discussing Rick. Josie must only recently have been standing beside him, but her conversation with the guest girls had caused her to turn her back to him, and he was now by himself, not conversing with anyone.

'He's a friend of Josie. Lives nearby,' a girl was saying behind me.

'We should be nice to him,' another girl said. 'It must be weird for him, being here with us.'

'Why'd Josie ask him? He must feel so weird.'

'How about we offer him something. Make him feel welcome.'

The girl – who was thin and had unusually long arms – picked up a metal dish filled with chocolates and went towards Rick. I also moved further into the room, and heard her say to him:

'Excuse me. Would you care for a bonbon?'

Rick had been watching Josie talking to the three guest girls, but now turned to the long-armed girl.

'Go ahead,' she said, raising the dish higher. 'They're good.'

'Thank you very much.' He looked into the dish and chose a chocolate wrapped in shiny green paper.

Though the voices continued all around the room, I realized that suddenly everyone – including Josie and her guest girls – was now watching Rick.

'We're all so pleased you came,' the long-armed girl said. 'Josie's neighbor, right?'

'That's right. I live next door.'

'Next door? That's a good one! Only your house and this one, that's all there is for miles!'

The three girls Josie had been talking to now joined the long-armed girl, all the time smiling at Rick. Josie herself though remained where she was, her eyes watching anxiously.

'I suppose so.' Rick laughed quickly. 'But that still makes me next door.'

71

'Sure does! Bet you like being out here. Must be peaceful.'

'Peaceful is correct. It's all quite perfect until you want to go to the movies.'

I knew Rick hoped everyone listening would laugh as the adults had done about the pizza deliveries. But the four girls just continued to look at him in a kindly way.

'So you don't watch movies on your DS?' one of them asked eventually.

'I do sometimes. But I like going to a real movie theater. Big screen, ice cream. My mother and I enjoy that. Trouble is it's such a long way to go.'

'We have a movie theater end of our block,' the long-armed girl said. 'But we rarely go.'

'Hey! He likes movies!'

'Missy, please? Sorry, you have to excuse my sister. So you enjoy movies. Help you relax, right?'

'I bet you like action movies,' said the girl called Missy.

Rick looked at her. Then he smiled and said: 'Those can be fun. But Mum and I like the old movies. Everything was so different then. If you watch those movies, you can see the way restaurants were once. The clothes people wore.'

'But you must like action, right?' said the long-armed girl. 'Car chases and stuff.'

'Hey,' another girl said behind me. 'He's saying he goes to the movies with his mom. That's kinda cute.'

'Doesn't your mom like you to go with your *friends*?'

'It's not like that exactly. It's just . . . it's something my mother and I like to do.'

'Did you go and see *Gold Standard*?'

'No way his mom would like *that*!'

Josie now stepped forward in front of Rick.

72

'Come on, Rick.' Her voice had anger in it. 'Tell them what you like to watch. That's all they're asking. What do you like to watch?'

Several more guests had by now gathered around Rick, partially blocking my view of him. But I could see at this moment something change within him.

'You know what?' He spoke not to Josie, but to all the others. 'I like movies in which horrible things happen. Insects coming out of people's mouths, things of that nature.'

'Really?'

'May I just ask,' Rick said, 'why all this curiosity about what kind of movies I like?'

'It's called conversation,' said the long-armed girl.

'Why doesn't he eat his chocolate?' Missy said. 'He's just holding it.'

Rick turned to her, then held out the chocolate still in its wrapping. 'Here. Perhaps you'd care for it yourself.'

Missy laughed but backed away.

'Look,' said the long-armed girl. 'This is like a friendly encounter, okay?'

Rick glanced quickly at Josie, who was staring at him, her eyes filling with anger. The next second he'd turned again to the guest girls.

'Friendly. Of course. I wonder if it would please you all to hear I like bug movies.'

'Bug movies?' someone else said. 'Is that like a genre?'

'Don't taunt him,' said the long-armed girl. 'Be nice. He's doing okay.'

A voice said: 'Yeah, he's doing okay,' and several people giggled. As Rick turned quickly towards them, Josie reached forward and took the chocolate from him.

73

'Hey, everyone,' Josie called out. 'I want you all to meet Klara. This here's Klara!'

She was signaling to me to come closer, and as I did so all the eyes turned my way. Rick too looked at me, but only for a second, then he walked off into a small clearing beside the corner desk. No one seemed to pay him further attention because they were now looking at me. Even the long-armed girl had lost interest in Rick and was staring at me.

'Now that's a smart-looking AF,' she said. She leaned towards Josie in a confidential manner, and I thought she was going to say something further about me, but what she said was:

'See Danny over there? First thing he comes in, he announces how he got detained by the police. No greeting, nothing. When we told him he had to greet correctly first, he still doesn't get it. Just keeps boasting about him and the police.'

'Wow.' Josie looked to the boys on the modular sofa. 'So he thinks it's smart to be a criminal?'

The long-armed girl laughed, and Josie became part of a shape the five girls made together.

'Then his brother over there gives it away. Too much beer, that's all it was.'

'Shush. He knows we're talking about him,' someone said.

'So much the better. The cops found him passed out on a bench and took him home. And he's telling us like he was arrested or something.'

'No greeting, nothing.'

'Hey, I didn't hear you give Josie a greeting just now, Missy. So you're just as bad as Danny.'

'I did. I said hello to Josie.'

'Josie? Did you hear my sister greet you when you came in?'

Missy became visibly upset. 'I did say hello. It's just that Josie didn't hear me.'

'Hey, Josie!' The boy called Danny – the one on the sofa with his leg extended over the cushions – was calling from the rear of the room. 'Hey, Josie, that your new AF? Tell her to come over here.'

'Go on, Klara,' Josie said. 'Go say hello to those boys.'

I didn't move at once, partly because I'd been surprised by Josie's voice. It was like the one she sometimes used when talking to Melania Housekeeper, but not like any voice she'd used before to me.

'What's up with her?' Danny got up off the sofa. 'Doesn't she take commands?'

Josie was giving me a stern look, so I began to make my way towards the boys on the sofa. But Danny, who was taller than anyone else in the room, came swiftly through the other guests and, before I was even halfway to the sofa, grasped me by both elbows, so I could no longer move freely. He looked me up and down, then said:

'So. Settling in?'

'Yes. Thank you.'

One of the other boys from the sofa at the rear shouted: 'Hey! She speaks! Rejoice!'

'Shut up, Scrub,' Danny shouted back. Then he asked me: 'So what do they call you again?'

'Her name's Klara,' Josie said from behind me. 'Danny, let go of her. She doesn't like being held that way.'

'Hey, Danny,' Scrub shouted again. 'Throw her over here.'

'You want to see her,' Danny said, 'get up off that sofa and come over here.'

'Just throw her over. Let's test her coordination.'

75

'She ain't your AF, Scrub.' Danny's hands were still tight around my elbows. 'You need to ask Josie about something like that.'

'Hey, Josie,' Scrub called. 'It's okay, right? My B3, you can swing her right through the air, lands on her feet every time. Come on, Danny. Throw her over onto the sofa. She won't get damaged.'

'So uncouth,' the long-armed girl said quietly, and several girls, Josie included, giggled.

'My B3,' Scrub continued, 'she'll somersault and land clean on her feet. Back straight, perfect. So let's see what this one can do.'

'You're not a B3, right?' Danny asked.

I didn't reply, but Josie behind me said: 'No, but she's the best.'

'Yeah? So can she do what Scrub says?'

'I have a B3 now,' a girl's voice said. 'You'll see him next meeting.'

Then another voice asked: 'Why didn't you get a B3, Josie?'

'Because . . . I liked this one.' Josie said this uncertainly, but then the strength returned to her voice. 'There's nothing any B3 can do Klara can't.'

There was movement behind me, and then the long-armed girl was standing beside Danny. He seemed to feel both excitement and fear to be near her, and let go of my elbows. But now the long-armed girl gripped my left wrist, though not nearly as roughly as Danny had been holding me.

'Hello, Klara,' she said, and looked me over carefully again. 'Now. Let's see. Klara, will you please sing for me the harmonic minor scale?'

I wasn't sure how Josie wished me to respond so I waited for her to speak. But she remained silent.

76

'Oh? You don't sing?'

'Come on,' the boy called Scrub called out. 'Throw her over. If she can't coordinate, I'll just catch her.'

'Not saying much.' The long-armed girl came closer and stared at my eyes. 'Maybe she's low on solar.'

'There's nothing wrong with her.' Josie said this so quietly, it was possible I was the only one to hear.

'Klara,' the long-armed girl said. 'Give me a greeting.'

I remained silent, waiting for Josie to speak again.

'No? Nothing?'

'Hey, Josie,' a voice said behind me. 'You could have got a B3, right? So why didn't you?'

Josie laughed and said: 'Now I'm starting to think I should have.'

This brought other laughs, then a new voice said: 'B3s are so amazing.'

'Come on, Klara,' the long-armed girl said. 'A little greeting at least.'

I'd by now fixed a pleasant expression on my face and was gazing past her, much as Manager had trained us to do in the store in such situations.

'An AF who refuses to greet. Josie, will *you* tell Klara to say something to us?'

'Throw her over here. That'll bring her to life.'

'Klara's got a great memory,' Josie said behind me. 'As good as any AF anywhere.'

'Oh really?' said the long-armed girl.

'And not just her memory. She notices things no one else does and stores them away.'

'Okay.' The long-armed girl kept holding my wrist. 'Okay, Klara. Here's what to do. Without turning to look. Tell me what my sister's wearing.'

I continued to stare beyond the long-armed girl at the bricks on the wall.

'Seems to have frozen. But she's cute, I'll give you that.'

'Ask her again,' Josie said. 'Go on, Marsha. Ask again.'

'Okay. Now, Klara, I know you can do it. Tell me what Missy's wearing.'

'I'm sorry,' I said, still looking past her.

'You're sorry?' Then the long-armed girl said to the room, 'What's that mean?' and people laughed. Then she glared at me and asked: 'What do you mean, Klara? What do you mean, you're sorry?'

'I'm sorry I'm unable to help.'

'She's not going to help.' The long-armed girl's look softened and at last she released my wrist. 'Okay, Klara. You can turn and look. Take a look at what Missy's wearing.'

Though it might look impolite, I didn't turn. Because if I did so, I'd not only see Missy – I knew of course what she was wearing down to her purple wristband and tiny bear pendant – but also Josie, and then we would have to exchange looks with each other.

'I give up,' the long-armed girl said.

'Okay,' Danny said. 'Then we'll do Scrub's test. Just to please him. Phil, come here and help me swing her. Scrub, stay where you are, get ready to catch. This is okay with you, Josie?'

Behind me, Josie remained silent, but a girl's voice said: 'Throwing AFs across the room. That's evil.'

'What's evil about it? They're designed to deal with it.'

'That's not the point,' the girl's voice said. 'It's just nasty.'

'You're being soft,' Danny said. 'Phil, take her arms. I'll get the legs.'

'What's that you have there in your pocket?' It was Rick who'd spoken and the room went silent.

'What d'you say, friend?'

Rick moved through the guests, stopping a little to my right. He showed no fear as he pointed at the breast pocket of Danny's shirt. I'd noticed the object earlier – a soft toy dog small enough for the pocket. I'd seen children of seven and eight carrying such toys in their pockets when they'd come into the store.

As everyone shifted positions to see what Rick was pointing at, Danny raised both hands to cover his pocket.

'A pet object, I'd say,' Rick said.

'It's not a pet object,' Danny said.

'I'd say it's your pet object. To help you feel calmer at gatherings like this one.'

'What's this bullshit? Who asked you anything?'

'If it's really nothing so special, perhaps you wouldn't mind showing it to me.' Rick held out his hand. 'Don't worry. I'll take good care of it.'

'Whether it's anything special or not, it's none of your business.'

'Do please let me borrow it. Just for a minute.'

'It's nothing to me, but I wouldn't hand it over to *you*.'

'No? Not even a little peek?'

'I'd never lend you anything. Why would I? You shouldn't even be here.'

Rick was still holding out his hand, and the room remained silent.

'It couldn't be you're perhaps a little soft yourself, Danny?' Rick said. 'At least, when it comes to cute little things for the pocket.'

'That's enough! You leave Danny be!'

79

The voice belonged to an adult, and the young people around me shrank back as the woman came striding into the room. 'And Danny's right,' she said. '*You* shouldn't be here at all.'

Then the Mother came hurrying in after her, and I saw other adults looking through the doorway into the Open Plan.

'Come on, Sara,' the Mother was saying. 'We don't interfere, remember?'

The Mother put an arm around the Sara woman, who continued to glare at Rick.

'Come on, Sara. Play by the rules. It's for the kids to sort out.'

Sara continued to look angry, but allowed herself to be led away out of the room and into the murmur of adult voices in the hall. One of the voices said: 'It's the only way they'll learn,' and then the adult voices receded, and there was silence in the Open Plan.

Danny was perhaps even more embarrassed about his adult's interference than he'd been about the small toy. He continued to cover his breast pocket with both hands as he returned to the sofa, his now slightly hunched back turned to the room.

'Okay,' the long-armed girl said brightly. 'How about we go outside for a while? It's turned nice out there. Look!'

A chorus of voices shouted approval, and I heard Josie's among them saying, 'Great idea. Let's do it!'

The children filed out, led by Josie and the long-armed girl. Danny and Scrub left with them, and then there was only Rick and myself in the Open Plan.

Rick looked around at the discarded jackets, displaced seat cushions, plates, soda cans, potato snack bags, magazines, but he didn't look towards me. I wondered if any adults would come in to tidy now that the children had left, but none of them came, and the blur of voices continued from the kitchen.

'You challenged that boy, I think, for my benefit,' I said eventually. 'Thank you.'

Rick shrugged. 'He was getting seriously annoying. In fact they all were.' Then he added, still not looking my way: 'I suppose it wasn't exactly enjoyable for you either.'

'It became uncomfortable for me and I was grateful for Rick's rescue. But it has also been very interesting.'

'Interesting?'

'It's important for me to observe Josie in many situations. And it was very interesting, for instance, to observe the different shapes the children made as they went from group to group.' When he said nothing to this, and continued to look the other way, I said: 'Perhaps Rick wishes to go out now and join them. Reconcile with them.'

He shook his head. Then he moved through the Sun's pattern – the Open Plan, I noticed, was no longer spatially segmented – and sat down on the modular sofa, stretching his legs out across the floorboards.

'I suppose they have a point though,' he said. 'I don't belong here. This is a meeting for lifted kids.'

'Rick came because Josie very much wanted him to come.'

'She insisted I came. But I suppose she's too busy now to come back in here, see how I'm enjoying this part of the party.' He leaned back into the sofa till the Sun's pattern was over his face, obliging him to close his eyes. 'The trouble is,' he went on, 'she doesn't stay the same. I thought if I came today – stupid, really – I thought she might not . . . change. Might stay the same Josie.'

When he said this, I saw again Josie's hands at various points during the interaction meeting – welcome hands, offering hands, tension hands – and her face, and her voice when someone had

81

asked why she hadn't chosen a B3 and she'd laughed and said, 'Now I'm starting to think I should have.' And Manager's words came into my mind, her warning about children who made promises at the window, yet never returned, or worse still, returned and chose another AF altogether. I thought about the boy AF I'd seen through the gap between the slow taxis, walking despondently along the RPO Building side, three paces behind his teenager, and I wondered if Josie and I would ever walk in such a way.

'Perhaps you can see now,' Rick said, opening his eyes despite the Sun's pattern. 'See how I need to save Josie from this lot.'

'I can see Rick is afraid Josie might become like the others. But even though she behaved strangely just now, I believe Josie is kind underneath. And those other children. They have rough ways, but they may not be so unkind. They fear loneliness and that's why they behave as they do. Perhaps Josie too.'

'If Josie hangs out with them much more, she soon won't be Josie at all. Somewhere she knows that herself, and that's why she keeps on about our plan. For ages she'd forgotten about it, but now she talks about it all the time.'

'I heard Josie mention this plan the other day. Is it a plan about Rick and Josie sharing a future together?'

He looked past me out of the Open Plan's window, and I thought his hostility towards me had returned. But then he said:

'It's just something we started when we were young. Before we realized how it would be. How all these things could get in our way. Even so, Josie still believes in it.'

'And Rick still believes in the plan too?'

He now looked directly at me. 'Like I say. Without the plan, she's going to end up becoming one of them. I'd better go.' He rose suddenly. 'Before those kids come back. Or that crazy mother.'

82

'I hope we can soon talk again about these matters. Because I believe in many ways Rick and I have similar goals.'

'Look, the other day. When I said about not wanting Josie to have an AF. It wasn't anything personal. It was just . . . well, it felt like something else that would get in our way.'

'I hope not. In fact now I understand more, I'd like to do my best to help with Rick and Josie's plan. Perhaps help remove the obstacles you talk about.'

'I'd better go. Check my mum's all right.'

'Of course.'

He walked past me, and out of the Open Plan. I took a few steps forward so I could watch him go out through the front door and into the Sun's brightness.

■

As I said to Rick that day, the interaction meeting had been a source of valuable new observations. I had, for one thing, learned about Josie's ability to 'change' – as Rick had put it – and I watched carefully for signs of her doing so again. I wondered too how much she really did wish she'd chosen a B3. Her remark had most likely been intended as a humorous one, to keep back the threat of disharmony during the meeting. Even so, it was true B3s had capabilities beyond my own, and I had to consider the possibility that Josie might sometimes entertain such ideas in her mind.

In the days following the meeting, I worried also about how Josie might view my failure to respond to the long-armed girl's questions. In the situation that had developed – and in the absence of clear signals from Josie – I'd taken the course I'd considered to be for the best. But it now occurred to me Josie might, after a period of reflection, become angry with me.

For all these reasons, I feared the interaction meeting might place shadows over our friendship. But as the days went by, Josie remained as cheerful and kind to me as she'd ever been. I waited for her to bring up the events of the meeting, but she never did so.

As I say, these were helpful lessons for me. Not only had I learned that 'changes' were a part of Josie, and that I should be ready to accommodate them, I'd begun to understand also that this wasn't a trait peculiar just to Josie; that people often felt the need to prepare a side of themselves to display to passers-by – as they might in a store window – and that such a display needn't be taken so seriously once the moment had passed.

I was happy then that nothing changed between us on account of the meeting. However, not long afterwards, something else came along which did for a time make our friendship less warm. This was the trip to Morgan's Falls, and it came to trouble me because I couldn't for a long time see how it had created coldness between us, or how I might have avoided such a thing happening.

■

Early one morning, three weeks after the interaction meeting, I looked over to Josie and could tell from her posture and her breathing that she wasn't sleeping in her usual way. I used the alarm button and the Mother came immediately. She phoned for Dr Ryan, and then I heard Melania Housekeeper calling him again a little later to ask him to hurry. When he did come, he checked Josie over carefully, then said there was nothing to worry about. The Mother was relieved, and once the doctor had left, her manner became brisk. She sat on the edge of Josie's bed and said to her: 'You have to quit that energy drink. I always said it was bad for you.'

Josie said, not lifting her head from her pillow: 'I knew there was nothing wrong with me. I got really tired, is all. You didn't have to worry about me. And now you're going to be late for work.'

'Worrying about you, Josie, that's my work.' Then she added: 'Klara's work too. She did well to raise the alarm.'

'I just need to sleep a little more. Then I promise I'll be fine, Mom.'

'Listen, honey.' The Mother leaned right over till she was talking into Josie's ear. 'Listen. You need to get well for me. Do you hear me?'

'Hear you, Mom.'

'Good. I wasn't sure you were listening.'

'Listening, Mom. I'm keeping my eyes shut, is all.'

'Okay. So here's the deal. Get better by the weekend and we'll go to Morgan's Falls. You still love that place, right?'

'Yes, Mom. I still love it.'

'Good. Then that's the deal. Sunday, Morgan's Falls. So long as you get well.'

There was a long silence, then I heard Josie say, as though into her pillow:

'Mom. If I get well, can we take Klara with us? Show her Morgan's Falls? She's only ever been outside once. And that was just around here.'

'Of course Klara can come. But you'll have to get well or none of this works. You understand, Josie?'

'I understand, Mom. I have to sleep some more now.'

■

She woke up just before lunch, and I was going to tell Melania Housekeeper as I'd been instructed to do, but Josie said tiredly:

'Klara? Have you been here the whole time I've been sleeping?'

'Of course.'

'Did you hear what Mom was saying about us going to Morgan's Falls?'

'Yes. And I'm very much hoping we'll be able to go. But your mother said we'd go only if you were well enough.'

'I'll be okay. If I wanted, I could go this afternoon. Just tired, that's all.'

'What is this Morgan's Falls, Josie?'

'Beautiful is what it is. You'll think it's amazing. I'll show you pictures later.'

Josie remained tired for much of the day. But in the late afternoon, once I raised the bedroom blinds to let the Sun's pattern fall over her, she became noticeably stronger. Melania Housekeeper came up to see her then, and said Josie could get dressed so long as she promised to spend the rest of the day quietly. That was how we came to still be in the bedroom as the evening approached, when Josie produced a cardboard box from under her bed.

'I'll show you,' she said, and tipped the box out. Many print photos of varying dimensions tumbled out onto the rug, some face up, others down. I understood that these were favorite images from Josie's past, kept near her bed so she could cheer herself up viewing them whenever she wanted. Many of the images were now overlapping, but I could see they were mostly of Josie when younger. Some photos showed her with the

Mother, some with Melania Housekeeper, others with people I didn't know. Josie continued spreading them across the rug, then picked one up and smiled.

'Morgan's Falls,' she said. 'This is where we're going on Sunday. What do you think?'

She gave me the photo – I was by now kneeling beside her – and I saw a younger Josie sitting outdoors at a table made from rough wooden planks. Even the seating was planks, and sitting beside her was the Mother, less thin and with her hair cut shorter than now. I was interested to see a third figure at the table, a girl who I estimated as eleven years old, wearing a short jacket made of light cotton. Because the stranger girl was sitting with her back to the photographer, I couldn't see her face. The Sun's patterns were visible over them all, falling across the tabletop. Behind Josie and the Mother was a blurred black-and-white pattern. I inspected this carefully, then said:

'This is a waterfall.'

'Yup. You ever seen a waterfall, Klara?'

'Yes. I saw one in a magazine at the store. And look! You're eating, right in front of the waterfall.'

'You can do that at Morgan's Falls. Have lunch while the spray covers you. You're eating your food then you realize your shirt's soaked at the back.'

'That can't be good for you, Josie.'

'It's okay when it's warm. But you're right. On a chilly day, you have to sit further away. There's plenty of seating though because people don't know about Morgan's Falls so much.' She reached out a hand, and I returned the photo to her. She looked at it again and said, 'Maybe it's only me and Mom think it's special. And that's why it's never crowded. But we always have a great day there.'

'I do hope you'll be strong enough this weekend.'

'Sunday's always the best day for Morgan's Falls. There's a good atmosphere on Sundays. It's like the waterfall knows about it being a Day of Rest.'

'Josie. Who is your companion in this photograph? The girl here with you and your mother?'

'Oh . . .' Her face became serious, then she said: 'That's Sal. My sister.'

She let the photo fall on top of the others, then began to pass both hands over the images, moving them around the rug. I saw images of children – in fields, in playgrounds, outside buildings.

'Yeah, my sister,' she said again after a long time.

'And where is Sal now?'

'Sal died.'

'How very sad.'

Josie shrugged. 'I don't remember her much. I was small when it happened. It's not like I miss her or anything.'

'How sad. Do you know what happened?'

'She got sick. Not the same sickness I have. Something much worse, and that's why she died.'

I thought Josie was searching for another photo with her sister's image, but she suddenly gathered the prints together and put them back into the cardboard box.

'You're so going to love it up there, Klara. Here's you, only once been outside, then suddenly you're up *there*!'

■

Josie became stronger each day, so that as the weekend approached there seemed no reason to suppose we wouldn't be able to go to the waterfall. On the Friday evening, the Mother came home late – long after Josie had finished her supper – and called me into the kitchen. Josie had by then gone up to her room, and the kitchen was in near-darkness, with only the light from the hall to illuminate it. But the Mother seemed happy to stand there before the large windows, staring out into the night as she drank her wine. I stood near the refrigerator where I could hear its hum.

'Klara,' she said after a while. 'Josie says you wish to come with us on Sunday. To Morgan's Falls.'

'If I wouldn't be in the way, I'd very much like to come. I believe Josie also wishes me to come.'

'She certainly does. Josie's become very fond of you. And if I may say so, so have I.'

'Thank you.'

'To tell you the truth, I wasn't sure at first what I'd feel. Having you around, moving through the house all day. But Josie's so much more calm, so much more cheerful since you got here.'

'I'm so glad.'

'You're doing very well, Klara. I want you to know that.'

'Thank you so much.'

'You'll be fine up at Morgan's Falls. Plenty of kids take their AFs up there. Even so, it goes without saying. You'll need to look out, both for yourself and for Josie. The terrain can be unpredictable. And Josie sometimes gets overexcited in places like that.'

'I understand. I'll be cautious.'

'Klara, are you happy here?'

'Yes, of course.'

'Curious thing to ask an AF. In fact, I don't even know if that question makes sense. Do you miss that store?'

She drank more wine and stepped towards me so I could see

one side of her face in the light from the hall, though the other side, including most of her nose, stayed in shadow. The one eye I could see looked tired.

'I sometimes think about the store,' I said. 'The view from the window. The other AFs. But not often. I'm very pleased to be here.'

The Mother looked at me for a moment. Then she said: 'It must be great. Not to miss things. Not to long to get back to something. Not to be looking back all the time. Everything must be so much more . . .' She paused, then said: 'Okay, Klara. So you're with us Sunday. But remember what I said. We don't want accidents up there.'

■

There must have been signals all along, because although what happened that Sunday morning made me feel sadness later, and reminded me again how much I had still to learn, it didn't come as a true surprise.

By the Friday, Josie was confident she'd be well enough for the expedition and spent many moments trying on different outfits, and studying herself in the long mirror inside the wardrobe. Occasionally she'd ask me what I thought, and I'd smile and be as encouraging as I could. But I must even then have been aware of the signals because when I praised her appearance, I was always careful to hold something back.

I knew already that Sunday breakfasts could become tense. On other mornings, even when the Mother stayed beyond her quick coffee, there was still the feeling that every exchange could be the last till the evening, and while this sometimes made both Josie and the Mother speak sharply to each other, the breakfast couldn't become loaded with signals. But on a Sunday, when the Mother wasn't about to go anywhere, there was the feeling that each question she asked could lead to an uncomfortable conversation. When I was still new in the house, I believed there were particular danger topics for Josie, and that if only the Mother could be prevented from finding routes to these topics, the Sunday breakfasts would remain comfortable. But on further observation, I saw that even if the danger topics were avoided – topics like Josie's education assignments, or her social interaction scores – the uncomfortable feeling could still be there because it really had to do with something *beneath* these topics; that the danger topics were themselves ways the Mother had devised to make certain emotions appear inside Josie's mind.

So I became concerned when, on that Sunday morning of the trip to Morgan's Falls, the Mother asked Josie why she liked to play a particular oblong game in which the characters continually died in car accidents. Josie had at first replied cheerfully: 'It's just the way the game's set up, Mom. You get more and more of your people in the superbus, but if you haven't figured out the routes, you can lose all your best people in a crash.'

'Why would you play a game like that, Josie? A game in which something awful like that happens?'

Josie continued for a while to answer the Mother patiently, but before long the smile left her voice. In the end she was repeating that it was just a game she enjoyed, while the Mother asked more and more questions about it and seemed to become angry.

Then the Mother's anger seemed all at once to vanish. She still didn't become cheerful, but she looked at Josie in a gentle way, and her kind smile transformed her entire face.

'I'm sorry, honey. I shouldn't be bringing this up today. I'm being so unfair.'

And she stepped off her highstool, went to the one Josie was on and held Josie in an embrace that seemed to go on and on, until the Mother was obliged to introduce a rocking motion to disguise how long it was lasting. Josie, I could see, didn't mind at all how long the hug lasted, and when they separated – I didn't turn from the refrigerator until I was sure they had – the rift between them had been mended.

So the breakfast I'd feared might pose a last obstacle to our going to Morgan's Falls ended in harmony, and my mind became filled with excitement. Only in the final moments, after the Mother and Melania Housekeeper had already gone out to the car, did I see Josie, as she placed her arms through the sleeves of her padded jacket, pause and allow weariness to pass through her. She finished putting on the jacket, and noticing me across the hall, smiled brightly. Then we heard the car outside and the wheels moving over the loose stones. Melania Housekeeper came back into the house holding her keys and gestured for us to go out. But now that I was aware, I was able to see another tiny signal, something in Josie's hurried step as she walked ahead of me out onto the loose stones.

The Mother was behind the wheel, watching us through the windshield, and a fear came into my mind. But Josie betrayed no more signs – she even managed a skip of happiness as she crossed the loose stones – and opened the front passenger door by herself.

I'd never been inside a car before, but Rosa and I had watched so many people get in and out of vehicles, their postures and maneuvers, how they sat once the vehicles began to move, that there was nothing that came as a surprise to me as I navigated into my rear seat. The cushion was softer than I'd expected, and the seat in front, the one Josie was now in, was very close so I could hardly see at all in front of me, but I created no delay. I had no time to make detailed observations of the car's interior because I became aware that the uncomfortable atmosphere had returned. In the front, Josie was silent, looking away from the Mother beside her, gazing towards the house and Melania Housekeeper coming across the loose stones carrying the shapeless bag that contained, among other things, Josie's emergency medicines. The Mother had both hands on the steering wheel as though eager to set off, and her head was turned in the same direction as Josie's, but I could tell the Mother wasn't looking at Melania Housekeeper's approach, or at the house, but straight at Josie herself. The Mother's eyes had grown large, and because the Mother's face was especially thin and bony, the eyes appeared even larger than they were. Melania Housekeeper put the shapeless bag in the trunk and thumped down the lid. Then she opened the rear door on her side and slid into the seat next to mine. She said to me:

'AF. Strap on belt. Or you get damaged.'

I was trying to understand the belt system, which I'd seen so many car passengers operating, when the Mother said:

'You think you have me fooled, don't you, girl?'

There was a silence, then Josie asked: 'What are you saying, Mom?'

'You can't hide it. You're sick again.'

'I'm not sick, Mom. I'm fine.'

'Why do you do this to me, Josie? Always. Why does it have to be this way?'

'I don't know what you're saying, Mom.'

'You think I don't look forward to a trip like this? My one

free day with my daughter. A daughter I happen to love very dearly, who tells me she's fine when she's really feeling sick?'

'That's not true, Mom. I really am fine.'

But I could hear the change in Josie's voice. It was as if the effort she'd been making until this point had been abandoned, and she was suddenly exhausted.

'Why do you pretend, Josie? You think it doesn't hurt me?'

'Mom, I swear I'm fine. Please drive us. Klara's never been to a waterfall and she's so looking forward to it.'

'*Klara's* looking forward to it?'

'Mom, please.'

'Melania,' the Mother said, 'Josie needs assistance. Get out the car. Go round her side, please, and help her. She may fall if she tries to get out herself.'

There was silence again.

'Melania? What's up back there? Are you sick too?'

'Maybe Miss Josie make it.'

'What's that?'

'I help her. AF too. Miss Josie all right. Maybe.'

'Let me get this right. Is this your assessment? That my daughter is well enough to spend the day out? At the falls? This gives me concern about you, Melania.'

Melania Housekeeper was silent, but still she didn't move.

'Melania? Am I to understand you're refusing to get out to help Josie disembark?'

Melania Housekeeper was looking out between the front seats at the road ahead. Her face looked puzzled, like something further up the hill was hard to identify. Then suddenly she opened her door and got out.

'Mom,' Josie said. 'Please can we go? Please don't do this.'

'Do you think I like this? Any of this? Okay, you're sick.

That's not your fault. But not telling anyone. Keeping it to yourself this way, so we all get in the car, the whole day before us. That's not nice, Josie.'

'It's not nice you telling me I'm sick when I'm easily strong enough . . .'

Melania Housekeeper opened the door beside Josie from the outside. Josie fell silent, then her face, full of sadness, looked round the edge of the car seat at me.

'I'm sorry, Klara. We'll go another time. I promise. I'm really so sorry.'

'It's all right,' I said. 'We must do what's best for Josie.'

I was about to get out also, but then the Mother said:

'Just a second, Klara. Like Josie says. You were looking forward to this. Well, why don't you stay right where you are?'

'I'm sorry. I don't understand.'

'Well, it's simple. Josie's too sick to go. She might have told us that earlier, but she chose not to. Okay, so she stays behind. Melania too. But no reason, Klara, why you and I can't still go.'

I couldn't see the Mother's face because the seat backs were high. But Josie's face was still peering round the edge of her seat at me. Her eyes had become dull, as if they no longer cared what they saw.

'Okay, Melania,' the Mother said in a louder voice. 'Help Josie out. Careful with her. She's sick, remember.'

'Klara?' Josie said. 'Are you really going with her to the falls?'

'The Mother's suggestion is very kind,' I said. 'But perhaps it would be best if this time . . .'

'Hold on, Klara,' the Mother cut in. Then she said: 'What is this, Josie? One moment you're concerned about Klara, how she's never seen a waterfall. Now you're trying to make her stay home?'

Josie went on looking at me, and Melania Housekeeper continued to stand outside the car, a hand held out for Josie to take. Finally Josie said:

'Okay. Maybe you should go, Klara. You and Mom. What's the sense in the whole day getting spoiled just because . . . I'm sorry. Sorry I'm sick all the time. I don't know why . . .' I thought tears would come then, but she held them back and went on quietly: 'Sorry, Mom. I really am. I must be such a downer. Klara, you go on. You'll love the waterfall.' Then her face disappeared from the edge of the seat.

For a second I was uncertain what to do. Both the Mother and Josie had now expressed the view that I should remain in the car and go on the outing. And I could see how likely it was, if I were to do so, that I would gain new, perhaps crucial insights concerning Josie's situation, and how I might best help her. And yet her sadness, as she walked back over the loose stones, was very clear. Her walk, now she had nothing to hide, was fragile, and she made no fuss about receiving Melania Housekeeper's support.

We watched Melania Housekeeper unlock the front door and the two of them go inside. Then the Mother started the car and we began to move.

■

Because it was my first time inside a car, I couldn't make a good estimate of our speed. It seemed to me the Mother drove unusually fast, and for a moment fear came into my mind, but I remembered she drove up the same hill every day, and so wasn't likely to cause dangers. I concentrated on the trees rushing by, and the large openings that would suddenly appear on one side then the other, through which I could see treetops from above. Then the road was no longer climbing, and the car crossed a large field, empty except for a barn in the far distance quite like the one visible from Josie's window.

Then the Mother spoke for the first time. Because she was driving, she didn't turn to me in the back, and if I hadn't been the only one present inside the vehicle, I might not have guessed she was addressing me.

'They always do this. Toy with your feelings.' Then a moment later she said: 'Maybe it looks like I'm being hard. But how else will they learn? They have to learn we have feelings too.' Then a while later: 'Does she think I *like* being away from her, day after fucking day?'

There were now other cars, and unlike outside the store, they were traveling in both directions. One would appear in the far distance and come speeding towards us, but the drivers never made errors and always managed to miss us. Soon the scenes were changing so rapidly around me I had difficulty ordering them. At one stage a box became filled with the other cars, while the boxes immediately beside it filled with segments of road and surrounding field. I did my best to preserve the smooth line of the road as it moved from one box into the next, but with the view constantly changing, I decided this wasn't possible, and allowed the road to break and start afresh each time it crossed a border. Despite all these problems, the scope of the view and the hugeness of the sky were very exciting. The Sun was often behind clouds, but I sometimes saw his patterns falling right the way across a valley or sweep of land.

When the Mother next spoke, it was more obvious she was speaking to me.

'It must be nice sometimes to have no feelings. I envy you.'

97

I considered this, then said: 'I believe I have many feelings. The more I observe, the more feelings become available to me.'

She laughed unexpectedly, making me start. 'In that case,' she said, 'maybe you shouldn't be so keen to observe.' Then she added: 'I'm sorry. I didn't mean to be rude. I'm sure you have all sorts of feelings.'

'When Josie was unable to come with us just now, I felt sadness.'

'You felt sadness. Okay.' She became silent, perhaps to concentrate on her driving and the cars coming in the opposite direction. Then she said: 'There was a time, not so long ago, when I thought I was getting to feel less and less. A little less each day. I didn't know if I was happy about that or not. But now, lately, I seem to be getting overly sensitive to everything. Klara, look over to your left. You okay back there? Look way over to your left and tell me what you can see.'

We were crossing land that neither rose nor fell, and the sky was still very large. I saw flat fields, empty of barns or farm vehicles, stretching into the distance. But near the horizon was what appeared to be a town created entirely out of metal boxes.

'You see it?' the Mother asked, not taking her own gaze from the road.

'It's far away,' I said. 'But I can see a kind of village. Perhaps the sort where cars or other such items are made.'

'Not a bad guess. Actually that's a chemical plant, and a pretty cutting-edge one. Kimball Refrigeration. Though they haven't had anything to do with a refrigerator for decades. It was the reason why we first came out here. Josie's father was employed there.'

Although the metal boxes village remained distant, I could now make out tubes connecting one building to the next, and other tubes pointing up at the sky. Something about it reminded me of the awful Cootings Machine, and a concern came into my mind about Pollution. But just then the Mother said:

'It's a good place. Clean energy in, clean energy out. Josie's father was once a rising star there.'

Then the metal boxes village was no longer visible, and I straightened in my seat again.

'We get along fine now,' the Mother said. 'You could almost say we're friends. That's a good thing for Josie, of course.'

'I wonder, does the Father still work at the refrigeration village?'

'What? Oh no. He was . . . substituted. Like all the rest of them. He was a brilliant talent. Still is, of course. We get along better now. That's the important thing for Josie.'

We traveled after that for some time without talking, the road now climbing steeply. Then the Mother slowed the car and we turned down a narrow road. When I next looked between the front seats, the new road appeared only slightly wider than the car itself. Before us, marked into the road's surface, were muddy parallel lines made by earlier wheels, and there were trees pressing in on us from both sides, like buildings in a city street. The Mother made the car continue down this narrow road, and though she drove more slowly, I wondered what would happen if another car came the other way. Then we turned another corner and came to a stop.

'This is it, Klara. From here we're on foot. Can you manage it?'

When we got out, I felt the chilly wind and heard the birds' noises. There were more wild trees around us as we climbed a path with rocks and clusters of mud. I had to take precautions, but I kept up behind the Mother, and after a time we went through a gap between two wooden posts onto another path. This one kept rising, and the Mother had frequently to stop to allow me to catch up. It occurred to me then she might have been correct after all in believing this trip too difficult for Josie.

Just at this point, I happened to look to my left, over the fence running beside us, and saw the bull in the field, watching us carefully. I had seen photos of bulls in magazines, but of course never in reality, and even though this one was standing quite far from us, and I knew it couldn't cross the fence, I was so alarmed by its appearance I gave an exclamation and came to a halt. I'd never before seen anything that gave, all at once, so many signals of anger and the wish to destroy. Its face, its horns, its cold eyes watching me all brought fear into my mind, but I felt something more, something stranger and deeper. At that moment it felt to me some great error had been made that the creature should be allowed to stand in the Sun's pattern at all, that this bull belonged somewhere deep in the ground far within the mud and darkness, and its presence on the grass could only have awful consequences.

'It's okay,' the Mother said. 'He can't touch us. Now come on. I need a coffee.'

I made myself look away from the bull and followed the Mother. Then quite soon we were no longer climbing and around us appeared the rough wooden tables I'd seen in Josie's photograph. I counted fourteen of them placed around the field, each one with benches attached on either side made from wooden planks. There were adults, children, AFs, dogs sitting at the tables, or running, walking and standing around them. Just beyond the tables was the waterfall. It was larger and fiercer than the one I'd seen in the magazine, filling eight boxes just by itself. I looked for the Sun, but couldn't see him in the gray sky.

'We'll sit here,' the Mother said. 'Go on, sit down. Wait for me. I need coffee.'

I watched her walk to a hut made of the same rough wood some twenty paces away. It had an open counter at the front so that it could function as a store, and passers-by were now standing in line there.

I was glad of the chance to sit down and orient myself, and as I waited at the rough table for the Mother to return, I found the surroundings settling into order. The waterfall no longer took up so many boxes, and I watched children and their AFs passing easily from one box to another with barely any interruption.

Although none of them looked my way with any interest, and each seemed very focused on their child, I felt pleased to be in the presence once more of other AFs, and for a moment watched them with happiness, following one then another with my gaze. Then the Mother returned and sat down in front of me, and I turned to face her fully, the waterfall moving fiercely behind her. Her coffee was in a paper cup and she raised it to her mouth. I remembered what Josie had said about sitting close to the waterfall, how your back could get wet without your noticing, and I wondered about mentioning this to the Mother. But something in her manner told me she didn't wish me to speak just yet.

She was gazing straight at my face, the way she'd done from the sidewalk when Rosa and I had been in the window. She drank coffee, all the time looking at me, till I found the Mother's face filled six boxes by itself, her narrowed eyes recurring in three of them, each time at a different angle. She said finally:

'So how do you like it here?'

'It's wonderful.'

'So now you've seen a real waterfall.'

'I'm grateful you brought me here.'

'That's odd. I was just thinking you didn't look so happy. I don't see your usual smile.'

'I apologize. I didn't mean to seem ungrateful. I'm very pleased to see the waterfall. But perhaps also regretful Josie couldn't be with us.'

'I am too. I feel bad about it.' Then she said: 'But I don't feel quite so bad because *you're* here.'

'Thank you.'

'Maybe Melania was right. Maybe Josie would have been fine.'

I said nothing. The Mother sipped her coffee and continued to look at me.

'What did Josie tell you about this place?'

'She said it was beautiful and she'd always enjoyed very much her trips here with you.'

'That's what she said? And did she tell you how we always came here with Sal? How much Sal loved it here?'

'Josie did mention her sister.' Then I added: 'I saw Josie's sister in the photograph.'

The Mother stared so intensely at me that I thought I'd made an error. But then she said: 'I think I know the one you mean. The one with the three of us sitting over there. I remember Melania taking it. We were over at that bench right there. Me, Sal, Josie. Something wrong, Klara?'

'I was very sad to hear Sal passed away.'

'Sad puts it pretty well.'

'I'm sorry. Perhaps I shouldn't have . . .'

'It's okay. It's a while now since she left us. Shame you didn't meet Sal. Different from Josie. Josie just says what she thinks. Doesn't care if she says the wrong thing. That gets irritating sometimes but I love her for it. Sal wasn't like that. Sal would have to think everything through before she came out with something, you know? She was more sensitive. Maybe didn't handle being sick so well as Josie's doing.'

'I wonder . . . why Sal passed away?'

The Mother's eyes changed and something cruel appeared around her mouth.

'What kind of a question is that?'

'I'm sorry. I was merely curious to know . . .'

'It's not your business to be curious.'

'I'm very sorry.'

'What's it to you? It happened, that's all.'

Then after a long moment, the Mother's face softened.

'I think it was right we didn't bring Josie today,' she said. 'She wasn't well. But now we're sitting here like this, I do miss her.' She looked around, turning to look at the waterfall. Then she turned back and her gaze went past me, to the passers-by, the dogs and AFs. 'Okay, Klara. Since Josie isn't here, I want *you* to be Josie. Just for a little while. Since we're up here.'

'I'm sorry. I don't understand.'

'You did it for me once before. The day we got you from the store. You haven't forgotten, have you?'

'I remember, of course.'

'I mean, you haven't forgotten how to do it. Walk like Josie.'

'I will be able to walk in her manner. In fact now I know her better, and have seen her in more situations, I'll be able to give a more sophisticated imitation. However . . .'

'However what?'

'I'm sorry. I didn't mean however.'

The Mother looked at me, then said: 'Good. But I wasn't going to ask you to do that walk anyway. We're sitting here, the two of us. A nice spot, a nice day. And I'd been looking forward to having Josie here. So I'm asking you, Klara. You're smart. If she were sitting here instead of you right now, how would she sit? I don't think she'd sit the way you're sitting.'

'No. Josie would be more . . . like this.'

The Mother leaned closer over the tabletop and her eyes narrowed till her face filled eight boxes, leaving only the peripheral boxes for the waterfall, and for a moment it felt to me her expression varied between one box and the next. In one, for instance, her eyes were laughing cruelly, but in the next they were filled with sadness. The sounds of the waterfall, the children and the dogs all faded to a hush to make way for whatever the Mother was about to say.

'That's good. That's very good. But now I want you to move. Do something. Don't stop being Josie. Let me see you move a little.'

I smiled in the way Josie would, settling into a slouching, informal posture.

'That's good. Now say something. Let me hear you speak.'

'I'm sorry. I'm not sure . . .'

'No. That's Klara. I want Josie.'

'Hi, Mom. Josie here.'

'Good. More. Come on.'

'Hi, Mom. Nothing to worry about, right? I got here and I'm fine.'

The Mother leaned even further across the table, and I could see joy, fear, sadness, laughter in the boxes. Because everything else had gone silent, I could hear her repeating under her breath: 'That's good, that's good, that's good.'

'I told you I'd be fine,' I said. 'Melania was right. Nothing wrong with me. A little tired, that's all.'

'I'm sorry, Josie,' the Mother said. 'I'm sorry I didn't bring you here today.'

'That's okay. I know you were worried for me. I'm okay.'

'I wish you were here. But you're not. I wish I could stop you getting sick.'

'Don't worry, Mom. I'm going to be fine.'

'How can you say that? What do you know about it? You're just a kid. A kid who loves life and believes everything can be fixed. What do you know about it?'

'It's okay, Mom, don't worry. I'll get well soon. I know how it'll happen too.'

'What? What are you saying? You think you know more than the doctors? More than I do? Your sister made promises too. But she couldn't keep them. Don't you do the same.'

'But Mom. Sal was sick with something different. I'm going to get well.'

'Okay, Josie. So tell me how you'll get well.'

'There's special help coming. Something no one's thought of yet. Then I'll be well again.'

'What is this? Who's this talking?'

Now, in box after box, I could see the cheekbones of the Mother's face very pronounced beneath her skin.

'Really, Mom. I'm going to be fine.'

'That's enough. Enough!'

The Mother stood up and walked away. I could then see the waterfall again, and its noise – as well as that of the people behind me – returned louder than ever.

The Mother stopped near the wooden rail marking where the ground finished and the waterfall began. I could see the mist hanging before her and I thought she would become wet in moments, but she continued standing with her back to me.

Then at last she turned and waved.

'Klara. Come on over here. Come and take a look.'

I got up from the bench and went to her. She'd called me 'Klara' so I knew I shouldn't attempt any more to imitate Josie. She gestured for me to come closer still.

'See, take a look. You've never seen a waterfall before. So take a look. What do you think?'

'It's wonderful. Much more impressive than in the magazine.'

'Something special, right? I'm glad you're seeing it. Now let's get back. I'm concerned about Josie.'

The Mother didn't speak for the entire way back down to the car. She walked quickly, always at least four paces ahead, and I had to take care not to make errors on the steep downhill path. As we passed the spot where we'd seen the bull, I looked over the field right into the distance, but the terrible creature was now nowhere to be seen, and I wondered if it had been taken back down into the ground.

■

When we reached the car, I began to get into my usual seat, but the Mother said:

'Travel in the front. You'll see better.'

So I got in beside her, and it was like the difference between mid-store and the window. We descended across the fields, the Sun visible between clouds, and I observed how the tall trees on the horizon gathered in tight groups of seven or eight, even though all around them there was emptiness. The car followed a long thin line across the land, and I saw that what at first had appeared to be part of a distant field's pattern was in fact sheep. We passed one field containing more than forty such creatures, and although we were moving very fast, I was able to see that each one of them was filled with kindness – the exact opposite of the terrible bull from earlier. My gaze fell in particular on four sheep that looked even more gentle than the others. They'd arranged themselves on the grass in a neat row, one after the other, as though proceeding on a journey. But I could tell, even though we were passing quickly, that they were in fact standing quite still, aside from the small movements of their mouths as they ate the grass.

'I'm grateful to you, Klara. Having you with me made it not so bad.'

'I'm so glad.'

'Maybe sometimes we'll do the same again. If Josie's too sick to come out.'

When I said nothing, she said: 'You don't mind, do you, Klara? If we do something like this again?'

'No, not at all. If Josie isn't able to come.'

'You know what? I think it's best we say nothing to Josie about this. Nothing about what you were doing up there. Imitating her. She might take it the wrong way.' Then after another moment, she asked: 'So we're agreed? Nothing to Josie about that.'

'As you wish.'

I could now see the metal boxes village in the distance again, this time to our right. I thought she might say something more about it, or about the Father, but she continued to drive in silence, and then the metal boxes village had disappeared. Only then did she say, quite suddenly:

'Kids can be hurtful sometimes. They believe if you happen to be an adult, nothing can possibly hurt you. Still, she's grown up some since you've been around. She's become more considerate.'

107

'I'm glad.'

'It's been noticeable. She's definitely more mindful of others these days.'

I could see a tree with a trunk that was in fact three thin trunks entwined together to look like a single one. I observed it carefully as we passed, turning in my seat to see it for longer.

'What you were saying earlier,' the Mother said. 'About her getting well. Some special kind of help coming along. You were just talking, right?'

'You must excuse me. I know that you, the doctor and Melania Housekeeper have all considered very carefully Josie's condition. It's very concerning. Even so, I'm hoping soon she'll get better.'

'Is that merely hoping? Or is this something more solid you're expecting? Something the rest of us haven't seen?'

'I suppose . . . it's merely a hope. But a real one. I believe Josie will soon become better.'

The Mother didn't speak for several moments after that, her eyes staring through the windshield with an expression so distant I wondered if she could see the road before us. Then she said quietly:

'You're an intelligent AF. Maybe you can see things the rest of us can't. Maybe you're right to be hopeful. Maybe you're right.'

■

When we got back to the house, Josie wasn't in the kitchen or the Open Plan. The Mother and Melania Housekeeper stood in the doorway of the kitchen and talked in low voices, and I could tell Melania Housekeeper was reporting that Josie had been fine in our absence. The Mother kept nodding, then walked across the hall to the bottom of the stairs and called up to Josie. When Josie called back with a single 'Okay', the Mother remained not moving at the foot of the stairs for some time. Then she shrugged and went off towards the Open Plan. I was now alone in the hall, so went up the stairs to Josie.

She was sitting on the rug, her back against the bed, her knees drawn up to rest a sketchpad against them. She was concentrating on what she was drawing with her pencil and so didn't look up when I greeted her. Scattered around her were several other sheets torn from the sketchpad, some abandoned after a few quick lines, others densely filled.

'I'm so glad Josie's been well,' I said.

'Yeah, I'm okay.' She didn't look up from her sketching. 'So how was the trip?'

'It was marvelous. Such a pity Josie couldn't come.'

'Yeah. That was too bad. Did you check out the waterfall?'

'Yes. It was wonderful.'

'Mom enjoy herself?'

'I believe so. Of course she very much missed having Josie there.'

At last she looked my way, glancing quickly over the top of her sketchpad, and I saw in her eyes an expression I'd never seen before. And I remembered again the voice, at the interaction meeting, asking Josie why she hadn't chosen a B3, and her replying with a laugh, 'Now I'm starting to think I should have.' Then her gaze fell away from me and she began to draw again. For a long time I remained standing at the spot where I'd first entered the room. Eventually I said:

'I'm very sorry if I did something to upset Josie.'

'Didn't upset me. What makes you think that?'

'So we're still good friends?'

'You're my AF. So we must be good friends, right?'

But there was no smile in her voice. It was clear she wished to be alone to get on with her sketching, so I left the room, to stand outside on the landing.

PART THREE

I hoped the shadows of the Morgan's Falls trip might be gone by the next morning, but I was disappointed, and Josie's cold manner continued for a long time afterwards.

Even more puzzling was the change Morgan's Falls made to the Mother's manner. I'd believed the trip had gone well, and that there would now be a warmer atmosphere between us. But the Mother, just like Josie, became more distant, and if she encountered me in the hall or on the landing, she'd no longer greet me in the way she'd done before.

Naturally then, in the days that followed, I thought often about why the interaction meeting should cast no shadows at all, but Morgan's Falls, despite my complying with Josie's and the Mother's wishes, had produced such consequences. Again, the possibility came into my mind that my limitations, in comparison to a B3's, had somehow made themselves obvious that day, causing both Josie and the Mother to regret the choice they'd made. If this were so, I knew my best course was to work harder than ever to be a good AF to Josie until the shadows receded. At the same time, what was becoming clear to me was the extent to which humans, in their wish to escape loneliness, made maneuvers that were very complex and hard to fathom, and I saw it was possible that the consequences of Morgan's Falls had at no stage been within my control.

As things turned out, however, I had little time to dwell on the Morgan's Falls shadows, because several days after the outing, Josie's health collapsed.

She became too weak to go down in the mornings to the Mother's quick coffee. So instead, the Mother would come up to the bedroom and stand over Josie's sleeping figure, her back remaining very straight even as she sipped her coffee and looked down at the bed.

Once the Mother left for the day, Melania Housekeeper would take over, moving the easy chair close to the bed and sitting with her oblong on her lap, eyes moving back and forth between the screen and the sleeping Josie. And it was on one such morning, as I was standing just inside the bedroom door in readiness to help, that Melania Housekeeper turned and said:

'AF. You behind me all the time. Creep me out. Go outdoors.'

She had said 'outdoors'. I turned to the door before asking quietly: 'Excuse me, housekeeper. Do you mean outside the house?'

'Outside room, outside house, who care? Come back quick if I send signal.'

I had never before gone into the outdoors on my own. But it was clear that as far as Melania Housekeeper was concerned there was no reason why I shouldn't do so. I went carefully down the staircase, excitement entering my mind despite the worries concerning Josie.

When I stepped out onto the loose stones, the Sun was high, but seemed weary. I was unsure about closing the house door behind me, but in the end, since there were no passers-by, and I didn't wish to disturb Josie by sounding the door chime on my return, I pulled the door nearly closed without engaging the lock mechanism. Then I stepped further into the outdoors.

To my left I could see the grass mound where I'd met Rick

flying his birds. Beyond the mound was the road along which the Mother left each morning – where I myself had traveled to Morgan's Falls. But I turned away from these sights and walked in the opposite direction, crossing the loose stones to where I had a clear view of the fields behind the house.

The sky was pale and large. Because the fields rose gradually into the distance, Mr McBain's barn was still visible despite my no longer having the benefit of the rear window's height. The blades of grass were easier to distinguish than from the bedroom, but the main change was that I could now see Rick's house rising out of the grass. I realized that if the rear window had been positioned just a little more to the left, Rick's house would have been visible also from the bedroom.

But I didn't consider Rick's house, because my mind had become filled once more with the Josie worries, and specifically the question of why the Sun hadn't yet sent his special help as he'd done for Beggar Man and his dog. I'd first expected the Sun to help Josie in the days when she'd become weak before Morgan's Falls. I'd then accepted that he'd perhaps been correct at that point to wait, but now with Josie so much weaker, and so many things concerning her future in uncertainty, it was puzzling why he continued to delay.

I'd already given much thought to this matter, but now I was outside on my own, the fields so close and the Sun high above me, I was able to bring several speculations together. I could understand that for all his kindness, the Sun was very busy; that there were many people besides Josie who required his attention; that even the Sun could be expected to miss individual cases like Josie, especially if she appeared well looked after by a mother, a housekeeper and an AF. The idea came into my mind, then, that for her to receive the Sun's special help, it might be necessary to draw his attention to Josie's situation in some particular and noticeable way.

I walked on the soft earth till I was beside the fence to the first field, and a wooden gate that resembled a picture frame. The gate could be opened simply by raising the loop of cord hung over its post, and I saw I could then move on into the field unimpeded. The grass in the field looked very tall – and yet Josie and Rick, while still small children, had managed to walk through it all the way to Mr McBain's barn. I could see the start of an informal trail, created by the feet of passers-by, leading into the grass, and wondered how possible it might be that I could undertake the same journey. I thought too about the time the Sun had given his special nourishment to Beggar Man and his dog, and considered the important differences between his circumstances and Josie's. For one thing, many passers-by had known Beggar Man, and when he'd become weak, he'd done so in a busy street, visible to taxi drivers and runners. Any of these people might have drawn the Sun's attention to his condition and that of his dog. Even more significantly, I remembered what had been happening not long before the Sun had given his special nourishment to Beggar Man. The Cootings Machine had been making its awful Pollution, obliging even the Sun to retreat for a time, and it had been during the fresh new era after the dreadful machine had gone away that the Sun, relieved and full of happiness, had given his special help.

I remained for a time in front of the picture frame gate, watching the grass lean one way then the other, wondering what other trails might be hidden within it, and how I might help to rescue Josie from her sickness. But I wasn't yet used to being outdoors alone, and could sense disorientation starting to set in. So I turned from the fields and made my way back to the house.

■

Dr Ryan visited frequently during this period, and Josie spent long stretches of the day asleep. The Sun would pour in his normal nourishment each day, his pattern often falling across her sleeping form, but there remained no sign of his special help. But here again, the Sun was perhaps correct to wait, for Josie did become gradually stronger, until eventually she was able to sit up in bed.

She'd been warned by Dr Ryan not to resume her oblong lessons, so there now came the days when, propped up on her pillows, she created many pictures with her sharp pencils and sketchpad. Each time she finished a picture, or decided to abandon one, she'd tear it out and toss it into the air, allowing it to float down onto the rug, and it became my job to gather these sheets together into ordered piles.

As Dr Ryan came less, Rick visited more. Melania Housekeeper had always been wary of Rick, but even she could see how much his visits raised Josie's spirits. So she allowed the visits, though insisting they last no more than thirty minutes. The first afternoon Rick was shown up to the bedroom, I started to leave in order to give privacy, but Melania Housekeeper stopped me on the landing, whispering: 'No, AF! You stay in there. Make sure no hanky-panky.'

So it became normal for me to remain during Rick's visits, even though he sometimes looked towards me with go away eyes, and almost never addressed me, even to say hello or goodbye. Had Josie also made such go away signals, I wouldn't have remained, even after Melania Housekeeper's instruction. But Josie seemed happy about my presence – I even thought she took comfort from it – though she never included me in their conversations.

I did my best to give privacy by remaining on the Button Couch and fixing my gaze over the fields. I couldn't help hearing what was being said behind me, and though I sometimes thought I shouldn't listen, I remembered it was my duty to learn as much about Josie as possible, and that by listening in this way, I might gather fresh observations otherwise unavailable to me.

Rick's visits to the bedroom during this time fell into three phases. In the first phase, he'd glance around nervously when he arrived, and behave throughout the thirty minutes as though any careless movement he made might damage the furniture. It was in this phase he took up the habit of seating himself on the floor just in front of the modern wardrobe, resting his back against its doors. From the Button Couch I could see their reflections in the window, and with Rick in this position, and Josie sitting up in bed, they looked almost as though they were seated side by side, except with Josie at a higher level.

Throughout this first phase, there was a gentle atmosphere and the thirty minutes often passed with nothing much of substance being said. The children would often share memories from when they were younger, and make jokes about them. It would take only a word or a single reference to trigger such a memory and then they'd become immersed in it. They conversed at such moments in a speech that was like a code, making me wonder if this was on account of my presence in the room, but I quickly understood it had simply to do with their familiarity with each other's lives, and that there was no intention to exclude my understanding.

Josie didn't at first draw pictures while hosting Rick. But as they became more relaxed, she often sketched throughout the entire thirty minutes, tearing out sheets as she went, and allowing them to float down to where he was sitting. And this was how – quite innocently at first – the bubble game began.

The coming of the bubble game marked the start of the next phase of Rick's visits. It's possible that the bubble game was one they'd invented a long time earlier in their childhoods. Certainly, when the game started this time round, there'd been no need for instructions between them. Josie had simply begun to throw down her sketches to Rick, even as they continued their rambling conversations, until at one point he'd scrutinized a picture and said:

'Okay. Is this now the bubble game?'

'If you want. Just if you want, Ricky.'

'I don't have a pencil. Throw me one of the dark ones.'

'I need all the dark ones here. Who's the artist here anyway?'

'How can I do the bubbles if you won't even lend me a pencil?'

Even with my back to them, it wasn't hard to guess the outline of this game. And once Rick left at the end of each half hour, I was able to observe the pages as I gathered them from the floor. And so it was I began to appreciate the growing importance this game had for them both.

Josie's sketches were skillful, usually showing one, two or occasionally three people together, their heads drawn deliberately too large for their bodies. During those earlier visits, the faces tended always to be kind, and were sketched only with black sharp pencil, while their shoulders and bodies, like the surroundings, had been done with color sharp pencils. In each picture, Josie left an empty bubble hovering above one head or the other – sometimes two bubbles over two heads – for Rick to fill with written words. I understood quickly that even when the faces didn't resemble Rick or Josie, within the world of this game, it was possible for all sorts of picture girls to stand for

Josie, and picture boys for Rick. Similarly, other figures could stand for others in Josie's life – the Mother, say, or children from the interaction meeting, as well as others I'd not yet encountered. Although for me it was difficult to understand who many faces stood for, Rick appeared to have no such problem. He never asked for clarification concerning the drawings that fluttered down to him, and would write his words into the bubbles without any hesitation.

I soon understood that the words Rick wrote inside the bubbles represented the thoughts, sometimes the speech, of the picture people, and that as such, his task carried some danger. From the start, I worried that something Josie drew, or something Rick wrote, would bring tension. But during this phase, the bubble game seemed to result only in enjoyment and reminiscences, and I'd see them reflected in the glass, laughing and pointing forefingers at each other. Had they concentrated solely on their game as they first played it – if they'd kept their conversation focused just on the pictures – perhaps the tensions wouldn't have leaked in. But as Josie continued to sketch, and Rick to fill the bubbles, they began to converse about topics unrelated to the pictures.

One sunny afternoon, with the Sun's pattern touching Rick's feet where he sat against the modern wardrobe, Josie said:

'You know, Ricky, I'm wondering if you're getting jealous. The way you always keep asking about this portrait.'

'I don't understand. You mean you're doing an actual portrait of me up there?'

'No, Ricky. I mean the way you keep bringing up *my* portrait. The one this guy's doing of me up in the city.'

'Oh that. Well, I did once mention it, I suppose. That's hardly bringing it up all the time.'

'You keep bringing it up. Twice just yesterday.'

Rick's writing hand paused, but he didn't look up. 'I suppose I'm curious. But how can anyone get jealous about your portrait getting done?'

'Seems dumb. But you definitely sound that way.'

For the next few moments they were silent, getting on with their respective tasks. Then Rick said:

'I wouldn't say I'm jealous. I'm concerned. This guy, this artist person. Everything you say about him sounds, well, *creepy*.'

'He's just doing my portrait, is all. He's always respectful, always anxious not to tire me out.'

'He never sounds right. You say I keep bringing this up. Well, that's because each time I do, you say something else to make me think, oh my God, this is getting creepy.'

'What's creepy about it?'

'For one thing, you've been to his studio, what, four times? But he never shows you anything. No rough sketches, nothing. All he seems to do is take photos up close. This piece of you, that piece of you. Is that what artists really do?'

'He prefers photos because that way I don't get exhausted sitting still for hours in the old-fashioned way. This way I'm only in there twenty minutes tops, each time. He takes the photos he needs stage by stage. And Mom's always there. Look, would my mom hire some pervert to do my portrait?'

Rick didn't respond. Then Josie went on:

'I think it *is* some kind of jealousy, Ricky. But you know what? I don't mind. Shows you've got the right attitude. You're being protective. Shows you're thinking about our plan. So don't worry.'

'I'm not worried. This is such a ridiculous accusation.'

'It's not an accusation. I'm not saying it's like sexual or

121

anything. What I'm saying is that this portrait, it's just part of the big world out there, and you're worried it could get in our way. When I say you might be jealous, I'm just meaning in that sense.'

'Fair enough.'

Their 'plan', though frequently mentioned, was rarely discussed in detail. Nevertheless, it was during this – still gentle – phase of the visits that I began to gather together their various remarks about it into a coherent observation. I came to understand that the plan wasn't anything they'd built carefully, but more a vague wish connected to their future. I realized too the significance of this plan for my own aims; that as the future unfolded, even if the Mother, Melania Housekeeper and I could remain near her at all times, without the plan, Josie might still not keep away loneliness.

■

There then came a point when the bubble game stopped bringing laughter and brought instead fear and uncertainty. In my mind today, this marks the third and last phase of those visits Rick made at that time.

It's hard now to establish which of them first altered the mood. In the earlier phases, Josie's sketches were often created purposefully to bring back amusing or happy incidents they'd shared in the past. This was one reason Rick was able to fill the bubbles quickly and with little hesitation. But there now came a change in Rick's reactions when the sheets floated down to him. Increasingly he would stare at them for long moments, sigh or frown. Then when he wrote his words, he'd do so slowly and with more concentration, often not replying to anything Josie said until he'd finished. And Josie's responses, once Rick had passed the sheets back up to her, became hard to predict. She might study a sheet with blank eyes, before placing it amidst her bedclothes without comment. Or sometimes she'd flick a completed sheet back onto the floor, this time to a spot beyond Rick's reach.

Every now and then, the mood might return to the way it was before, and they'd laugh or argue in a friendly way. But increasingly, either Josie's picture or Rick's words would cause an unkind exchange. Even so, a comfortable atmosphere would usually have returned by the time Melania Housekeeper called up the end of the thirty minutes.

■

Once, Rick reached forward and picked up a sheet, regarded it carefully, then put down his sharp pencil. He went on looking at the picture for some time, till Josie, noticing from the bed, stopped her sketching.

'Something up, Ricky?'

'Hmm. I was just wondering what these were supposed to be.'

'What do they look like?'

'These folks surrounding her. Am I to assume they're aliens? It almost looks like instead of a head, they have, well, a giant eyeball. I'm sorry if I have this all wrong.'

'You haven't got it all wrong.' There was a coldness in her voice, and also a small fear. 'Well, at least not really. They're not aliens. They're just . . . what they are.'

'All right. They're an eyeball tribe. But what's rather troubling is the way they're all staring at her.'

'What's troubling about it?'

The silence continued behind me and, in the window reflections, I saw Rick continuing to stare at the sheet.

'So what's troubling about it?' Josie asked again.

'I'm not sure. This is an extra large bubble you've made for her too. I'm not sure what I should write.'

'Write whatever you think she's thinking. No different from the others.'

There was another silence. The Sun on the glass made it hard to see the reflections, and I was tempted to turn around, even though this might reduce privacy. But before I could, Rick said:

'Their eyes are really quite creepy. And what's even creepier. It looks like she wants them to keep staring at her.'

'That's sicko, Rick. Why would she want something like that?'

'I don't know. You tell me.'

'How can I tell you?' Josie's voice was now annoyed. 'Whose job is it to do the bubbles?'

'She's half smiling. Like she's pleased on the inside.'

'No, Ricky, that's wrong. That's just sick.'

'I'm sorry. I must be misinterpreting.'

'Misinterpreting's right. So hurry up and do her bubble. The next one's here, nearly finished. Rick? You there?'

'Perhaps I might pass on this one.'

'Oh come on!'

The Sun had retreated now, and I could see Rick, in the glass, tossing the sheet gently onto the floor to join the untidy pile accumulating closer to Josie's bed.

'I'm disappointed, Rick.'

'Then don't draw pictures like that one.'

There was another silence. I could see Josie on the bed, pretending to be absorbed in her next sketch. I could no longer see

124

Rick very well in the reflection, but I knew he'd remained quite still against the modern wardrobe, and was staring past me out of the rear window.

■

After Rick's visits finished, Josie would usually be tired, and toss her sharp pencils, sketchpad and loose pages onto the floor, turn onto her front and rest. At these moments, I'd come off the Button Couch to pick up the many items by now scattered over the floor, and I'd then have the chance to see what they'd been discussing during the visit.

Josie, even with her cheek pressed into the pillow, wouldn't actually be asleep, and often she'd continue to make remarks with her eyes closed. So she was fully aware I was observing the pictures as I gathered them, and clearly didn't mind. In fact, it's likely it was her wish that I look at each and every one of them.

Once, while performing this tidying, I happened to pick up a sheet, and though I glanced at it only fleetingly, established straight away that the two main faces in the picture were supposed to represent Missy and the long-armed girl from the interaction meeting. There were, of course, various inaccuracies, but Josie's intention was obvious. The sisters were at the front of the picture, with unkind expressions, while other less finished faces crowded around them. And although there were no furniture details I knew the setting was the Open Plan. Had it not been for a large bubble above it, it would have been easy not to notice the small, featureless creature squeezed into the gap between the sisters. In contrast to the Picture Missy and the Picture Long-Armed Girl, this creature lacked the usual human features, such as face, shoulders, arms, and resembled more one of the water blobs that formed on the surface of the Island near the sink. In fact, if not for the bubble above it, a passer-by might not even have guessed this shape was intended to represent a person at all. The sisters were ignoring the Water Blob Person completely, despite the person's closeness. Inside the bubble, Rick had written:

'The smart kids think I have no shape. But I do. I'm just keeping it hidden. Because who wants them to see?'

Although I only glimpsed this picture for a second, Josie knew I'd taken it in, and she said from the bed in a sleepy voice:

'Don't you think that's a weird thing for him to write?'

When I gave a small laugh and carried on tidying, she went on:

'Do you suppose he thinks I meant that to be him? The little guy between the two nasties? Do you suppose that's why he filled the bubble that way?'

'It's possible.'

'But you don't think so. Do you, Klara?' Then she said: 'Klara, you listening? Come on. Can we have a comment here?'

'It's perhaps more likely he assumed the small person was Josie.'

She said nothing else while I ordered the various sheets into piles and placed them with the previous ones in a space beneath the dressing table. I thought she'd fallen asleep, when she said suddenly:

'What makes you say that?'

'It's only an estimate. I think that Rick thought the small person was Josie. And I believe Rick was trying to be kind.'

'Kind? Why is that being kind?'

'I believe Rick worries about Josie. How she sometimes appears to change in different situations. But in this picture,

126

Rick is being kind. Because he's suggesting Josie is being clever to protect herself and isn't really changing.'

'So what if I sometimes want to act different? Who wants to be the same all the time? The trouble with Rick is he always gets accusing when I'm any way he doesn't like. It's because he wants me to stay the way I was when we were small kids.'

'I don't really think that's what Rick wishes.'

'Then what's all this? All this no shape, hiding stuff? I don't see what's kind about it. That's Rick's problem. He doesn't want to grow up. At least, his mother doesn't want him to and he goes along with it. The idea is he lives with his mom for ever and ever. How's that going to help our plan? Any time I show any sign of trying to grow up, he gets sulky.'

I said nothing to this, and Josie continued to lie there with her eyes closed. She did fall asleep then, but just before she did, she said quietly:

'Maybe. Maybe he did mean it to be kind.'

I wondered if Josie would bring up this particular picture – and the words inside the bubble – during Rick's next visit. But she didn't, and I realized there was a kind of rule between them not to talk directly about any of the pictures or bubble words once they'd been completed. Perhaps such an understanding was necessary in allowing them to draw and write freely. Even so, as I have said, I considered from the start that their bubble game was filled with danger, and it was what brought about the sudden end to Rick's thirty-minute visits.

■

It was a rainy afternoon, but the Sun's patterns still came faintly into the bedroom. There'd been around then a run of fairly

127

relaxed visits, and the mood that day had also been quite comfortable. Then twelve minutes into the visit – they were again playing the bubble game – Josie said from the bed:

'What's going on down there? Haven't you finished yet?'

'I'm still thinking.'

'Ricky, the idea's you *don't* think. You write down the first thing that comes to you.'

'Fair enough. But this one requires more thought.'

'Why? What's different about it? Hurry it up. I've nearly finished this next one.'

In the window reflections, I could see Rick at his usual place on the floor, knees drawn up so that he could rest the picture on them, both hands down at his sides. He was staring at the picture before him with a puzzled expression. After a while, without pausing from her drawing, Josie said:

'You know, I always meant to ask. Why is it your mom won't drive any more? You still have that car, right?'

'No one's started it up in years. But yeah, it's still in the garage. Maybe once I get my license, I'll get it checked over.'

'Is it like she's afraid of accidents?'

'Josie, we've talked about this already.'

'Yeah, but I don't remember. Is it because she got too scared?'

'Something like that.'

'*My* mom, she's the reverse. Drives way too fast.' When Rick didn't respond, she asked: 'Ricky, you still haven't filled that in?'

'I'll get there. Just give me a moment.'

'Not driving's one thing. But doesn't your mom mind not having friends?'

'She has friends. That Mrs Rivers comes all the time. And she's friends with your mum, isn't she?'

'That's not really what I mean. Anyone can have one or two *individual* friends. But your mom, she doesn't have *society*. My mom doesn't have so many friends either. But she does have society.'

'Society? That sounds rather quaint. What's it mean?'

'It means you walk into a store or get into a taxi and people take you seriously. Treat you well. Having society. Important, right?'

'Look, Josie, you know my mother's not always so well. It's not as if she made a decision about it.'

'But she does make decisions, right? One thing, she made a decision about *you*. Back whenever.'

'I don't know why we're talking about this.'

'You know what I think, Ricky? Stop me if this is unfair. I think your mom never went ahead with you because she wanted to keep you for herself. And now it's too late.'

'I don't see why we're talking about this. And what does it matter? Who wants this society anyway? None of it needs to get in the way of anything.'

'It all gets in the way, Ricky. Gets in the way of our plan for one thing.'

'Look, I'm doing my best . . .'

'But you're *not* doing your best, Ricky. You keep talking about our plan, but what really are you doing? Each day goes by we get older, stuff keeps coming up. I'm doing all I can, but not you, Rick.'

'What am I not doing I should be doing? Going to more of your interaction meetings?'

'You could at least try more. You could do like we said. Study harder. Try for Atlas Brookings.'

'What's the point in talking about Atlas Brookings? I don't even have an outside chance.'

'Of course you've got a chance, Ricky. You're smart. Even my mom says you stand a chance.'

'A theoretical chance. Atlas Brookings may make a big thing of it, but it's less than two percent. That's all. Their intake of unlifteds is less than two percent.'

'But you're smarter than any of the other unlifteds trying to get in. So why won't you go for it? I'll tell you. It's because your mom wants you to stay with her forever. She doesn't want you going out there and turning into a real adult. Hey, are you still not finished down there? The next one's ready.'

Rick was silent, gazing at the picture. Josie, despite her announcement, continued to add to her picture.

'Anyway,' she went on, 'how's this going to work? Our plan, I mean. How's it going to work if I've got society and you haven't? My mom drives too fast. But at least she's got courage. It goes wrong with Sal, but even after that she finds the courage to go ahead with me all over again. That takes courage, right?'

Rick suddenly leaned forward and started to write on the picture. He often used a magazine to press on, but this time I could see the page was directly against his thigh, and starting to crinkle. But he went on writing quickly, then stood up, dropping his sharp pencil to the floor. Rather than hand the picture to Josie, he tossed it towards the bed, making it land on the duvet in front of her. He then stepped back till he was near the door, all the time watching her with large eyes that were both angry and fearful.

Josie turned to him in surprise. Then she put down her own sharp pencil and reached forward for the sheet. For a long moment, she looked at it with blank eyes, while Rick kept watching from the door.

'I can't believe you'd write this,' she said finally. 'Why would you do this?'

I turned around on the Button Couch, estimating the tension had reached a level that could no longer justify complete privacy. Perhaps Rick had forgotten about my presence, because my turning round appeared to startle him. His gaze came to me for a second, still filled with fear and anger, then he strode out of the room without a word. We listened to his steps going down the stairs.

Once the front door noise came, Josie yawned, threw everything off the bed and lay down on her front, as though the visit had ended like any other.

'He can be so exhausting sometimes,' she said into her pillow.

I came off the Button Couch and began to tidy the room. Josie's eyes stayed closed, and she said nothing more, but I could tell she hadn't fallen asleep. As I went on tidying, I naturally glanced at the sheet that had caused the tension.

As expected, the picture showed versions of Josie and Rick. There were many inaccuracies, but also enough resemblances to leave no doubt about the intended identities. Picture Josie and Picture Rick appeared to be floating in the sky, the trees, roads and houses far below reduced to miniature sizes. Behind them, in one section of sky, were seven birds flying in formation. Picture Josie was holding up with two hands a much larger bird, offering it as a special gift to Picture Rick. Picture Josie had a large smile, and Picture Rick a look of thrilled amazement.

There was no bubble for Picture Rick. The only one was for Picture Josie's thoughts, and inside it Rick had written:

'I wish I could go out and walk and run and skateboard and swim in lakes. But I can't because my mother has Courage. So

131

instead I get to stay in bed and be sick. I'm glad about this. I really am.'

I added this picture to the collection I was gathering in my hands, making sure it wasn't near the top. Josie remained quiet and still, her eyes closed, but I knew she wasn't asleep. In the days before Morgan's Falls I would perhaps have spoken to her at this point, and Josie would have responded with honesty. But the mood between us was different now, and so I decided to say nothing. I went to the dressing table, reached down and placed this latest pile beside the others in the space underneath.

∎

Rick didn't come back the next day or the day after. But when Melania Housekeeper asked, 'Where boy go? Get sick?' Josie just shrugged and said nothing.

As the days continued and there was still no visit from Rick, Josie grew more quiet, and her signals became keep away ones. She still continued with her drawings in bed, but without Rick and the bubble game, her enthusiasm would quickly drain away, and often she'd toss unfinished pictures onto the floor, stretch out on the bed and stare at the ceiling.

One afternoon when she'd been staring in this way, I said to her: 'If you liked, Josie, we could play the bubble game. If Josie would draw the pictures, I'd do my best to think of suitable words.'

She went on staring up at the air. Then she turned and said: 'Look. That's just not going to work. I don't mind you listening in. But there's no way you could do that instead of Rick. No way at all.'

'I see. I'm sorry. I shouldn't have suggested . . .'

'No. You shouldn't have.'

As more days passed without a Rick visit, Josie grew lethargic, and I was concerned she was also growing weak again. It occurred to me this was the ideal time for the Sun to send his special help, and whenever his pattern in the bedroom altered suddenly, or when he burst out in the sky following an overcast spell, I'd watch with particular keenness. But though he continued unfailingly to send his normal nourishment, his special help didn't come.

■

One morning I returned to the bedroom after taking down her breakfast tray, and found her propped up on her pillows, sketching busily with something like her old enthusiasm. She also had a serious expression I'd not seen before while working on a picture, and when I tried to make conversation, she didn't reply. Once, as I was tidying the room and came near the bed, she adjusted her posture to prevent me glimpsing any part of her sheet.

After a time she tore out the page, screwed it into a tight ball and dropped it into a crevice in her duvet between herself and the wall. She then began a fresh drawing, her eyes large and tense. I sat on the Button Couch, this time facing towards her so she would know I was ready to converse whenever she wished to do so.

After almost an hour, she put down her sharp pencil and stared at her picture for some time.

'Klara? See down there, bottom left drawer? Could you get me an envelope? One of the large padded ones?'

As I was crouching down by the drawer, I saw Josie raise her sharp pencil again, and from its movements I knew she was no longer drawing, but writing words. Then she folded the picture down the middle, placing a blank sheet between the halves to prevent smudging, took the padded envelope from me and carefully slid the picture inside. Peeling off the thin paper tape, she sealed the envelope, pressing its edge to make sure.

'Glad that's done,' she said, turning the envelope in her hands as though it brought her comfort to do so. But as I began to move away from the bed, she suddenly held it towards me. 'Would you put this in the same drawer you found the envelope? Lower left?'

'Of course.' I took it from her, but didn't go immediately to the drawer. Instead I stood in the middle of the room, holding the envelope, and looked at her. 'I wonder if this picture is a special gift from Josie to Rick.'

'What makes you say that?'

'It was just an estimate.'

'Well, your estimate's right. I wanted it to be for Rick. For when he next comes here.'

There was silence while she watched me, and I was uncertain if she was simply impatient for me to place the envelope in the drawer as she'd requested, or if she was waiting for me to say something more about Rick and his visits. In the end I said:

'Perhaps he'll come again soon.'

'Perhaps he will. No sign of it though.'

'I think Rick will be pleased to see the picture. He'll see Josie took special care with it.'

'I didn't take special care.' She flashed angry eyes. 'I got bored and drew another picture. That's all. But you're right. It's for Rick. Problem is, he'd have to come here to get it. And he doesn't come any more.'

She went on staring at me. I remained standing in the middle of the room.

'Josie,' I said after a while. 'If you like, I could take the drawing to him.'

Her eyes became surprised and also excited. 'You mean, you'll take it over to him? To his house?'

'Yes. It's only the neighbor house after all.'

'I guess it wouldn't be so weird you taking this to him. Other people's AFs go on errands all the time, right?'

'I'd be happy to go. I believe I'll be able to find the correct trail to his house.'

'And would you do it today? Before lunch?'

'Whenever Josie wishes. If you like, I could take it to him now. Right away.'

'You think that's a good idea?'

I raised the padded envelope slightly. 'I'd very much like to take Josie's picture to Rick. It would be good for me to explore the outside. And if Rick receives this special picture, he may forgive Josie and be her best friend again.'

'What do you mean, "forgive"? It's for *me* to forgive *him*. That's really dumb, Klara. I don't think I want you to take this to him now.'

'I'm sorry. It's my error. I don't understand yet the rules about forgiveness. Even so I think it will be best to take him the picture. I think he'd like it.'

Her anger faded from her face. 'Okay. Go ahead. Take it.' Then as I turned, she added quietly: 'You're probably right. I guess it *is* him who needs to forgive me.'

'I'll take it to him and we can see what he does.'

'Okay.' Then she smiled. 'If he's rude about it, you just tear it up, right?' Her smile was almost like the smiles from before

Morgan's Falls. I smiled too then, and said: 'I hope that won't be necessary.'

She fell back onto her pillow in a jokey way. 'Okay, go. I need a rest now.'

But as I was leaving the bedroom, the padded envelope held closely to me, she said suddenly: 'Hey, Klara?'

'Yes?'

'It must be dull, right? Living here with a sick kid.'

She was still smiling, but I saw fear beneath the smile.

'It's never dull to be with Josie.'

'You waited all that time for me in the store. I bet you're wishing now you'd gone with some other kid.'

'I've never wished such a thing. It was my wish to be Josie's AF. And the wish came true.'

'Yeah, but . . .' She made a small laughing sound full of sadness. 'But that was before you got here. I promised it would be great.'

'I'm very happy here. I have no wish other than to be Josie's AF.'

'If I get better, we can go outside together all the time. We could go to the city, see my dad. Maybe he could take us to the other cities.'

'Those are possibilities for the future. But Josie must know. I couldn't have a better home than this one. Or a better child than Josie. I'm so glad I waited. That Manager allowed me to wait.'

Josie thought about this. Then when she smiled again, it was full of kindness, with no fear behind it. 'So we're friends, right? Best friends.'

'Yes, of course.'

'Okay. Good. So remember. Don't take any shit from Rick.'

I smiled too then, and held up the padded envelope to show I would take good care of it.

■

Melania Housekeeper expressed no objection to my going alone on an errand to Rick's house. Nevertheless, as I crossed the loose stones towards the picture frame gate, she remained at the front door watching me, and only as I stepped into the first field did she go back inside.

I followed the informal trail and the ground soon became hard to predict, a soft step often coming straight after a hard one. The grass came up to my shoulders, and a fear entered my mind that I would lose my bearings. But this part of the field had been divided into orderly boxes, so that as I passed from one box into the next, I was able to see clearly those lined up ahead of me. Less helpful was the way the grass frequently sprang across me from one side or the other, but even this I quickly learned to control by holding out an arm. If I'd had both arms free, I'd have made even faster progress, but of course I was holding Josie's envelope in one hand and couldn't risk harming it. Then the tall grass finished around me and I was standing in front of Rick's house.

While viewing from a distance, I'd already estimated that Rick's house wasn't as high-rank as Josie's. Now I could see that many of its white paint boards had become gray – even brown in some places – and three of the windows were dark rectangles with no curtains or blinds within them. I went up a stairway of planks, each one bending under my tread, then onto a platform constructed from more such planks, this time with gaps between them through which I could see the muddy ground below. Near the house front door, pushed over to one side, was a refrigerator, its back fully exposed to passers-by, and I saw how spiders had made their homes within the complicated metal bracing. I'd paused to observe their delicate cobwebs when the front door opened – though I hadn't pressed any button – and Rick came out onto the platform.

'Excuse me,' I said quickly. 'I didn't wish to take your privacy. I came on an important errand.'

He didn't seem angry, but said nothing and went on watching me.

'AFs often do important errands,' I said. 'Josie sent me on this one.' I raised the envelope.

Excitement appeared suddenly in Rick's face, then vanished again. 'It's good you came then,' he said.

Perhaps he expected me simply to hand him the envelope, then go away. But I'd anticipated this possibility and made no move to offer it to him. We went on standing on the planks like that, facing one another, the wind moving through the gaps.

'In that case,' he said eventually, 'I suppose you ought to come in. Be warned. It's not fancy in here.'

The hallway had a dark wood floor, and we walked past an open trunk in which items such as broken lamps and single shoes had been placed. Rick led the way into a large room with a wide window looking out over the fields. The furniture wasn't modern, and didn't interconnect like that in the Open Plan: there was a heavy dark wardrobe, floor rugs with faded patterns, hard and soft chairs in different shapes and sizes. Of the many small pictures on the walls, some were photographs, others drawn by sharp pencil, and here too spiders had made homes in the corners of frames. There were books, round-face clocks, low tables. I could see navigation wouldn't be easy, so selected a spot where the floor was relatively open, went to it and stood there with my back to the wide window.

'Okay, so this is where we live,' Rick said. 'My mother and me.'

'It's kind of you to allow me in.'

'I was watching you coming from upstairs. I'll need to go back up soon.' He gestured with just his eyes towards the ceiling. Then he said with sadness: 'I suppose you noticed the smell.'

'I'm not able to smell.'

'Oh sorry, I didn't realize. I assumed smell would be an important faculty. I mean for safety. Burning, things like that.'

'Perhaps for that reason B3s have been given limited smell. But I have none.'

'Well that's lucky for you just now. Because this place still smells. Even though I did the hall this morning. Did it over and over and over.' Tears had appeared in his eyes, but he went on looking at me.

'Rick's mother isn't well?'

'You could say that. Though she's not sick in the way Josie's sick. I'd rather not talk about Mum if you don't mind. How's Josie these days?'

'I'm afraid she's no better.'

'Worse?'

'Perhaps not worse. But I believe her condition may be a very serious one.'

'That's what I was thinking.' He sighed and sat down on the sofa facing me. 'So she sent you here on an errand.'

'Yes. She wanted me to give you this. She worked especially hard on it.'

I held out the envelope in such a way that he could receive it while still sitting on the sofa. But he rose to his feet, even though

139

he'd only just sat down, and, taking the envelope, opened it carefully.

He gazed at the picture for some time, his face on the edge of smiling. 'Rick and Josie forever,' he said finally.

'Is that what it says? Inside the bubble?'

'Oh, I thought you'd seen it.'

'Josie put it in the envelope without showing me.'

He went on looking at it for another moment, then turned the drawing for me to see.

It was unlike any I'd seen during the bubble games. Much of the sheet was filled with sharp-looking objects, many with angry protruding points, that had become tangled together into an impenetrable mesh. Josie had used pencils of many colors to create the mesh, but its overall effect was dark and forbidding. However, a clear tranquil space had been kept in the lower left-hand corner, where the figures of two small people could be seen, their backs to passers-by, walking away hand in hand. They were too stick-like to be identifiable other than as a boy and girl, but they seemed happy and lacking worries. There was a bubble just above them, but because it was without the usual tail or bubble dots, the words inside seemed more like a poster slogan, or taxi door ad, than the thoughts from either person's mind.

'So what do you think?' he asked.

'It's very nice. I think it's a kind picture.'

'Yes. I suppose it is. And a kind message.'

Suddenly music and electronic voices came loudly from upstairs and annoyance appeared in Rick's face. He rushed out of the room, still holding Josie's picture.

'Mum!' he shouted out in the hall. 'Mum! For God's sake turn that down please!'

A voice from upstairs said something, then Rick called up more gently: 'I'll come up in a minute. Now please. Turn it down.'

The electronic sounds grew quieter, and when Rick came back into the large room, he was again looking at Josie's picture.

'Yes, it's a kind picture. Say thanks to Josie for me.'

'I think Josie was hoping Rick would come in person to say thank you.'

His smile faded. 'But it's not that simple, is it?' he said. 'You're always there, taking it all in. So you know as well as I do. The way she keeps getting at me. There's no reason a person has to take all that. She pushes it too far, then thinks it can all be fixed with a nice picture. Send the AF over with it. Well she has to understand. Things aren't always that easily fixed.'

'If Rick came to visit once more, I believe Josie may wish to apologize.'

'Really? Look, I know Josie and my guess is she's pretty convinced I'm the one who needs to do the apologizing.'

'Josie and I have already had that very discussion. I believe she's wishing to apologize to Rick.'

'I suppose I was out of order too. But she can't just keep saying all that about my mum. It's not fair. My mother's doing her best and she's getting better.'

Although the version of Rick who'd opened the door and faced me on the platform had been much like the one who'd ignored me throughout his visits, it was interesting to see he'd now become much closer to the person I'd talked to at the interaction meeting after the other children had gone outside. In fact it was almost as if this version of Rick was meeting me for the first time since that afternoon and continuing the conversation we'd then started.

141

'I agree Josie's words were sometimes unkind,' I said. 'But that might be because Josie feels Rick's mother holds Rick too closely. Too closely to allow Rick and Josie's plan to become possible in the future.'

'But why does Josie blame Mum all the time? It's not fair.'

'Josie worries about the plan. I think she believes Rick's mother is reluctant to let Rick go because she fears the loneliness that would result for her.'

'Look, you might be a very intelligent AF. But there's a lot you don't know. If you only ever listen to Josie's side of things, you'll never get the whole picture. And it's not just about Mum. Josie's always trying to trap me now.'

'Trap you?'

'You must have heard. She's always doing it now. Either she accuses me of thinking about that stuff too much. Or she's offended because I don't think about her enough in that way. Always trapping me, whatever I say. She claims I'm always lusting after these girls I can see on my DS, then the next time she brings it up, and I don't react, she says there's something wrong with me, I'm not being natural. She keeps talking about how we knew each other too well when we were children and so the whole sex thing might not even work with us. Whatever I try to say or do, it's wrong and I get trapped. And the way she goes on about Mum. It's going too far. Plan or no plan, that's just not fair.'

He sat down again, the Sun's pattern falling across him. He placed Josie's drawing carefully on the sofa space beside him, and though the sheet was face down, kept staring at it.

'Anyway,' he said quietly, 'Josie's ill now. None of this, our plan, none of it will count if she doesn't get better soon. And the way it's going . . . I don't know what to think these days.' He looked up at me. 'Look, Klara. You're supposed to be super-intelligent. So what's your, you know, estimate? How ill *is* Josie?'

'I believe, as I've said, that Josie's illness is serious. It's possible she could become so weak she will have to pass away, just as her sister did. But I believe there's a way for her to become well again that the adults haven't yet considered. I believe also that the situation is now urgent and we can't keep waiting. Even if it seems rude, and taking privacy, it's perhaps time to be active. I came here today, of course, because of my important errand. But I was also hoping Rick would give me some useful advice.'

'You're super-intelligent and I'm an idiot kid who hasn't even been lifted. But okay. If you want, I'll try and give you advice. Fire away.'

'I wish to go across the fields to Mr McBain's barn. I think Rick has been there at least once. Josie told me about it.'

'You mean that barn over there? We did go there once when we were pretty young still. Before she got ill. I've been there other times since, just on my own. It's nothing special. A place to sit in the shade if you happen to be taking a walk out there. How's that going to help Josie?'

'I shouldn't confide just now, in case it's necessarily a secret. I may even be taking things too far simply by going to Mr McBain's barn. But I feel I must now try.'

'You want to speak to Mr McBain? About Josie's health? You'd be lucky to run into him out there. He lives five miles away on his main spread. Hardly ever comes around here these days.'

'It wasn't Mr McBain I wished to talk to. But please, I mustn't confide or we'll risk the special help Josie may yet receive. All I wish from Rick is some useful advice.' I turned myself until we were both looking out of the wide window. 'Please tell me. Is there an informal trail through the grass that will take me to the barn, like the one that brought me here to Rick's house?'

He rose to his feet and walked to the window. 'There's a path of sorts. It's easier some days than others. As you said yourself, it's informal. No one keeps it specially cleared or anything. Sometimes you go that way and everything's overgrown. But if one path's blocked or soaked, you can usually find another. There's always some way through, even in the winter.' He was suddenly looking me up and down, as if regarding me in earnest for the first time. 'I don't know much about AFs. So I don't know how hard it'll be for you. If you want, I could come with you. If it's really going to help Josie, though we're not even speaking just now, I'd be pleased to help.'

'That's very kind of Rick. But I think I'd better go alone. As I say, there's a possibility . . .'

'Oh God . . .' Rick suddenly turned and moved towards the door.

I'd already been aware of the footsteps moving within the building, but now they were out in the hallway. Then Miss Helen – though I didn't yet know her name – came into the room. Her gaze moved all around her, but she appeared not to notice me. She had a light coat around her shoulders – the sort office workers wear outdoors – into which she hadn't yet put her arms, and she clutched at it to stop it slipping as she strode to a wooden trunk under the window ledge.

'Where could it be? How silly of me.' She raised the trunk lid and began to go through its contents.

'Mum, what are you looking for?'

Rick sounded annoyed, as if his mother had broken a rule. He came and stood beside me, and we both watched Miss Helen bending over the box.

'I know, I know,' she said. 'We have a visitor. I'll attend in just one moment.'

When she straightened to face us, she was holding a shoe, its companion dangling from it on a piece of tangled shoelace.

'I'm sorry,' she said, now looking directly at me. 'I have dreadful manners. Welcome.'

'Thank you.'

'One never knows how to greet a guest like you. After all, are you a guest at all? Or do I treat you like a vacuum cleaner? I suppose I did as much just now. I'm sorry.'

'Mum,' Rick said quietly.

'Don't fuss, darling. Let me get to know our new visitor in my own way.'

The shoe that had been dangling dropped into the trunk of its own weight. Miss Helen stared at it, the other shoe still in her hand. I saw Rick was becoming increasingly uncomfortable, and I wanted to leave to give privacy, but Miss Helen then went on speaking to me.

'I know who you are. Josie's little companion. What a great success you've been! I've heard all about it from Chrissie. She comes here quite often, you know. Doesn't she, Rick? Won't you sit down?'

'You're very kind. But I feel I should be returning.'

'Not on my account, I hope. I came down looking forward to a nice chat.'

'Mum, Klara has responsibilities. And you're probably still tired.'

'I'm feeling fine, thank you, darling.' Then to me, she said: 'Apparently I wasn't at my best last night. Now, Klara. I expect you're curious about me. Chrissie says you're curious about everything. If so, you must have noticed that I'm English. Are

145

you equipped to identify accents? Or perhaps you can see deep into me, right through to my genetics.'

'Mum, please.'

'English people often came into the store,' I said, smiling. 'So all the AFs became familiar with your way of speaking. We thought it very pleasant and Manager, the lady who looked after us, always encouraged us to learn from it.'

'The thought of all you robots receiving elocution lessons! How delightful!'

'Mum . . .'

'Speaking of lessons. Klara. Your name is Klara, isn't it? Speaking of lessons, there's an idea that's been brewing here in this household.'

'Mum. Definitely no. Klara isn't interested in . . .'

'Let me speak, darling. Here she is in person, so let's seize our chance. I must say, darling, you've developed a tendency these days to rule the roost. It's most irritating. Klara, are you willing to listen to our idea?'

'Of course.'

Rick began to walk away as if to leave the room in disgust. But he stopped at the doorway, so that from where I was standing, I could see just a part of his back and the rear of his elbows.

'I'm not party to this,' he called out, as though to someone in the hallway.

Miss Helen smiled at me, then sat down on the sofa Rick had occupied earlier. She adjusted her light coat with one hand, her shoe still in the other.

'Rick used to go to a school, you know. I mean a real, old-fashioned one. It was rather lawless, but he made some nice friends there. Didn't you, dear?'

'I'm not participating.'

146

'Then why are you still hovering there like that? You do look odd, darling. Do either leave or stay.'

Rick didn't move, keeping his back to us, his shoulder now leaning on the doorframe.

'Well, the long and short of it is that Rick left the school to take up home tutoring like all the smarter children. But then, well, as you may already know, things grew complicated.'

Miss Helen became suddenly silent and stared past my shoulder. I thought she'd seen something through the wide window behind me, and was about to turn, when she said:

'There's nothing out there, Klara. I was just lost in thought. Recalling an incident. I get that way at times. Rick will tell you. I require someone to give me a little nudge when I get like that.'

'Mum, for God's sake . . .'

'Where were we? Ah yes, so the plan was for Rick to be home-tutored by screen professors like all the other smart children. But of course, you probably know, it all became complicated. And here we are. Darling, would you like to tell the tale from here? No? Well, the long and short of it. Even though Rick was never lifted, there still remains one decent option for him. Atlas Brookings takes a small number of unlifted students. The only proper college that will still do so. They believe in the principle and thank heavens for that. Now there are only a few such places available each year, so naturally the competition is savage. But Rick is clever and if he applied himself, and perhaps received just a little expert guidance, the sort I can't give him, he has a good chance. Oh yes you do, darling! Don't shake your head! But the long and short of it is we can't find screen tutors for him. They're either members of TWE, which forbids its members to take unlifted students, or else they're bandits demanding ridiculous fees which we of course are in no position to offer. But then we heard you'd arrived next door, and I had a marvelous idea.'

'Mum! I mean it. We're not going any further with this!' Rick came back into the room, striding towards his mother as if to pick her up and carry her off.

'Very well, darling, if you feel so strongly, we shan't continue.'

Rick had now come right up to the sofa and was glaring down at Miss Helen. She adjusted her posture slightly so that she could go on looking at me past him.

'Just now, Klara, when I appeared to be in a dream. It wasn't any dream, you know. I was looking out there' – she pointed the shoe behind me – 'and I was recalling. Turn and look all you like, I assure you there's nothing there just now. But once, some time ago, I was looking out there and I did see something.'

'Mum,' Rick said again, but now that Miss Helen had changed topic, his voice had lost urgency. He half turned to me, stepping back so he was no longer obstructing his mother's view.

'It was a nice day,' Miss Helen was saying. 'Around four in the afternoon. I called Rick and he came and he saw it too, didn't you, dear? Though he claimed he was too late.'

'It could have been anything,' Rick said. 'Anything at all.'

'What I saw was Chrissie, Josie's mother, that is. I saw her come out of the grass, just over there, holding someone by the arm. I'm explaining myself rather poorly. What I mean is, it was as if this other person had been trying to run away, and Chrissie had been after her. And she'd caught hold of her, but hadn't been able quite to stop her. So they'd both of them tumbled out, so to speak. Just over there, out from the grass onto our land.'

'Mum wasn't perhaps in the best condition that day to see things accurately.'

148

'I was able to see perfectly well. Rick doesn't like this story, so he tries to insinuate all kinds of things.'

'Do you mean,' I asked, 'that you saw Josie's mother come out of the grass with a child? One other than Josie?'

'Chrissie was trying to hold back this person and then she did manage to impose some control. Just out there. Chrissie had both arms around the girl. Rick got here in time to see that part. Then they both vanished back into the grass.'

'It could have been anyone.' Rick, now more relaxed, sat down beside his mother, and he too looked past me out of the window. 'Okay, one was Josie's mum. I'll allow that. But the other one . . .'

'The other one looked like Sal,' Miss Helen said. 'Josie's sister. That's why I called Rick. This being a good two years *after* Sal is supposed to have died.'

Rick laughed, and putting his arm around her shoulders, squeezed his mother affectionately, tilting her light coat. 'Mum has some weird theories. Like one about Sal still living in that house, hiding in some cupboard.'

'I didn't say that, Rick. I've never suggested such a thing seriously. Sal passed away, it was a great tragedy, and we shan't play foolish games with her memory. What I'm saying is that the person I saw, trying to run away from Chrissie, *looked like* Sal. That was all I said.'

'But this is such a strange story,' I said.

'I was just thinking, Klara,' Rick said, 'Josie might be wondering what's happened to you.'

'Ah, but our little friend can't go yet,' Miss Helen said. 'I've just remembered what we were discussing. We were discussing Rick's education.'

'No, Mum, that's enough!'

'But darling, Klara's here and I mean to talk to her about this. And what do we have here?' Miss Helen had noticed Josie's picture, which Rick had left on the sofa, face down on the envelope.

'That's enough!' Before Miss Helen could reach it, Rick had snatched up the picture and risen quickly.

'There you go again, darling. Trying to rule the roost. You must stop it.'

With his back to Miss Helen to shield what he was doing, he put Josie's picture back into the envelope with some care. Then he walked out of the room, this time not stopping at the threshold. We heard his firm strides in the hallway, the front door opening, then slamming shut.

'A little air will do him good,' Miss Helen said. 'He gets cooped up. And now he's even stopped going to visit Josie.'

She was again looking past me out of the wide window, and this time when I turned, I saw Rick's figure outside on the boards, leaning on the rail where the plank stairs descended from the platform. He was gazing out over the fields, the Sun's pattern over him. The wind was disturbing his hair, but he remained quite still.

Miss Helen rose from the sofa and came a few steps towards me until we were side by side before the window. She was taller than the Mother by two inches. However, when she was standing, she didn't do so in the upright way the Mother did, but with a gentle curve forward, as if she, like the tall grass outside, was being pushed by the wind. She wasn't at that moment partitioned at all, and in the window light, I could see the tiny white hairs around her chin.

'I didn't introduce myself properly,' she said. 'Please call me Helen. My manners have been awful.'

'Not at all. You've been very kind. But I'm afraid my coming may have caused friction.'

'Oh, but there's always friction. Incidentally, before you ask. The answer is yes. I do miss England. In particular I miss the hedges. In England, the part of it I'm from anyway, you can see green all around you, and always divided by hedges. Hedges, hedges everywhere. So ordered. Now look out there. It just goes on and on. I suppose there are fences somewhere in the midst of it all, but who can tell?'

She became quiet, so I said: 'I believe there are indeed fences. It's really three separate fields, fences dividing them.'

'You can tear down a fence in a moment,' she said. 'Then put up another somewhere else. Change the entire configuration of the land in a day or two. A land of fences is so temporary. You can change things as easily as a stage set. I used to act, you know. Sometimes in decent theaters. Wretched theaters too. Fences, what are they? Stage design. That's the nice thing about England. Hedges give a sense of history properly set down in the land. When I was acting, I never forgot my lines. My fellow actors did forget all the time. They weren't much good on the whole. But I never forgot. Not a single line. I've often thought over the years to ask Chrissie about what I saw. She comes to visit from time to time and we always have a good chat. I've often thought about asking her, but then I stop myself. I think, no, better not to. What business is it of mine anyway?'

'I believe Rick's mother was just now wishing to discuss Rick's education.'

'Please call me Helen. Yes, that was it. As you see, Rick is reluctant even to raise the topic. About getting you to help, I mean. I suppose I should really ask Chrissie about it first. Or even Josie. I've no idea. It's so unclear, the etiquette. If one was borrowing a vacuum cleaner . . . But it's not like that, I know. You must forgive me. What dreadful manners. All Rick needs is a little guidance. I've bought the best textbooks for him. They're from an era before children were lifted and they're just right for him. But they all assume there's some sort of tutor lurking around. He has a genuine ability, especially with physics, engineering, that sort of thing, but then he comes across something he doesn't understand, there's no one to explain, and that's when he gets discouraged. I used to tell him to ask Josie, but of course he gets so cross about that.'

'So Miss Helen wishes me to help Rick with his textbooks?'

'Just an idea. Those textbooks would be child's play for you. It's just to get him through these exams. You see, he really does need to get into Atlas Brookings. It's his only chance. I wasn't suggesting anything more long-term. I suppose I really should ask Chrissie first.'

'If Rick could go to the Atlas Brookings college that would be a good thing. In which case, yes, I'd very much like to assist Rick, so long as it didn't disturb at all my looking after Josie. Perhaps if Rick resumed his visits, he could sometimes bring his books with him.'

I could see my response hadn't satisfied Miss Helen. She went on looking at Rick out on the board platform – he hadn't moved at all – then said:

'I suppose if I'm honest, that's not the true issue. Yes, some tutoring would help. But the real obstacle is that for the moment, the way things stand, *Rick doesn't wish to try*. If only he'd give it his all, then I know he has such a chance. Especially, you see, since I have a secret weapon to help him. To give him a little extra push, this being Atlas Brookings. But he won't try, not properly. He won't try because of me.'

152

'Because of you?'

'He's convinced himself he can't go away and leave me here. Of course, I can manage perfectly well. But he likes to pretend I'm quite helpless, likely to get up to all sorts of mischief in his absence.'

'Is the Atlas Brookings college far away?'

'A day's drive. But distance is beside the point. He's convinced an hour is about as much as he can leave me on my own. Now how will he grow up and go out into the world if he can't leave me for more than an hour at a time?'

Outside, Rick began to step down the boards towards the grass. He did so slowly, as if daydreaming, and I could tell from the way he kept one arm stiffly to his chest that he was still holding Josie's drawing. As his head and shoulders descended out of view, Miss Helen went on:

'What I really wished to ask you, Klara. The real request, the deeper one. Would you ask Josie to try and persuade Rick? She's the one person who might change his stance. He's very stubborn, you see, and also – I suspect this – rather afraid. And who can blame him? He knows the world out there won't be easy. But Josie's the one capable of getting him to see this differently. Will you speak to her? I know you have a big influence on her. Would you do this for me? Mention it to her not just the once, but over and over, so she'll exert a real pressure on him?'

'Of course I'd be pleased to do so. But I believe Josie has already spoken to Rick in just these terms. The current rift between them may in fact have to do with Josie expressing herself too forcefully on this very topic.'

'That's interesting to know. If what you say is correct, then it's more important than ever, what I'm asking you. Josie may feel she has to relent in order for them to make up. She may come to feel she was wrong ever to take the attitude she did. Well, you must speak with her. Tell her she must persevere, never mind what temper tantrums he throws. Is something the matter, dear?'

'I'm sorry. It's just that I'm a little surprised.'

'Oh? Why are you surprised, dear?'

'Well, I . . . Frankly, I'm surprised because Miss Helen's request concerning Rick appears very sincere. I'm surprised someone would desire so much a path that would leave her in loneliness.'

'And that's what surprises you?'

'Yes. Until recently, I didn't think that humans could choose loneliness. That there were sometimes forces more powerful than the wish to avoid loneliness.'

Miss Helen smiled. 'You really are a sweet one. You don't say as much, but I can tell what you're thinking. A mother's love for her son. Such a noble thing, to override the dread of loneliness. And you might not be wrong. But let me tell you, there are all kinds of other very good reasons why, in a life like mine, one might prefer loneliness. I've often made such a choice in the past. I did so, for instance, rather than stay with Rick's father. *Late* father, very sadly, though Rick has no memory of him. Even so, he was for a while my husband, and not an entirely useless one at that. It's thanks to him we're able to get by this way, even if we don't exactly live in splendor. Here's Rick coming back again. Oh, he's not. He wishes to stay out there and sulk further.'

Indeed, Rick had come walking up the plank steps and glanced towards the house, but had then sat down on the top step, his back turned to us once more.

'I must return to Josie,' I said then. 'It was very kind of Miss

Helen to take me into her confidence. I'll do as you ask and speak with Josie.'

'And speak with her repeatedly. This is Rick's only chance. And as I say, I have a secret weapon. A contact. Perhaps the next time Chrissie takes Josie into the city, perhaps when she next sits for her portrait, Rick and I could cadge a ride. Then Rick could meet my secret weapon, hopefully impress him. Chrissie and I have already spoken about it. But all of this is useless until Rick changes his attitude.'

'I understand. Then goodbye. I must go now.'

When I stepped out onto the platform, I could feel the wind blowing through the gaps of the planks more strongly than before. The fields were no longer divided into boxes, so I could see a single clear picture all the way to the horizon. Despite the altered angles, Mr McBain's barn was where I expected it to be, though now a slightly changed shape to the one from Josie's rear window.

I walked past the cobweb refrigerator to the top plank where Rick was seated. I thought he might still be angry and ignore me, but he looked up with gentle eyes.

'I'm sorry if my visit caused friction,' I said.

'Hardly your fault. It often gets like that.'

We both looked at the fields before us, and I realized after a moment that his gaze, like mine, was on Mr McBain's barn.

'You were saying something,' he said. 'Before Mum came down. You were saying how you wanted to go out to that barn for some reason.'

'Yes. And it will have to be in the evening. It's essential to time such a trip accurately.'

'And you're sure you don't want me to go with you?'

'It's very kind of Rick. But if there are informal trails leading

155

to Mr McBain's barn, it's best I go alone. It's important I don't take anything for granted.'

'Okay. If you say so.' He was squinting up at me, partly on account of the Sun's pattern on his face, but also, I realized, because he was once again studying me carefully, perhaps assessing my ability to make such a journey. 'Look,' he said eventually. 'I don't really understand what this is about. But if it's going to help Josie to get better, then, well, good luck.'

'Thank you. Now I must return to the house.'

'You know, I've been thinking about it,' he said. 'Perhaps you could tell Josie I really liked her picture. That I was grateful. And that if it's okay with her, I'd like to come over soon and tell her that myself.'

'Josie will be so happy when she hears.'

'Maybe tomorrow even.'

'Yes, of course. Well then, goodbye. It was a very interesting trip for me. Thank you for your useful advice.'

'See you, Klara. Go carefully.'

■

The timing of my journey to Mr McBain's barn, as I'd told Rick, was crucial, and when I crossed the loose stones towards the picture frame gate for the second time that day, a fear came into my mind that I'd miscalculated. The Sun was already low before me – and I couldn't assume the second and third fields would be as easy to navigate as the first.

My journey began reassuringly, the informal trail to Rick's house similar to what it had been in the morning. This time I had both hands to push away the grass, and as I did so, evening insects flew up. I saw more insects hovering before me in the air, nervously exchanging positions, but unwilling to abandon their friendly clusters.

My fear of not reaching Mr McBain's barn in time caused me to give only a brief glance at Rick's house as I passed it, and then I was further along the informal trail, beyond any point I'd been. I went through another picture frame gate, then the grass became too tall to see the barn any more. The field became partitioned into boxes, some larger than others, and I pressed on, conscious of the contrasting atmospheres between one box and another. One moment the grass would be soft and yielding, the ground easy to tread; then I'd cross a boundary and everything would darken, the grass would resist my pushes, and there would be strange noises around me, making me fearful that I'd made a serious miscalculation, that there was no justifiable reason to disturb his privacy in the manner I was hoping to do, that my efforts would have gravely negative consequences for Josie. While crossing one particularly unkind box, I heard around me the cries of an animal in pain, and a picture came into my mind of Rosa, sitting on the rough ground somewhere outdoors, little pieces of metal scattered around her, as she reached out both hands to grasp one of her legs stretched out stiffly before her. The image was in my mind for only a second, but the animal carried on making its noise, and I felt the ground collapsing beneath me. I remembered the terrible bull on the walk up to Morgan's Falls, and how in all probability it had emerged from beneath the ground, and for a brief moment, I even thought the Sun wasn't kind at all, and this was the true reason for Josie's worsening condition. Even in this confusion, I was convinced that if I could only pull myself through into a kinder box, I'd become safe. I'd also been aware of a voice calling to me, and I now spotted an object – shaped like one of the overhaul men's traffic cones – placed in the grass a little ahead of me. The voice was coming from behind this cone, and when I tried to move towards it, I realized it was in fact two cones, one inserted into the other, allowing the higher one to perform a rocking motion, perhaps to draw the attention of passers-by.

'Klara! Come on! Over here!'

I came closer, then realized these weren't cones at all, but Rick, holding back the grass with one hand and reaching the other towards me. Now that I'd recognized him, I had even more incentive to move towards him, but my feet sank further, and I knew if I attempted another step I'd lose balance and fall deep into the ground. I knew too that despite Rick appearing to be within touching distance, he was not in reality so near because of the fierce border separating our boxes. Even so, he continued to reach out towards me, and where his arm crossed into my box, it appeared elongated and bent.

'Klara, come on!'

But I'd accepted now that I would soon fall into the ground, that the Sun was angry with me, and perhaps unkind, and that Josie was disappointed with me. I began to lose orientation, even as Rick's arm grew longer and more crooked till it touched me. It stopped me falling, and my feet steadied a little.

'Okay, Klara. This way.'

He was guiding – almost carrying – me across, and then I was in a kind box, the Sun's generous pattern over me, and my thoughts found order once more.

'Thank you. Thank you for coming to help.'

'I saw you from my window. Are you okay?'

'Yes, everything is fine again. The field posed more problems than I expected.'

'I suppose these little ditches can get tricky. I have to say, from up there, you looked like one of those flies that buzz around blindly on the window pane. But that's unkind, I'm sorry.'

I smiled and said: 'I feel so foolish.' Then remembering, I looked up to check the Sun's position. 'This journey is so important,' I said, looking at him again. 'But I estimated incorrectly and now I won't get there in time.'

The grass was still too high to see Mr McBain's barn in the distance, but Rick was looking straight in its direction, a hand shielding his eyes, and it occurred to me he was tall enough to see it.

'I should have left the house earlier,' I said, 'regardless of the awkwardness when I returned. But I was waiting till Josie fell asleep, and to allow Melania Housekeeper to believe I was going on another errand to Rick's house. I thought there'd be sufficient time, but the fields were more complex than I'd imagined.'

Rick was still looking towards Mr McBain's barn. 'You keep saying you won't get there in time,' he said. 'But when exactly did you want to be there?'

'Just as the Sun is arriving at Mr McBain's barn. But before he disappears for his rest.'

'Look, I don't understand any of this. And I appreciate you can't let me in on it for whatever reason. But if you want, I'll take you there.'

'That's very kind. But even with Rick guiding, I believe it's now too late.'

'I wouldn't guide you. I'll carry you. Piggyback. We've got a way to go yet, but if we hurry, I think we can make it.'

'You'd do that?'

'You keep saying it's important. Important for Josie. So yes, I'd like to help. This is over my head, but then I'm used to that. If we're going, we have to hurry.'

He turned and lowered himself into a crouching position. I understood I was to climb on his back, and immediately I did so – clasping my arms and legs around him – he began to move.

■

Now I was higher, I could see better the evening sky, and the roof of Mr McBain's barn ahead of us. Rick moved confidently, crashing through the grass, and since his arms were occupied holding me, most of the impact was taken by his head and shoulders. I felt sorry about this, and that there was so little I could do myself to push back the grass.

Then I looked up past Rick's head and saw that the sky had become divided into segments of irregular shape. Some segments were glowing orange or pink, while others showed pieces of the night sky, sections of the moon visible at a corner or edge. As Rick moved forward, the segments kept overlapping and displacing one another, even as we passed through another picture frame gate. After that the grass, instead of being delicate and waving, came towards us as flat shapes, possibly made from heavy board such as the sort used for street advertising, and I feared they would cause Rick injury as he plunged into them. Then the sky and the field were no longer in segments, but one broad picture, and Mr McBain's barn was looming before us.

The uneasy thought that had been growing in my mind could now no longer be set aside. Even before Rick had come to my aid, I'd started to wonder if the Sun's resting place really was inside the barn itself. Of course, I'd been the one, not Josie, who'd first suggested such a thing, that time we'd gazed out together from the rear window, so any such error was entirely my own. Certainly, there was no question of Josie having misled me at any stage. Even so, it was a discouraging thought that the Sun was about to descend not into the place I was making such an effort to reach, but somewhere further away still.

What I now observed obliged me to accept that my fear was justified. Mr McBain's barn was unlike any building I'd seen. It resembled the outer shell of a house the men hadn't yet finished. There was a gray roof with a facing triangle in the usual manner, supported to the left and right by walls of a darker shade. But apart from the sections enclosing the roof, the structure had no walls front or rear. The wind, I knew, was even then blowing right the way through with barely any obstruction. And the Sun, I saw, had now fallen behind the barn's structure, and was sending his rays through the rear opening back out to us as we approached.

We'd meanwhile come into a clearing not unlike the one upon which Rick's house was built. There was grass here, but it had been cut, perhaps by Mr McBain himself, to just above feet level. The cutting had been performed skillfully, so that a pattern could be seen weaving towards the barn entrance, and because the Sun was now shining straight through the barn, its shadow was spreading across the grass towards us.

Though it seemed discourteous, I signaled urgently to Rick by tightening my arms and legs. 'Please stop!' I whispered into his ear. 'Stop! Please let me down!'

He lowered me carefully, and we both gazed at the scene before us. Although I now had to accept the barn couldn't be the Sun's actual resting place, I allowed myself an encouraging possibility: that regardless of where the Sun ultimately settled, Mr McBain's barn was a place he made a point of calling at last thing each evening, just as Josie always visited her en suite before retiring to bed.

'I'm so grateful,' I said, keeping my voice low, despite the outdoor acoustics. 'But from here, it's best Rick leaves me and I go alone.'

'Whatever you say. If you like, I'll wait here for you. How long do you suppose you'll be?'

'It's best Rick returns to his house. Miss Helen will worry otherwise.'

'Mum will be fine. I think I'd better wait. Remember how it was going before I came on the scene? And your journey back will probably be in the dark.'

'I'll have to manage. Rick has been too kind already. And it's best I enter alone. As it is, standing here like this, it might already be stealing too much privacy.'

Rick looked again at Mr McBain's barn, then shrugged. 'Okay. I'll leave you to it. Whatever this is you have to do.'

'Thank you.'

'Good luck, Klara. I mean it.'

He turned and walked back into the tall grass, and soon I could no longer see him.

Once alone, I began to place my thoughts fully on the task before me. It occurred to me that if a passer-by had stood directly before the barn even five minutes earlier, they would have been able to see not only the evening sky through the rear, and the continuation of the field, but also a lot more of the barn's shadowy interior. But now, with the Sun's rays coming straight towards me, I could make out only some blurred box-like shapes stacked one on top of the other. And the thought returned to me with more certainty than ever that, even accounting for the Sun's great generosity, what I was about to do carried risk, and would require all my concentration. I heard behind me the breeze in the grass and the cries of distant birds, and ordering my thoughts, I walked across the cut grass towards Mr McBain's barn.

■

The interior was filled with orange light. There were particles of hay drifting in the air like evening insects, and his patterns were falling all across the barn's wooden floor. When I glanced behind me my own shadow looked like a tall thin tree ready to break in the wind.

There were some curious features about my surroundings. On first entering the barn, I'd encountered such sharply contrasting divisions of brightness and shadow that my sight had taken a few moments to adjust. Nevertheless, I'd established quickly that the blocks of hay, whose shapes I'd noted from outside, were now to my left, stacked one on top of the other to form a kind of platform – one as tall as my shoulders – upon which passers-by could climb or even lie down and rest. But the hay blocks had been stacked so as to allow a gap between them and the wall behind – perhaps so that Mr McBain could gain access from that side. Peering over the hay platform, I now saw, fixed to this wall and running all along it, the Red Shelves from our store, complete with the ceramic coffee cups displayed upside down and in a line.

On my other side – to my right – where the shadows were at their deepest, I saw a section of wall almost identical to the front alcove. In fact I felt sure that if I went over to it, I'd discover amidst the shadows an AF standing there proudly at the spot where – no matter what else was said – customers were most likely to look first.

Also on my right, though not as far over as the alcove, was the only item in the barn that could be counted as furniture: a small metal foldaway chair, now in its open position, at present bisected by a diagonal separating its brightly lit area from its shadowy one. This chair too was reminiscent of the chairs Manager kept in the back room and occasionally unfolded in the store, except that its paint had started to flake, revealing patches of metal underneath.

I decided, after some reflection, that it wouldn't be discourteous to sit down on this chair while waiting for the Sun. When I did so, I fully expected to see a revised picture of my surroundings due to the altered angle, but was surprised to find that everything had instead become partitioned – and not just into the usual boxes, but into segments of irregular shape. Inside some segments I could see certain parts of Mr McBain's farming tools – a spade handle, the lower half of a metal ladder. In another segment was what I knew to be the mouths of two plastic buckets placed side by side, but owing perhaps to the difficult light conditions, they were presented simply as two intersecting ovals.

I knew the Sun was now very near me, and although I thought at times I should stand up, as when receiving a customer, something else suggested I would steal less privacy – and be less likely to cause annoyance – if I remained seated. So I aligned my own shape as closely as I could with that of the foldaway chair and waited. The Sun's shafts became more pronounced, and more orange, and I even thought these shafts might be causing pieces of hay to come loose from their blocks and float into the air, for there were now many more drifting particles in front of me.

Then the thought came to me that if I was correct, and the Sun was now passing through Mr McBain's barn on his way to his real resting place, I couldn't afford to be overly polite. I'd have to seize my chance boldly, or all my efforts – and Rick's help – would come to nothing. So I gathered my thoughts and began to speak. I didn't actually say the words out loud, for I knew the Sun had no need of words as such. But I wished to be as clear as possible, so I formed the words, or something close to them, quickly and quietly in my mind.

'Please make Josie better. Just as you did Beggar Man.'

I raised my head a little and saw, alongside the fragments of farming tools and blocks of hay, a section of a traffic signal, and part of the wing from one of Rick's drone birds, and I remembered Manager's voice saying, 'That's not going to be possible,' and Boy AF Rex saying, 'You're so selfish, Klara.' And I said:

'But Josie's still a child and she's done nothing unkind.'

And I remembered the Mother's eyes scrutinizing me across the picnic bench at Morgan's Falls, and the bull, staring angrily, as though I'd no right to be passing before his field, and I realized I may have angered the Sun by intruding in this way, just when he was needing his rest. I formed an apology in my mind, but the shadows were now even longer, so that were I to spread my fingers out before me, I knew their shadows would reach right the way back to the entrance of the barn. And it was clear the Sun was unwilling to make any promise about Josie, because for all his kindness, he wasn't yet able to see Josie separately from the other humans, some of whom had angered him very much on account of their Pollution and inconsideration, and I suddenly felt foolish to have come to this place to make such a request. The barn filled even more intensely with orange light, and I saw again Rosa, on the hard ground wearing an expression of pain, reaching forward to touch her outstretched leg. I bowed my head right down and curled myself into the smallest shape I could within the shape of the foldaway chair, but then remembered again how any chance to make an appeal would be fleeting, and so, finding courage, I said in almost-words, forcing them through my mind in a split moment:

'I understand how forward and rude I've been to come here. The Sun has every right to be angry, and I fully understand your refusal even to consider my request. Even so, because of your great kindness, I thought I might ask you to delay your journey for one more instant. To listen to one more proposal. Supposing I could do something special to please you. Something to make you particularly happy. If I could achieve such a thing, then would you consider, in return, showing special kindness to Josie? Just as you did that time for Beggar Man and his dog?'

As these words moved through my mind, something distinctly changed around me. The red glow inside the barn was still dense, but now had an almost gentle aspect – so much so that the various segments into which my surroundings were still partitioned appeared to be drifting amidst the Sun's last rays. I spotted the lower half of the Glass Display Trolley – I recognized its castors – rising slowly until it became obscured behind a neighboring segment, and though I raised my head and looked all around me, I could no longer see any trace at all of the terrible bull. I knew then that I'd gained a vital advantage, but couldn't waste even a tiny moment, and so pressed on, no longer forming half-words, for I knew I didn't have the time.

'I know how much the Sun dislikes Pollution. How much it saddens and angers you. Well, I've seen and identified the machine that creates it. Supposing I were able somehow to find this machine and destroy it. To put an end to its Pollution. Would you then consider, in return, giving your special help to Josie?'

The inside of the barn was getting darker, but it was a friendly darkness, and soon the segments had gone, leaving the interior no longer partitioned. I knew the Sun had moved on, and rising from the foldaway chair, I walked for the first time over to the back opening of Mr McBain's barn. I saw then how the field continued into the mid-distance until it met a line of trees – a kind of soft fence – and behind it, the Sun, tired and no longer intense, was sinking into the ground. The sky was turning into night, with stars visible, and I could tell that the Sun was smiling towards me kindly as he went down for his rest.

Out of gratitude and respect, I continued to stand at the back opening until his last glow had vanished into the ground. Then I walked through the dark interior of Mr McBain's barn, leaving the same way I'd come.

■

The tall grass moved gently around me as I re-entered it. Getting across the fields in the darkness was a daunting prospect, but I was so encouraged by what had just occurred, I felt hardly any fear. Even so, with the unevenness of the ground reminding me of the dangers in front of me, I was pleased to hear suddenly Rick's voice somewhere close by.

'Is that you, Klara?'

'Where are you?'

'Over this way. To your right. I ignored your advice about going straight home.'

I moved towards the voice, the grass fell away and I found myself in a clearing. It was as though a vacuum cleaner had created it – a small circular area in which the grass was again shoe height and the night sky above had a curving slice of the moon. Rick was sitting there, apparently on the ground, but when I came nearer, I saw he was seated on a large stone that was mostly submerged into the earth. He looked calm and smiled at me.

'Thank you for waiting,' I said.

'Just self-interest. Suppose you'd got stuck out here all night and got damaged. I'd be in deep shit then for bringing you out here.'

'I think Rick waited out of kindness. I'm very grateful.'

'Did you find what you went in there for?'

'Oh yes. At least, I believe so. And I believe there's now reason for hope. Hope for Josie. Hope that she'll get better. But first I must perform a task.'

'What kind of task? Perhaps I can help with it.'

'I'm sorry, I'm not able to discuss this matter with Rick. Tonight I believe an understanding was achieved. A contract, if you like. But it might be jeopardized if I speak about it freely.'

'Okay. I don't want to put anything at risk. Still, if there's anything you think I could do . . .'

'If I may speak frankly. The most important thing Rick can do is to try hard to go to the Atlas Brookings college. Then Josie and Rick can remain side by side and the wishes expressed in the kind picture will remain possible.'

'God, Klara, it's obvious Mum's been working on you. She makes it sound so easy. But you've no idea what it takes for someone like me to get into a place like that. And even if I did, what happens to Mum? I just leave her out here on her own?'

'Miss Helen may be stronger than Rick supposes. And even if Rick isn't lifted, he has special talents. If he tried very hard, I believe he could be accepted by the Atlas Brookings college. Besides, Miss Helen has said she has a secret weapon to assist him.'

'Her secret weapon? Some creep she knows who helps run

that place. An old flame of hers. I don't want any part of it. Look, Klara, we should be getting back.'

'You're right. We've been out a long time. Miss Helen might be concerned. And if I could return before Josie's mother comes in, that would avoid awkward questions.'

■

The next day, when the doorbell rang towards the middle of the morning, Josie seemed to guess who it was and, leaving her bed, hurried out onto the landing. I followed her, and as Rick stepped past Melania Housekeeper into the hall, Josie turned to me with an excited smile. But then she made her expression completely blank as she went to the top of the staircase.

'Hey, Melania,' she called down. 'Do you know who this weird guy is?'

'Hello, Josie.' Rick, looking up at us, had on a cautious smile. 'I heard this rumor we might be friends again.'

Josie seated herself on the top step, and though I was behind her, I knew she now had on her kindest smile.

'Oh really? That's strange. Wonder who put that out there.'

Rick's own smile became more confident. 'Just gossip, I suppose. By the way, I really liked that picture. I put it in a frame last night.'

'Yeah? One of those frames you make yourself?'

'To be honest, I used one of Mum's old ones. There are so many lying around. I took out a picture of a zebra and put yours in there instead.'

'Great swap.'

Melania Housekeeper had walked away into the kitchen, and Rick and Josie went on grinning at each other from either end of the staircase. Then Josie must have given a signal, for they both moved quickly at once, she rising to her feet, he reaching for the banister.

As they went together into the bedroom, I remembered Melania Housekeeper's instruction from before and followed them in. And for a while after that, it was like the old days, with me on the Button Couch facing the rear window, Rick and Josie behind me, laughing about silly things. At one point I heard Josie say:

'Hey Rick. I'm wondering if this is the correct way you hold one of these.' In the reflection I saw her holding up a table knife left behind from breakfast. 'Or is it more like this?'

'How would *I* know?'

'I thought you might, being English and all. My chemistry professor said you should hold it *this* way. But what does she know?'

'What would I know either? And why do you keep saying I'm English? I've never actually lived there, you know that.'

'It was you yourself, Rick. Two, three years ago? You kept insisting how English you were.'

'I did? Must have been a phase.'

'Oh yeah, went on for months. You were like, pray this, pardon me that. That's why I thought you might know about the knife thing.'

'But why would an English person know any more than anyone else?'

A few minutes later, I heard Rick moving around the bedroom, and he said:

'You know one reason I like this room so much? The place smells of you, Josie.'

'What? I can't believe you said that!'

'I meant in an entirely nice way.'

'Rick, that's so not what you can say to a girl!'

'I wouldn't say it to any girl. I'm just saying it to you.'

'Excuse me? So I'm not a girl any more?'

'Well, not *any* girl. What I'm trying to say, all I'm saying, is that I haven't been here for a while, and so I've forgotten some things about this room. The way it looks, the way it smells.'

'Jesus, that's so offensive, Rick.'

But there was laughter in her voice, and after a quiet moment, Rick said:

'At least we're not cross with each other any more. I'm glad about that.'

There was further quiet, then Josie said: 'Me too. I'm glad too.' Then she added: 'I'm sorry I kept saying stuff, about your mom and all. She's a good person and I didn't mean any of that. And I'm sorry about being sick all the time. Making you worry.'

I saw Rick, in the glass, take a step closer to Josie and put an arm around her. Then after a second, he put his other arm around her too. Josie let herself be held, though she didn't raise her own arms up in return, the way she did to the Mother when they said goodbye.

'This so you can smell me better?' she asked after a while.

Rick didn't reply to this, but he said: 'Klara? Are you there?'

When I turned, they'd pulled apart slightly and were both looking at me.

'Yes?'

'Maybe you should, you know. Give privacy, as you always say.'

'Oh yes.'

They watched as I came off the Button Couch and went past them. At the door, I turned and said:

'I always wanted to give privacy. It's just that there was concern about hanky-panky.' They both looked puzzled, so I went on: 'I was instructed to ensure against hanky-panky. That's why I always remained in the room, even during the bubble game.'

'Klara,' Josie said, 'Rick and I are not about to engage in sex, okay? We've got a few things to say to each other, that's all.'

'Yes, of course. Then I'll leave you.'

With that I walked out onto the landing, closing the door behind me.

■

Over the days that followed, I often thought about the Cootings Machine and how I might be able to find and destroy it. I experimented in my mind with various pretexts on which I could accompany the Mother into the city, and once there, be left to my own devices for a sufficient period, but none of these seemed at all convincing. Josie, noticing my frequent inattentiveness, would say something like: 'Klara, you're zoning out again. Maybe you're low on solar.' I even considered taking the Mother into my confidence, but rejected this option not only because of the danger of angering the Sun, but also because I felt the Mother would neither understand nor believe in the agreement I'd entered into. But then an opportunity presented itself without any initiative on my part.

One evening, an hour after the Sun had gone to rest, I was standing in the kitchen beside the refrigerator, listening to its comforting sounds. The ceiling lights hadn't been switched on, so I was there in the semi-light coming from the hallway. The Mother had returned late from her office not long before, and

I'd come down to the kitchen to allow her privacy with Josie up in the bedroom. After a time, her footsteps came down the staircase, then towards the kitchen. Her silhouette appeared in the doorway, making the kitchen even darker, and she said:

'Klara, I wanted to give you a heads up. After all, this involves you.'

'Yes?'

'Next Thursday, I've taken time off work. I'm going to drive Josie into town and we'll be staying overnight. We were just talking about it. Josie has an appointment.'

'An appointment?'

'As you know, Josie was in the process of getting her portrait done. The times she came by your store, that's why we were in town. There's been a long break on account of her health, but she's stronger now and so I want her to go in for another sitting. Mr Capaldi's been very patient and kept everything on hold.'

'I see. So will Josie be required to sit still for a long time?'

'Mr Capaldi's good at not tiring her. He's able to take photographs and work from those. Even so, he needs her to come in from time to time. I'm telling you this because I want you to accompany Josie on this trip. I think she'd like you with her.'

'Oh yes. I'd like that very much.'

The Mother stepped further into the kitchen and now I could see just one edge of her face illuminated by the hall light.

'I want you, Klara, to be with her when she goes in to see Mr Capaldi. In fact, Mr Capaldi is keen to meet you. He takes a special interest in AFs. You could call it his passion. That okay with you?'

'Of course. I'll look forward to meeting Mr Capaldi.'

'He may have a few questions for you. To do with his research. Because as I say, he's fascinated by AFs. You won't mind that?'

'No, of course not. And I believe a trip into the city would be good for Josie now she's a little stronger.'

'Good. Oh and we may well have passengers. In the car I mean. Our neighbors are needing a ride.'

'Rick and Miss Helen?'

'They have some business of their own in town and she doesn't drive any more. Don't worry, there's room enough for us all. You won't have to travel in the trunk.'

I heard more about this trip the following Sunday when not only Rick but his mother visited the house during the early part of the afternoon. I'd once more stepped onto the landing to give Rick and Josie privacy in the bedroom. Standing beside the banister rail, gazing down onto the hallway, I could hear the Mother's and Miss Helen's laughter coming from the kitchen. I couldn't hear their words well, except when one or the other exclaimed something loudly. Once, Miss Helen called out, 'Oh Chrissie, that's quite outrageous!' and laughed. A little later, I heard the Mother, also with laughter, say loudly: 'It's true, it's true, it's absolutely true!'

Because I couldn't hear many words, or see the Mother's expressions, I wasn't able to make a reliable estimate, but my impression was that the Mother was at that moment the most lacking in tension I'd witnessed since my arrival. I was trying to listen more closely when the bedroom door opened and Rick came out.

'Josie's in the bathroom,' he said, coming over to me. 'Thought it only good manners to come out here in the meantime.'

'Yes, that's considerate.'

He followed my gaze over the rail, then nodded down towards the adults' voices.

'They've always got on,' he said. 'A shame Mrs Arthur isn't

174

around more. It's so good for Mum, having someone to talk to like that. She always cheers up around Mrs Arthur. I do my best. But I can never get her to laugh that way. I suppose, me being her son, it's hard to relax.'

'Rick must be a wonderful companion for Miss Helen. But as you can see, if you weren't with her, she'd be able to find other companions to laugh and talk with.'

'I don't know. Maybe.' Then he said: 'Look, I've been thinking all this over. What you said the other night. And I've agreed now. I promised Mum I'll try. Try my best, my very best, to get into Atlas Brookings.'

'That's wonderful!'

He was now leaning over even more, perhaps trying to catch words, and I was concerned he might topple over because of his greater height. But then he straightened, resting both hands on the rail.

'I've even agreed to meet this . . . *man*,' he said, lowering his voice. 'Her old flame.'

'The secret weapon person?'

'Yeah, Mum's secret weapon. She reckons he can pull strings for me. I've even agreed to that.'

'But this might result in the best solution. The wishes in Josie's kind picture could come closer to reality.'

'Maybe they're talking about that down there right now. How I've come round to Mum's way of thinking after all this time. Maybe that's what they're finding so amusing.'

'I don't think they're laughing unkindly. I think Miss Helen must be happy because of Rick's promise. And hopeful.'

He was silent for a moment, listening to the voices below. Then he said: 'I think we're getting a lift into the city with Josie and Mrs Arthur.'

175

'Yes, I know. And I've been asked to come too.'

'Well, that's good. Then you and Josie can both give me moral support. Because I'm not looking forward to begging this character for help.'

Josie's voice suddenly called from the bedroom: 'Great! So everyone's deserted me!' Then as Rick turned back towards the door: 'Hey, Klara, you can come back in here too. It's okay. We're not performing any big sex acts.'

■

Two days later, I was to hear yet more about the trip to the city, and this time in a surprising way.

It was a rainy weekday with no visitors. Josie had gone into the Open Plan after lunch for an oblong tutorial, and I'd gone up to the bedroom. I was sitting on the floor, surrounded by magazines, when Melania Housekeeper appeared in the doorway. She stared down at me, her face neither kind nor frowning, and I thought she'd come to reprimand me for the times I'd left Rick and Josie unattended in the bedroom despite her warnings about hanky-panky. But she stepped further inside, then said in a kind of harsh whisper:

'AF. You wish help Miss Josie right?'

'Yes, of course.'

'Then you listen. Ma'am take Miss Josie city Thursday. I say I want go with them, Ma'am reply no. I say yes, Ma'am still say no. She say no because she see damn well I onto something. She say she want take AF instead. So you listen. You keep damn good eye Miss Josie in city. Hear me?'

'Yes, housekeeper.' I also spoke quietly, though there was no chance Josie could hear us. 'But please explain further. What is

176

it you're worried about?'

'Listen, AF. Ma'am take Miss Josie see Mr Capaldi. Portrait guy. That Mr Capaldi one creep son bitch. Ma'am say you good observe. Then you damn good observe Mr Son Bitch. You want help Miss Josie. We same side.' She glanced back at the door, though there were no sounds of Josie emerging from her lesson downstairs.

'But housekeeper, isn't Mr Capaldi just wishing to paint Josie's portrait?'

'Paint portrait fuck. AF, you watch close Mr Son Bitch or something bad happen Miss Josie.'

'But surely . . .' I lowered my voice even further. 'Surely the Mother would never . . .'

'Ma'am love Miss Josie. But Miss Sal die and mess Ma'am up bad. Get me, AF?'

'Yes. Then I'll observe very carefully as you say, especially around Mr Capaldi. But . . .'

'What you *but* about now, AF?'

'If Mr Capaldi is as you say. Will it be enough for me just to observe?'

The way Melania Housekeeper was staring down at me, a passer-by might have thought she was threatening me, but I now understood she was filled with fear.

'How fuck I know enough? I want go with Miss Josie, Ma'am say no way. Take AF instead. Can't figure it. So you stick close Miss Josie, specially when Mr Son Bitch around. You do best, AF. We same side.'

'Housekeeper,' I said. 'I have a plan, a special plan to help Josie. I'm not able to speak openly about it. But if I can go to the city with Josie and her mother, I may have the opportunity to carry it out.'

'Plan? Listen, AF. You make things worse, I fuck come dismantle you.'

'But if my plan works, Josie will become strong and well. She'll be able to go to college and become an adult. Unfortunately I'm not free to tell you more. But if I can get to the city, I'll have a chance.'

'Okay. Main thing, AF, you keep good eye Miss Josie in city Thursday. Hear me?'

'Yes, housekeeper.'

'And AF. Your big plan. If it make Miss Josie worse I come dismantle you. Shove you in garbage.'

'Housekeeper,' I said, smiling confidently at her for the first time since coming to the house, 'thank you for this talk and for your warning. And thank you for trusting me. I'll do everything I can to protect Josie.'

'Okay, AF. We same side.'

■

There was one further incident of note during this period before the trip to the city, and it was one that provided me with an important lesson. It occurred deep in the night when I was brought awake by Josie making a noise. The bedroom was dark, but because Josie disliked complete darkness, the blind covering the front window was one third raised, and the moon and stars were making patterns on the wall and floor. When I looked towards the bed, I saw Josie had created a mound shape there with her duvet, and a humming noise was coming from within it, as if she were trying to remember a tune and hadn't wished to disturb the rest of the house.

I moved closer to the mound shape, then when I was standing

over it, touched it gently. Immediately it erupted, the duvet disintegrating into the surrounding darkness, and the room became filled with Josie's sobbing.

'Josie, what's the matter?' I kept my voice low, but urgent. 'Has the pain come back?'

'No! No pain! But I want Mom! Get Mom! I need her here!'

Not only was her voice loud, it was as if it had been folded over onto itself, so that two versions of her voice were being sounded together, pitched fractionally apart. I'd never before heard her produce such a voice and for a second became hesitant. She brought herself up into a kneeling position and now I saw the duvet hadn't disintegrated after all, but was in a large ball behind her.

'Get Mom!'

'But your mother needs to rest.' I kept my voice a whisper. 'I'm your AF. This is exactly why I'm here. I'm always here.'

'I didn't say you. I need Mom!'

'But Josie . . .'

There was movement behind me, and I was pushed aside so that I almost lost balance. When I recovered, I saw before me, on the near edge of the bed, a large shifting shape, made additionally complex by the patches of blackness and moonlight moving over its surface. I realized the shape was the Mother and Josie embracing – the Mother dressed in what looked like pale running clothes, Josie in her usual dark blue pajamas. As well as their limbs, their hair had become mingled, and then their shape began gently to rock, in a way not unlike when their goodbyes became extended.

'Don't want to die, Mom. I don't want that.'

'It's okay. Okay.' The Mother's voice was soft, at just the same level mine had been.

'I don't want that, Mom.'

'I know. I know. It's okay.'

I moved quietly away from them towards the doorway, then out onto the dark landing. I stood at the rail, looking at the strange night patterns on the ceiling and the hallway below, and turned over in my mind the implications of what had just occurred.

After a while, the Mother came quietly out of the bedroom and, without looking my way, turned into the darkness of the short corridor that led to her own room. There was now silence from behind Josie's door, and when I returned to the bedroom, the duvet and the bed were orderly, and Josie was sleeping, her breaths peaceful again.

PART FOUR

The Friend's Apartment was inside a townhouse. From the window of its Main Lounge I could see similar townhouses on the opposite side of the street. There were six of them in a row, and the front of each had been painted a slightly different color, to prevent a resident climbing the wrong steps and entering a neighbor's house by mistake.

I made this observation aloud to Josie that day, forty minutes before we set off to see the portrait man, Mr Capaldi. She was lying on the leather sofa behind me, reading a paperback she'd taken down from the black bookshelves. The Sun's pattern was falling across her raised knees, and she was so engrossed in her reading, she made only a vague noise in reply. I was pleased about this because earlier she'd been getting very tense with the waiting. She'd relaxed noticeably once I'd gone to stand at the triple window, knowing I'd alert her the moment the Father's taxi drew up outside.

The Mother too had been getting tense, though whether on account of the coming meeting with Mr Capaldi or because of the Father's imminent arrival, I couldn't be certain. She'd left the Main Lounge some time before, and I could hear her voice from the next room on the phone. I could have listened to her words by putting my head to the wall, and I even considered doing so, given the possibility she was talking to Mr Capaldi. But I thought this might make Josie even more anxious, and in any case, it occurred to me the Mother was more likely to be speaking to the Father to give street directions.

Once I'd understood Josie was depending on me to look out for the Father's taxi, I put aside plans to learn further the Friend's Apartment and concentrated on the view from the triple window. I didn't mind this, particularly since there was always the chance the Cootings Machine would go by, and even if I couldn't very well chase after it, such a sighting would be an important step forward.

But by then I'd come to accept that the chances of the Cootings Machine passing the Friend's Apartment were slight. Earlier, during our drive into the city, I'd become overly hopeful because, while still on the outskirts, we'd passed numerous overhaul men, and even when the men weren't to be seen, their barriers were there closing off one street or another. That was when I'd begun to think the Cootings Machine would appear at any moment. But though I kept looking from my side window, and though twice we passed other kinds of machines, it never appeared. Then the traffic became slower and there were fewer overhaul men. The Mother and Miss Helen, in the front, were talking to one another in their usual relaxed way, while beside me in the back, Josie and Rick pointed things out to each other in soft voices. Sometimes one would nudge the other as we passed something, and they'd laugh together, even though no words had been exchanged. We passed a pink blossoming park, then a building with a sign that said 'No Standing Except Trucks', and in the front Miss Helen and the Mother were also laughing, though both had caution in their voices. 'Just be strict with him, Chrissie,' Miss Helen said. Next came Chinese signs, and bicycles chained to posts, then it began to rain – though the Sun kept trying his best – and umbrella couples appeared and tourists with magazines over their heads, and I saw an AF hurrying for shelter beside his teenager. 'Rick, that's ridiculous,'

Josie said about something and giggled. The rain stopped as we came into a street with buildings so tall the sidewalks on both sides were in shadow, and there were undershirt men sitting on their front steps talking and watching us go by. 'Really, Chrissie, please drop us off anywhere,' Miss Helen was saying. 'We've already taken you much too far out of your way.' I saw two gray buildings side by side that weren't the same height, and some-one had made a cartoon painting on the wall of the taller build-ing where it stood above its neighbor, perhaps to make their discrepancy less awkward. My mind filled with happiness each time I saw a Tow-Away Zone sign though these were slightly different to the ones outside our store. Josie leaned forward and made a humorous remark and both adults laughed. 'We'll see you both tomorrow then at the sushi place,' the Mother said to Miss Helen. 'It's right next to the theater. You can't miss it.' And Miss Helen said, 'Thank you, Chrissie, I know it'll help me greatly. It will help Rick too.' We drove through a fountain square, then a park filled with leaves where I spotted two more AFs, then into a busy street with high buildings.

'He's late,' Josie said from the sofa, and I heard the dull thump of her paperback falling onto the rug. 'But I guess that's not unusual.'

I realized she was trying to make a joke of it, so laughed and said: 'But I'm sure he's very anxious to see Josie again. You must remember how slowly the traffic moved when we were coming here. The same is probably happening to him now.'

'Dad never gets places on time. And after Mom promised to pay for his taxi. Okay. I'm going to forget everything about him for a while. Definitely doesn't deserve fussing over.'

As she reached down for her fallen paperback, I turned again to the triple window. The view of the street from the Friend's

Apartment was quite different to the one from the store. Taxis were rare, but other kinds of cars – in every size, shape and color – went by quickly, coming to a stop at the far left of my view, where a long-arm traffic signal hung over the street. There were fewer runners and tourists here, but more headset walkers – and more pedal cyclists, some carrying items in one hand while steering with the other. Once, not long after Josie's remark about the Father's lateness, a cyclist went by holding under his arm a large board shaped like a flattened bird, and I feared the wind would catch the board and make him lose balance. But he was skillful and darted around the cars till he was at the front, right under the hanging traffic signal.

The Mother's voice in the next room had grown anxious, and I knew Josie could hear it, but when I glanced around, she appeared still to be engrossed in her paperback. A dog lead woman went past, then a station wagon with 'Gio's Coffee Shop Deli' on its side. Then a taxi slowed down directly outside. The Main Lounge was higher than the sidewalk, so I couldn't see into the interior of the taxi, but the Mother's voice stopped, and I was certain this was the Father arriving.

'Josie, here he is.'

At first she went on reading. Then she took a deep breath, sat up and let the book fall to the rug again. 'Bet you think he's a dork,' she said. 'Some people think he's a dork. But actually he's super-smart. You have to give him a chance.'

I saw a tall but stooping figure in a gray raincoat emerge from the taxi holding a paper bag. He looked uncertainly up at our townhouse, and I supposed that he was confused as to which one it was, those on our side being as similar as those on the other. He kept holding the paper bag carefully, the way people carry a small dog too tired to walk. He chose the correct steps, and might even have seen me, though I'd moved back into the room once I'd given Josie my warning. I thought the Mother would now come back into the Main Lounge, and her footsteps sounded, but she remained out in the hall. For what seemed a long time, Josie and I – and the Mother in the hall – waited in silence. Then the bell rang and we heard again the Mother's footsteps, then their voices.

They were speaking to one another softly. The door between the hall and the Main Lounge was partly open, and Josie and I – both standing in the center of the room – watched carefully for signs. Then the Father came in, no longer in his raincoat, but still holding his paper bag in both hands. He had on a fairly high-rank office jacket, but under it a tired brown sweater that came up to his chin.

'Hey, Josie! My favorite wild animal!'

He clearly wished to greet Josie with an embrace, and looked around for somewhere to put down the paper bag, but Josie stepped forward and placed her arms around him, paper bag and all. As he received her embrace, his gaze wandered around the room and fell on me. Then he looked away and closed his eyes, letting his cheek rest against the top of her head. They stayed like that for a time, keeping very still, not even rocking slowly the way the Mother and Josie did sometimes during their morning farewells.

The Mother was equally still, standing a little way behind, a black bookshelf at each shoulder, her face unsmiling as she watched. The embrace continued, and when I glanced again at the Mother, that whole section of the room had become partitioned, her narrowed eyes repeated in box after box, and in some boxes the eyes were watching Josie and the Father, while in others they were looking at me.

At last they loosened their embrace, and the Father smiled and raised the paper bag higher, as though it were in need of oxygen.

'Here, animal,' he said to Josie. 'Brought you my latest little creation.'

He passed the bag to Josie, holding its bottom till she was doing the same, and they sat down side by side on the sofa to peer inside it. Rather than remove the item from the bag, Josie tore the paper away at the sides to reveal a small, rough-looking circular mirror mounted on a tiny stand. She held it on her knee and said: 'So what's this, Dad? For doing make-up?'

'If you want. But you're not looking at it. Take another look.'

'Wow! That's sensational. What's going on?'

'Isn't it strange how we all tolerate it? All these mirrors that show you the wrong way round? This one shows you the way you really look. No heavier than the average compact.'

'That's brilliant! Did you invent this?'

'I'd like to claim it, but the real credit goes to my friend Benjamin, one of the other guys in the community. He came up with the idea, but he didn't know quite how to pull it off in real-world terms. So I did that part. Fresh out the oven, only last week. What do you think, Josie?'

'Wow, it's a masterpiece. I'm going to be checking my face in public the whole time now. Thanks! You're such a genius. Does this thing run on batteries?'

For the next few moments the Father and Josie went on talking about the mirror, breaking off to exchange jokey greetings as if they were only meeting for the first time at that moment. Their shoulders were touching, and as they talked they often pressed further into one another. I remained standing in the middle of the room, the Father sometimes glancing towards me, and I thought at any moment Josie would introduce us. But the Father's arrival had made her excited, she continued to talk rapidly to him, and soon the Father ceased glancing my way.

'My new physics tutor, Dad, I bet he doesn't know even half what you do. And he's weird. If he wasn't mega-accredited, I'd be like, Mom, we have to get this guy arrested. No, no, don't panic, he isn't improper. It's just so obvious he's fixing something in his shed, you know, to blow us all up. Hey, how's the knee?'

'Oh, much better, thanks. In fact it's just fine.'

'You remember that cookie you had the last time we went out? The one that looked like the president of China?'

Even though Josie's speech was fast and seamless, I could tell she was testing her words in her mind before speaking them. Then the Mother – who'd gone out into the hall – came back wearing her coat, and she was also holding up in the air Josie's thicker jacket. Cutting straight into the talk between Josie and the Father, she said:

'Paul, come on. You haven't said hello to Klara. This here's Klara.'

The Father and Josie fell silent, both looking at me. Then the Father said: 'Klara. Hello.' The smile he'd had since entering the apartment had vanished.

'Hate to rush you guys,' the Mother said. 'But you got here late, Paul. We have an appointment to keep.'

The Father's smile returned, but there was now anger in his eyes. 'I haven't seen my daughter in nearly three months and I don't get to talk with her for five minutes?'

'Paul, it's you who insisted on coming with us today.'

'I think I have a right to come, Chrissie.'

'No one's denying that. But you don't make us late.'

'Is this guy so busy . . .'

'Don't make us late, Paul. And you behave while we're there.'

The Father looked at Josie and shrugged. 'See, in trouble already,' he said and laughed. 'Come on then, animal, we'd better get going.'

'Paul,' the Mother said, 'you haven't spoken to Klara.'

'I just said hello.'

'Come on. Speak to her some more.'

'Part of the family. Is that what you're saying?'

The Mother stared at him, then seemed to change her mind about something and shook Josie's jacket in the air.

'Come on, honey. We need to go.'

■

While we were waiting outside for the Mother's car, the Father – wearing his raincoat again – stood with his arm around Josie. They were at the front edge of the sidewalk while I stood further back, almost at the townhouse's railings, the pedestrians passing between us. Because of our positions and the unusual outdoor acoustics, I had difficulty hearing their words. At one point the Father turned towards me, but continued speaking to Josie even as his eyes examined me. Then a black-skinned lady with large earrings passed between us, and when she'd gone, the Father's back was turned once more.

When the Mother's car arrived, Josie and I got into the back, and as we set off, I tried to catch her eye, to give reassurance in case she was anxious about posing for her portrait. But she was looking out of the window on her own side and didn't turn my way.

The Mother's car made slow progress, leaving one traffic line only to get held up in another. We passed shuttered doorways and buildings with crossed-out windows. It began to rain again, the umbrella couples appeared and the dog lead people moved in a hurry. Once there appeared on my side – close enough that I might have touched it had I lowered my window – a soaked wall covered in angry cartoon writing.

'It's not so bad,' the Mother was saying to the Father. 'There aren't enough of us. Budget per campaign's down almost forty percent. We're in chronic conflict with the PR people. But otherwise, yes. It's fine.'

'Steven still making his presence felt?'

'Certainly is. Same congenial figure he always was.'

'You know, Chrissie. I really do wonder if it's worth it. You hanging on this way.'

'I'm not sure I understand. What is it I'm hanging onto?'

'Goodwins. Your law department. This whole . . . world of work. Your every waking moment determined by some contract you once signed.'

'Please let's not go over this again. I'm sorry about what happened to you, Paul. I'm sorry and I'm still angry. But I keep *hanging on*, as you put it, because on the day I stop, Josie's world, *my* world, would collapse.'

'Why are you so sure of that, Chrissie? Look, it's a big step, I know. I'm only suggesting you think about it further. Try viewing things from a fresh perspective.'

'Fresh perspective? Come on, Paul. Don't start claiming you're happy about the way it turned out. All that talent. All that experience.'

'Honestly? I think the substitutions were the best thing that happened to me. I'm well out of it.'

'How can you say that? You were top-flight. Unique knowledge, specialist skills. How is it right no one can make use of you?'

'Chrissie, I have to tell you, you're much more bitter about it than I am. The substitutions made me take a completely fresh look at the world, and I really believe they helped me to distinguish what's important from what isn't. And where I live now, there are many fine people who feel exactly the same way. They all came down the same road, some with careers far grander than mine. And we all of us agree, and I honestly believe we're not kidding ourselves. We're better off than we were back then.'

'Really? Everyone thinks that? Even that friend of yours, the one who was the judge in Milwaukee?'

'I'm not saying it's always easy. We all have our bad days. But compared to what we had before, we feel like . . . we're really living for the first time.'

'That's good to hear from an ex-husband.'

'Sorry. Look, never mind this. I have some questions. About this portrait.'

'Not now, Paul. Not here.'

'Hmm. Okay.'

'Hey, Dad,' Josie called out beside me. 'You go ahead and ask what you want. I'm not listening.'

'Like hell you're not listening,' the Father said and laughed.

'No more arguments about the portrait, Paul,' the Mother said. 'You owe me that.'

'I owe you? I don't quite see why I owe you anything, Chrissie.'

'Not now, Paul.'

It was just then I realized that the Tow-Away Zone sign we were passing was the very one I knew so well, and in that same instant, the RPO Building appeared on Josie's side, and the familiar taxis were all around us. But when I turned with excitement towards our store, I could see something was not correct.

192

Of course I'd never seen the store from the street, but even so, there were no AFs and no Striped Sofa in the window. Instead there was a display of colored bottles and a sign saying 'Recessed Lighting'. I turned right around to continue looking just as Josie said:

'Hey, Klara, you know where we are?'

'Yes, of course.' But we were already beyond the pedestrian crossing, and I hadn't even looked to see if the birds were perched up on the traffic signal. In fact I'd been so startled by the store's new appearance, I'd not observed the surroundings nearly as much as I'd have liked. And then we were in a different section of the street altogether, and I turned again to see, through the rear windshield, the RPO Building growing smaller.

'You know what I think?' There was concern in Josie's voice. 'I think maybe your old store's moved on.'

'Yes. Perhaps.'

But I had no more time to think about the store, for what I saw next – between the two front seats – was the Cootings Machine. I recognized it before we were close enough to see the name on its body. There it was, throwing out Pollution from three funnels the way it had always done. I knew I should feel anger, but coming on it after the surprise about the store, I felt something almost like kindness towards the terrible machine. Then we'd passed it, the Mother and the Father continuing to speak with tension, and Josie said beside me: 'These stores, the way they keep changing. That day I came looking for you, that's what I was afraid of. That the store would have gone, you and all your friends with it.'

I smiled at her, but didn't say anything. In the front the adults' voices grew louder.

193

'Look, Paul, we've been over and over this. Josie, Klara and I are going in there and we're proceeding just as planned. You agreed to it, remember?'

'I agreed to it, but I can still comment, can't I?'

'Not here you can't! Not now and not in this goddam car!'

Josie, all this time, had been saying something to me, but she'd become distracted. Now, as the adults fell silent, she said: 'If you want, Klara, we can go look for it tomorrow provided we've time.'

I almost thought she meant the Cootings Machine, then realized she was referring to whatever new premises Manager and the other AFs might have gone to. I thought she was being hasty in assuming they'd definitely moved, simply because the window had looked different, and was about to say so, when she leaned forward to the adults.

'Mom? Just if there's time tomorrow? Klara wants to go find out what's happened to her old store. Could we do that?'

'If you want, honey. That was the deal. Today we go and see Mr Capaldi and you do what he asks. Tomorrow we do what you want.'

The Father shook his head and turned to his own window, but because Josie was sitting directly behind him, she didn't see his expression.

'Don't worry, Klara.' She reached over to touch my arm. 'We'll find it tomorrow.'

■

The Mother steered the car off the street into a small yard enclosed by wire mesh. There was an anti-parking sign fixed to a fence, but she stopped the car facing it beside the only other

194

car present. When we got out, the ground was hard and cracked in many places. Josie began her cautious walk beside the Father towards a brick building overlooking the yard, and perhaps because of the uneven ground, the Father took her arm. The Mother, standing at the car, watched this and didn't move for a moment. Then to my surprise, she came up to me and took my own arm, and we began to walk together, as though in imitation of the Father and Josie.

There were no other adjoining buildings to either side, and I designated it a building rather than a house because the brick-work was unpainted and dark fire escapes rose up in zigzags. There were five stories ending at a flat rooftop, and I had the impression the reason there were no neighbor buildings was because something unfortunate had happened, and they'd had to be cleared away by the overhaul men. As I stepped over the cracks, the Mother leaned closer towards me.

'Klara,' she said quietly. 'Remember. Mr Capaldi will want to ask you some questions. In fact, he may have quite a few. You just answer them. Okay, honey?'

It was the first time she'd called me 'honey'. I replied, 'Yes, of course,' and then the brick building was there before us, and I saw that each window had within it a graph-paper pattern.

There was a door at ground level beside two trash cans, and when Josie and the Father reached it, they turned and waited, as though it was up to the Mother to lead us in. Seeing this, she let go of me and went up to the door by herself. She stood there quite still for a moment, then pressed the door button.

'Henry,' she said into the wall speaker. 'We're here.'

■

The interior of Mr Capaldi's house was nothing like its outside. In his Main Room the floors were almost the same shade of white as his huge walls. Powerful spotlights fixed to the ceiling shone down on us, making it hard to look up without being dazzled. There was very little furniture for such a large space: one large black sofa, and in front of it, a low table on which Mr Capaldi had laid out two cameras and their lenses. The low table, like the Glass Display Trolley in our store, had wheels to allow it to move smoothly across the floor.

'Henry, we don't want Josie getting tired,' the Mother was saying. 'Maybe we can get started?'

'Of course.' Mr Capaldi waved towards the far corner, where two charts were fixed side by side to the wall. I could see, on each chart, many ruled lines criss-crossing at various angles. A light metal chair had been left in front of the charts, and also a tripod-stand lamp. Just now the tripod-stand lamp wasn't switched on, and the far corner looked dark and lonely. Josie and the Mother gazed towards it apprehensively, then Mr Capaldi, perhaps noticing, touched something on the low table and the tripod-stand lamp came to life, brightly illuminating the entire corner, but creating new shadows.

'This will be totally relaxed,' Mr Capaldi said. He had a balding head, and a beard that almost hid his mouth. I estimated fifty-two years old. His face was constantly on the brink of smiling. 'Nothing strenuous. So if Josie's ready, let's maybe get started. Josie, if you'd care to come this way?'

'Henry, wait,' the Mother said, her voice echoing in the space. 'I was hoping to see the portrait first. What you've done so far.'

'Of course,' Mr Capaldi said. 'Though you must understand, it's still work in progress. And it's not always easy for a layperson to understand the way these things slowly take shape.'

196

'I'd like to take a look all the same.'

'I'll take you up. In fact, Chrissie, you know you don't need my permission. You're the boss here.'

'It's kind of scary,' Josie said, 'but I'd like to take a peek too.'

'Uh uh, honey. I promised Mr Capaldi you wouldn't see anything yet.'

'I tend to agree,' Mr Capaldi said. 'If you don't mind, Josie. In my experience, if the subject sees a portrait too early, things get messy. I need you to remain totally unselfconscious.'

'Unselfconscious about what exactly?' the Father asked, his voice loud and echoing. He'd kept on his raincoat, even though Mr Capaldi had twice invited him to hang it on one of the pegs inside the entrance. He had now drifted towards the charts and was studying them with a frown.

'What I mean, Paul, is that if the subject, in this case Josie, becomes too self-conscious, she may start posing unnaturally. That's all I was meaning.'

The Father kept staring at the wall charts. Then he shook his head in the same way he had in the car.

'Henry?' the Mother said. 'May I go now to your studio? See what you've been doing?'

'Of course. Follow me.'

Mr Capaldi led the Mother over to a metal staircase rising to a balcony. I watched their ascending feet through the gaps between the steps. Arriving on the balcony, Mr Capaldi pressed a keypad beside a purple door, there was a short hum, and they both went in.

The Purple Door closed behind them, and I went to the black sofa where Josie was sitting. I wanted to make a humorous remark to relax her, but the Father spoke first from the illuminated corner.

'I guess the idea, animal, is that you get photographed over and over in front of these charts.' He stepped in closer. 'See this. Measurements marked along every line.'

'You know, Dad,' Josie said. 'Mom told us you were cool about coming today. But maybe it wasn't such a great idea. We could have met up somewhere else. Done something different.'

'Don't worry, we'll do something else later. Something better than this.' Then he turned and smiled at her gently. 'This portrait. Let's say it gets finished. What bothers me is that I won't get to have it with me. Because your mom will want it with her.'

'You could come see it any time,' Josie said. 'It could be like your excuse. To come more often.'

'Look, Josie, I'm sorry. The way everything's turned out. I wish I could be with you more. A lot more.'

'That's okay, Dad. It's all working out now. Hey, Klara. What do you think of my dad here? Not such a crazy, huh?'

'It's been a great pleasure to meet Mr Paul.'

The Father went on looking at the charts as though I hadn't spoken, making a pointing gesture towards a detail. When at last he turned to face me, his eyes had lost their smiling folds.

'Pleasure to meet you too, Klara,' he said. Then he looked at Josie. 'Tell you what, animal. Let's get done with all of this quickly. Then just the two of us, we can go somewhere, get something to eat. There's a place I'm thinking you'd like.'

'Yeah, sure. If that's okay with Mom and Klara.'

She turned to look over her shoulder, and just at that moment, up on the balcony, the Purple Door opened and Mr Capaldi came out. He called back into his studio through the doorway:

'You're welcome to stay in there as long as you want. I'd better go and see to Josie.'

I heard the Mother's voice say something, then she too came out onto the balcony. She had lost her usual straight-backed posture and Mr Capaldi extended a hand, as though ready to catch her if she fell over.

'You okay there, Chrissie?'

The Mother pushed past Mr Capaldi and started down the steps, holding onto the rail. Midway down, she paused to push back her hair, then she came down the rest of the way.

'So what do you think?' Josie asked with anxious eyes.

'It's okay,' the Mother said. 'It'll be okay. Paul, you want to see it, go ahead.'

'Maybe in just a minute,' the Father said. 'Capaldi, I'd appreciate you getting finished with us quickly today. I want to take Josie out for a coffee and cake.'

'That's okay, Paul. We have everything under control. You sure you're okay there, Chrissie?'

'I'm fine,' the Mother said, but she hurried to reach the black sofa.

'Josie,' Mr Capaldi said. 'Just before we do this, what I'd really like is for Klara here to do me a little favor. I have a small assignment for her. I was thinking maybe she could be getting on with it while we took our photos. That okay?'

'Fine by me,' Josie said. 'But you should ask Klara.'

But Mr Capaldi now addressed the Father. 'Paul, maybe as a fellow scientist, you'll agree with me. I believe AFs have so much more to give us than we currently appreciate. We shouldn't fear their intellectual powers. We should learn from them. AFs have so much to teach us.'

'I was an engineer, never a *scientist*. I think you know that. In any case, AFs were never in my territory.'

Mr Capaldi shrugged, and raising a hand to his beard, appeared to be checking its texture. Then he turned to me, saying: 'Klara, I've been devising a survey for you. A kind of questionnaire. It's up there on the screen ready to go. If you wouldn't mind completing it, I'd be so grateful.'

Before I could say anything, the Mother said: 'It's a good idea, Klara. Give you something to do while Josie gets through her sitting.'

'Of course. I'd be happy to help.'

'Thanks! It's nothing difficult, I swear. In fact, what I'd like, Klara, is for you to make no special effort. The whole thing works best if you respond spontaneously.'

'I understand.'

'They're not even questions as such. But why don't we just go up there and I'll show you? Folks, Josie, this won't take a minute. I'll get Klara settled, then come right back down. Josie, you look so well today. This way, Klara.'

I thought he might take me also to the Purple Door, but we went to the opposite side of the room, where a different metal staircase climbed to its own section of balcony. Mr Capaldi went first up the steps, then I followed, taking each step carefully. When I glanced back down, I saw Josie, the Mother and the Father looking up at us, the Mother still seated on the black sofa. I waved towards Josie, but no one below moved. Then Josie called up: 'Be good, Klara!'

'This way please, Klara.' The balcony was narrow, made from the same dark metal as the staircase. Mr Capaldi was holding open a glass door leading into a room smaller even than Josie's en suite, dominated by a padded desk chair facing a screen. 'Please sit down in there. It's all waiting for you.'

I seated myself with a white wall at my shoulder. Beneath the screen was a narrow ledge offering three control devices.

The room wasn't large enough for Mr Capaldi to come in too, so the glass door remained open while he gave me his instructions, reaching over sometimes to manipulate the devices. I listened to him carefully, even though I became aware that below, the Mother and the Father were once again using tense voices. Behind Mr Capaldi's words, I heard the Mother saying: 'No one's insisting you stay, Paul.'

'It's not consistent,' the Father was saying. 'I'm merely pointing out the inconsistency.'

'I'm not trying to be consistent. I'm just trying to find a way forward for us. Why make it harder than it is, Paul?'

Beside me, Mr Capaldi laughed, broke off from his instructions and said: 'Oh my. Looks like I'd better go down there and referee! You all straight here, Klara?'

'Thank you. Everything's quite clear.'

'I appreciate it. Anything puzzles you, please call down.'

When he closed the door it actually nudged my shoulder, but I could see sufficiently through its glass to watch Mr Capaldi descending beneath the balcony level. Then I allowed my gaze to go beyond, across the empty air, over to the opposite balcony and the Purple Door from which the Mother had recently emerged.

I began Mr Capaldi's questionnaire. Sometimes a question would come on the screen as writing. At other times there were shifting diagrams, or the screen would darken and sounds with many layers emerge from the speakers. A face – Josie's, the Mother's, a stranger's – would appear then vanish. At first, short responses of around twelve digits and symbols were appropriate, but as the questions grew more complex, I found myself giving longer answers, some running to over a hundred digits and symbols. All the time, the voices from below remained tense, but with the glass door closed, I could no longer hear their words.

Halfway through my assignment, I caught movement through the glass and saw on the opposite balcony Mr Capaldi leading the Father up onto it. I continued my assignment, but having grasped its central purpose, I no longer needed to give it much attention, and was able to watch the Father, nervously drawing the raincoat around him, approaching the Purple Door. He had his back to me and I was looking through frosted glass, so I couldn't be sure, but he looked as though he'd become suddenly ill.

But Mr Capaldi, on the balcony beside him, seemed unconcerned, smiling and talking cheerfully. Then he reached up to the keypad beside the Purple Door. From inside my cubicle I couldn't hear the unlocking hum, but the next time I glanced their way, the Father had gone inside and Mr Capaldi was leaning in through the doorway, saying something. Then I saw Mr Capaldi move suddenly backward, and the Father came out and, though I couldn't be sure through the frosted glass, he looked no longer ill but filled with a new energy. He seemed not to mind that he'd almost knocked Mr Capaldi aside, and started down the metal steps at reckless speed. Mr Capaldi, watching him, shook his head as a parent would do when a child has a tantrum in a store, then closed the Purple Door.

The images on the screen were changing ever faster now, but my tasks remained obvious, and after several minutes, without losing focus, I pushed partially ajar the glass door beside me. I could then hear more clearly the voices below.

'What you're emphasizing here, Paul,' Mr Capaldi was saying, 'is how any work we do brands us. That's your point, am I right? It brands us, and sometimes brands us unjustly.'

'That's a very smart way of misunderstanding my point, Capaldi.'

'Paul, come on,' the Mother said.

'I'm sorry, Capaldi, if this sounds impolite. But frankly? I think you're deliberately misconstruing what I'm saying.'

'No, Paul, you're genuinely not coming through here. There are always ethical choices around any work. That's true, whether we get paid for it or we don't.'

'That's very considerate of you, Capaldi.'

'Paul, come on,' the Mother said again. 'Henry's just doing what we asked him. No more, no less.'

'It's no wonder, Capaldi – *Henry*, sorry – a guy like you would struggle to understand what I'm saying here.'

I pushed back my chair on its castors, rose and passed through the glass door onto the balcony. I'd already established that the balcony was a rectangular circuit touching all four walls. Now, choosing the rear half of it, I kept close to the white wall, taking care not to cause the metal mesh to ring under my feet, or to cross spotlight beams in any way that could create moving shadows below. I reached the Purple Door unnoticed and keyed in the code I'd observed twice already. There came the usual short hum, but this too went unnoticed by those below. I was then inside Mr Capaldi's studio and closed the door behind me.

The room was L-shaped, the section before me turning a corner into an extension beyond the normal boundary of the building. Leading towards this corner were two counters attached to each wall, busy with shapes, fabrics, small knives and tools. But I had no time to focus on these, and went on towards the corner, remembering to tread cautiously, because the floor was still of the same metal mesh.

I turned the corner of the L and saw Josie there, suspended in the air. She wasn't very high – her feet were at the height of my shoulders – but because she was leaning forward, arms outstretched, fingers spread, she seemed to be frozen in the act of falling. Little beams illuminated her from various angles, forbidding her any refuge. Her face was very like that of the real Josie, but because there was at the eyes no kind smile, the upward curve of her lips gave her an expression I'd never seen before. The face looked disappointed and afraid. Her clothes weren't real clothes, but made from thin tissue paper to approximate a T-shirt on her top half, loose-fitting shorts on the lower. The tissue was pale yellow and translucent and under the sharp lighting made this Josie's arms and legs look all the more fragile. Her hair had been tied back in the manner the real Josie wore it on her ill days, and this was the one detail that failed to convince; the hair had been made from a substance I'd never seen on any AF, and I knew this Josie wouldn't be happy with it.

Having made my observations, my intention was to return to the cubicle before my absence from it was noticed. I walked carefully back past the two work counters and opened the Purple Door a small way. It made the usual humming noise, but I could tell from the voices below that no one had heard it. I could tell too that the mood was now even more filled with tension.

'Paul' – the Mother's voice was almost shouting – 'you've been determined to make this difficult from the start.'

'Come on, Josie,' the Father said. 'Let's go. Right now.'

'But Dad . . .'

'Josie, we leave right now. Believe me, I know what I'm doing.'

'I don't think you do,' the Mother said, and Mr Capaldi said over her, 'Paul, come on, take it easy. If there's been a misunder-standing, I take full responsibility and I apologize.'

'How much more information do you need anyway?' the Father asked, and now he was shouting too, but that could per-haps have been because he was moving across the floor. 'I'm surprised you're not requesting a sample of her blood.'

'Paul, be reasonable,' the Mother said. The Father and Josie were saying something at the same time, but then Mr Capaldi said over them:

'It's okay, Chrissie, let them go. Let them go, it doesn't change anything.'

'Mom? Why don't I go with Dad just now? Then at least you can all stop yelling. If I stay here, it's just going to get worse.'

'I'm not angry at you, honey. I'm angry at your father. He's the child here.'

'Come on, animal. Let's go.'

'I'll see you later, Mom, okay? See you, Mr Capaldi . . .'

'Let them go, Chrissie. Just let them go.'

When the entrance door closed behind them, its sound echoed all around the building. I remembered then that the car belonged to the Mother, and wondered if the Father had money for a taxi to take him and Josie to where he now intended them to go. It felt a little strange Josie hadn't thought to take me with her, but the Mother was still here, and I remembered the day we'd gone to Morgan's Falls.

I stepped out onto the balcony, now making no effort to con-ceal myself or to soften my footsteps. Leaning over the steel rail, I saw the Mother had sat down where earlier Josie had been sit-ting – on the metal chair in front of the charts. Mr Capaldi came across the floor till he was directly below me, and I could see the top of his bald head, but not his expression. He then continued to walk slowly towards the Mother, as if slowness were a mark of his kindness, and stopped beside the tripod-stand lamp.

'I can see you're having misgivings,' he said in a new, soft voice. 'Let me tell you. I've seen this kind of thing happen many times before. And it's the ones who stick with it, keep faith, who win out.'

'Damn right I'm having misgivings.'

'You mustn't let Paul sway you. Remember. You've thought this through and he hasn't. Paul is confused.'

'It's not Paul. To hell with Paul. It's that . . . that portrait up there.'

As she said this, she glanced up in my direction and saw me. She stared past the dazzle of the ceiling lights, then Mr Capaldi also turned and looked up at me. Then he looked at the Mother questioningly. The Mother continued to gaze at me, her hand now raised to her forehead.

'Okay, Klara,' she said finally. 'Come on down.'

As I descended the metal steps, I was interested to see that instead of anger, the Mother showed anxiety. I crossed the floor but stopped while still several strides away. It was Mr Capaldi who spoke first.

'What do you think, Klara? Am I doing a good job?'

'She resembles Josie quite accurately.'

'Then I guess that's a yes. By the way, Klara, how did you get on with the survey?'

'I completed it, Mr Capaldi.'

'Then I'm grateful for your cooperation. And you stored the data safely?'

'Yes, Mr Capaldi. My responses are stored.'

There was a silence, while the Mother continued to stare at me from her chair and Mr Capaldi from beside his tripod light.

I realized they were waiting for me to say something further, so I continued:

'It's a pity Josie and the Father have left. Mr Capaldi's work on the portrait may be temporarily impeded.'

'It's okay,' he said. 'Not a serious setback.'

'I need to hear,' the Mother said. 'I need to hear, Klara, what you think. About what you saw.'

'I apologize for examining the portrait without permission. But in the circumstances, I felt it best to do so.'

'Okay,' the Mother said, and again I saw she was fearful rather than angry. 'Now tell us what you thought. Or rather, tell us what you think you saw up there.'

'I'd suspected for some time that Mr Capaldi's portrait wasn't a picture or a sculpture, but an AF. I went in to confirm my speculation. Mr Capaldi has done an accurate job of catching Josie's outward appearance. Though perhaps the hips should be a little narrower.'

'Thank you,' Mr Capaldi said. 'I'll bear that in mind. It's still a work in progress.'

The Mother suddenly lowered her face into her hands, letting her hair hang over them. Mr Capaldi turned to her with an expression of concern, but didn't move from his spot. The Mother wasn't crying though, and she said through her hands, her voice muffled:

'Maybe Paul's right. Maybe this whole thing's been a mistake.'

'Chrissie. You mustn't lose faith.'

She brought her head back up and her eyes were now angry. 'It's not a matter of faith, Henry. Why are you so fucking sure I'll be able to accept that AF up there, however well you do her? It didn't work with Sal, why will it work with Josie?'

'What we did with Sal is no comparison. We've been through

207

this, Chrissie. What we made with Sal was a doll. A bereavement doll, nothing more. We've come a long, long way since then. What you have to understand is this. The new Josie won't be an imitation. She *really will be Josie*. A *continuation* of Josie.'

'You want me to believe that? Do *you* believe that?'

'I do believe it. With everything I'm worth, I believe it. I'm glad Klara went in there and looked. We need her on board now, we've needed that for a long time. Because it's Klara who'll make the difference. Make it very, very different this time round. You have to keep faith, Chrissie. You can't weaken now.'

'But will I believe in it? When the day comes. Will I really?'

'Excuse me,' I said. 'I'd like to say there's a chance you'll never need the new Josie. The present one may become healthy. I believe there's a good chance of this. I'll need, of course, the opportunity, the chance to make it so. But since you're so distressed, I'd like to say this now. If ever there comes such a sad day, and Josie is obliged to pass away, I'll do everything in my power. Mr Capaldi is correct. It won't be like the last time with Sal because this time you'll have me to help. I now understand why you've asked me, at every step, to observe and learn Josie. I hope the very sad day will never come, but if it does, then I'll use everything I've learned to train the new Josie up there to be as much like the former one as possible.'

'Klara,' the Mother said in a firmer voice, and suddenly she'd become partitioned into many boxes, far more than at the Friend's Apartment when the Father had first come in. In several of the boxes her eyes were narrow, while in others they were wide open and large. In one box there was room only for a single staring eyeball. I could see parts of Mr Capaldi at the edges of some boxes, so I was aware that he'd raised his hand into the air in a vague gesture.

'Klara,' the Mother was saying. 'You've made your deductions well. And I'm grateful for what you've just said. But there's something you need to hear.'

'No, Chrissie, not yet.'

'Why not? Why the hell not? You said yourself we need Klara on board. That she's the one who'll make the difference.'

There was a moment of silence, then Mr Capaldi said: 'Okay. If that's how you want it. Tell her.'

'Klara,' the Mother said. 'We came here today, the main reason. It wasn't so Josie could sit more. We came here because of you.'

'I understand,' I said. 'I understood about the survey. It was to test how well I've come to know Josie. How well I understand how she makes her decisions and why she has her feelings. I think the results will show I'm well able to train the Josie upstairs. But I say again, it's wrong to give up hope.'

'You still don't quite understand,' Mr Capaldi said. Although he was standing there before me, his voice seemed to come from the edges of my vision, because all I could see still were the Mother's eyes. 'Let me explain to her, Chrissie. It'll be easier coming from me. Klara, we're not asking you to train the new Josie. We're asking you to *become* her. That Josie you saw up there, as you noticed, is empty. If the day comes – I hope it doesn't, but if it does – we want you to inhabit that Josie up there with everything you've learned.'

'You wish me to inhabit her?'

'Chrissie chose you carefully with that in mind. She believed you to be the one best equipped to learn Josie. Not just superficially, but deeply, entirely. Learn her till there's no difference between the first Josie and the second.'

'Henry's telling you this now,' the Mother said, and suddenly she was no longer partitioned, 'like it was carefully planned. But

209

it was never like that. I didn't even know if I believed any of this would work. Maybe once I believed it could. But seeing that portrait up there, I don't know any more.'

'So you see what's being asked of you, Klara,' Mr Capaldi said. 'You're not being required simply to mimic Josie's outward behavior. You're being asked to continue her for Chrissie. And for everyone who loves Josie.'

'But is that going to be possible?' the Mother said. 'Could she really continue Josie for me?'

'Yes, she can,' Mr Capaldi said. 'And now Klara's completed the survey up there, I'll be able to give you scientific proof of it. Proof she's already well on her way to accessing quite comprehensively all of Josie's impulses and desires. The trouble is, Chrissie, you're like me. We're both of us sentimental. We can't help it. Our generation still carry the old feelings. A part of us refuses to let go. The part that wants to keep believing there's something unreachable inside each of us. Something that's unique and won't transfer. But there's nothing like that, we know that now. *You* know that. For people our age it's a hard one to let go. We *have* to let it go, Chrissie. There's nothing there. Nothing inside Josie that's beyond the Klaras of this world to continue. The second Josie won't be a copy. She'll be the exact same and you'll have every right to love her just as you love Josie now. It's not faith you need. Only rationality. I had to do it, it was tough but now it works for me just fine. And it will for you.'

The Mother stood up and began walking across the room. 'You may be right, Henry, but I'm too tired to think any more. And I need to talk to Klara, talk with her alone. I'm sorry things got messy here.' She went to where she'd left her bag hanging from one of the entrance hooks.

'I'm really glad Klara knows,' Mr Capaldi said. 'In fact, I'm relieved.' He was following behind the Mother, as if reluctant to be left alone. 'Klara, the data may possibly highlight where you still need to put in a little more effort. But I'm glad we can speak more openly.'

'Come on, Klara. Let's go.'

'So Chrissie. We're still okay about all this?'

'We're fine. But I need a break from it now.'

She touched Mr Capaldi's shoulder, then we left through the main entrance, which he hurried to open for us. He followed us to the elevator and gave a cheerful wave before the doors closed.

On the descent, the Mother took her oblong from her bag and stared at it. She put it away again as the elevator doors opened, and we walked out across the cracked concrete where the Sun was making his evening patterns through the wire fences. I'd thought there might be a chance Josie and the Father would be waiting there for us, but there was nobody, only a tree's shadow falling across the Mother's car, and the sounds of the city nearby.

'Klara, honey. Get in the front.'

But when we were seated side by side, looking through the windshield at the anti-parking sign, the Mother didn't start the car. I looked at Mr Capaldi's building, the Sun's patterns on its wall and its fire escapes, and I thought it curious the building could be so dirty on the outside. The Mother was again looking at her oblong.

'They've gone to some burger place. Josie says she's fine. And that *he's* fine too.'

'I hope they're enjoying themselves.'

'I've things to say to you. But let's get out of this place.'

When we drove out of the yard into the neighborhood, we had to stop for a lady on a basket bicycle crossing our path.

211

We stopped again a few minutes later under a long-arm traffic signal, even though there were no other cars in sight. Soon after the signal changed, we passed a large brown building set back from the sidewalk with no windows at all, but with a large central chimney, then we moved through an under-bridge area full of shadows, puddles and jump-skaters. We emerged out in the Sun's patterns beside a building with a 'Hiring Now' sign, and soon we were among pedestrians, and the sidewalk had small trees. Eventually the Mother slowed, then stopped beside a sign saying 'We Grind Our Own Beef'. The other cars had to pass noisily around us, but there was no anti-parking sign. Through the windshield, we could see another under-bridge area in front of us, and the cars that passed us were forming a line to enter it.

'This is the place. They're inside there.' Then she said: 'Paul does have a point. They need to be by themselves sometimes. Just them. They need that. We shouldn't always be with them. You see that, Klara?'

'Of course.'

'She misses her father. That's natural. So let's just sit out here for a while.'

Up ahead the signal color changed and we watched the cars move into the darkness beneath the bridge.

'This must all be a shock for you,' she said. 'You must have questions.'

'I think I understand.'

'Oh? You understand? You understand what I'm asking of you? And it *is* me asking. Not Capaldi and not Paul. In the end it's me. That's who it comes down to. I'm asking you to make this work. Because if it happens, if it comes again, there's going to be no other way for me to survive. I came through it with Sal, but I can't do it again. So I'm asking you, Klara. Do your best

212

for me. They told me in the store you were remarkable. I've watched you enough to know that's maybe true. If you set your mind to it, then who knows? It might work. And I'll be able to love you.'

We didn't look at each other, but kept gazing out through the windshield. Beside me, on my side, an apron man had emerged from the Grind Our Own Beef building and was sweeping the sidewalk.

'I don't blame Paul. He's entitled to his feelings. After Sal, he said we shouldn't risk it. So what if Josie doesn't get lifted? Plenty of kids aren't. But I could never have that for Josie. I wanted the best for her. I wanted her to have a good life. You understand, Klara? I called it, and now Josie's sick. Because of what I decided. You see how it feels for me?'

'Yes. I'm sorry.'

'Feeling sorry's not what I'm asking of you. I'm asking you to do what's within your power. And think what it'll mean for you. You'll be loved like nothing else in this world. Maybe one day I'll take up with another man. Who knows? But I promise you I'll never love him the way I'll love you. You'll be Josie and I'll always love you over everything else. So do it for me. I'm asking you to do it for me. Continue Josie for me. Come on. Say something.'

'I did wonder. If I were to continue Josie, if I were to inhabit the new Josie, then what would happen to . . . all this?' I raised my arms in the air, and for the first time the Mother looked at me. She glanced at my face, then down at my legs. Then she looked away and said:

'What does it matter? That's just fabric. Look, there's something else you might consider. Maybe it doesn't mean so much to you, me loving you. But here's something else. That boy.

213

Rick. I can see he's something to you. Don't speak, let me speak. What I'm saying is that Rick worships Josie, always has done. If you continue Josie, you'll have not just me but him. What will it matter that he's not lifted? We'll find a way to live together. Away from . . . everything. We'll stay out there, just ourselves, away from all of this. You, me, Rick, his mother if she wants. It could work. But you have to pull it off. You have to learn Josie in her entirety. You hear me, honey?'

'Until today,' I said. 'Until just now. I believed it was my duty to save Josie, to make her well. But perhaps this is a better way.'

The Mother turned in her seat slowly, reached out her arms and started to hug me. There was car equipment separating us, which made it hard for her to embrace me fully. But her eyes were closed in just the way they were when she and Josie rocked gently during a long embrace, and I felt her kindness sweeping through me.

■

The drivers wishing to enter the under-bridge area were annoyed at having to pass around the Mother's car. Many gave me unfriendly stares as they went past, even though they could see I was a passenger and not responsible.

My concern however wasn't the passing cars or their unfriendly drivers, but what was going on at that moment inside the Grind Our Own Beef. Had my mind not been momentarily filled by the Mother's words and her embrace, I might have been able to dissuade her from going inside. But no sooner had the embrace finished – and despite her remarks about Josie and the Father needing time to themselves – she'd suddenly vanished from my side, slamming the car door behind her.

214

As the minutes went by, I recalled the tense moments in Mr Capaldi's building, and wondered if, despite the discourtesy, my own arrival inside the Grind Our Own Beef might be required in order to divert proceedings from scenes of similar upset for Josie. But before I could decide, the Father appeared on the sidewalk on the other side of my window. He pointed the key device at the car, and when nothing happened, examined it more closely then pressed again. This time there were release noises around me – the Mother must have locked me in – and walking around to the traffic side, he quickly entered the car. He settled himself in the driving seat, but hardly glanced my way, staring instead towards the under-bridge area. Then he placed a hand on the steering wheel and began drumming his fingers on it.

'Amazing how she still has this vehicle,' he said. 'I helped her choose it. For a while she was keen on a German car, but I told her this one would be more dependable. Well, I wasn't wrong. At least, it's outlasted *me*.'

'Since Mr Paul is an expert engineer,' I said, 'he must be very good at advising when choosing cars.'

'Not really. Car engines were never my field.' He went on touching the steering wheel, now with some sadness.

'Are Josie and the Mother about to come out too?' I asked.

'What? Oh no. No, they're not. I don't think they'll come out any time soon.' Then he said: 'In fact Chrissie suggested I drive off somewhere. She wants me far away while she talks more with Josie.' He seemed less angry than in Mr Capaldi's building; indeed he was now almost dreamy. 'To be honest, I wasn't unhappy when Chrissie came in. You'd think I wouldn't be pleased, her interrupting like that. But the truth is, Josie and I weren't exactly having a light-hearted conversation. In fact I was in a tight spot. Look' – at last he looked at me – 'I'm sorry

215

if I've behaved badly towards you. I have a feeling I may have been impolite.'

'Please don't worry. I now understand very well why Mr Paul may have been reluctant to greet me warmly.'

'I've never been good at, well, relating to your kind. You have to excuse me. No, I didn't mind Chrissie breaking in on us. Because Josie was in the middle of asking some tough questions, and I'd no idea, no idea at all, how to answer her. No fool, that Josie.' He looked out again to the under-bridge area, and went on drumming his fingers on the steering wheel. 'After that *visit*, I wanted us to have a relaxing time. A coffee, something to eat. But then she asks me. Since Capaldi is trying to help us, as I've been claiming, why do I hate him so much?'

'How did Mr Paul reply?'

'I've always been useless at lying to her. So I guess I was, you know, prevaricating. And I knew she could see right through me. That was when Chrissie came in.'

'Does Josie suspect about . . . about this plan? The one in case she has to pass away?'

'I don't know. Maybe she suspects it, but doesn't dare look at it. But she's no fool. All these tough questions. Why was I so against someone doing her portrait? Well, let Chrissie have a go at answering.' Suddenly he placed the key device into the ignition slot. 'We've been instructed to get lost for a while. Until, to be precise' – he looked at his watch – 'five forty-five. Then we're to rendezvous at this sushi place. All of us, apparently. Josie, Chrissie, the neighbors too. So unless you want to sit in a parked car for an hour, I suggest we drive around.'

He started the engine, but the traffic line had become so extended we couldn't yet move. I put on the safety belt and waited. Then the lights changed up ahead and the car lurched forward.

216

■

Shadow and light patterns moved all around us, then we came out from the under-bridge area into an avenue of tall brown buildings. We drove past a large creature with numerous limbs and eyes, then even as I watched, a crack appeared down its center. As it divided itself, I realized it had been, all along, two separate people – a runner and a dog walk woman – moving in opposite directions who for an instant happened to be passing one another. Then came a store with a sign saying 'Eat In Take Out' and in front of it, a lost baseball cap on the sidewalk.

'Was there anyplace special you wanted to go?' the Father asked. 'Josie mentioned something about your old store. She said we'd passed it earlier today.'

As soon as I heard him say this I recognized the opportunity it represented, and exclaimed perhaps too loudly: 'Oh yes!' Then controlling myself, I said more quietly: 'If you don't mind, I'd very much like that.'

'She was saying it may not be there any more. That it might have moved on.'

'I'm not certain. Even so, if Mr Paul could take us to the area, it would make me very happy.'

'Fine. We've time to kill.'

At the next intersection, he turned to the right, saying as he did so: 'I wonder how Chrissie's getting on. What they're talking about right now. Maybe she managed to change the topic.'

There was now more traffic and we moved slowly behind other vehicles. The Sun was sometimes visible, but he was already getting quite low and the tall buildings often blocked his view. The sidewalks were busy with office workers at the end of their work, and we passed a man on a ladder, doing something to a shiny red notice that said 'Rotisserie Chicken'. The pedestrian crossings and Tow-Away Zone signs went by, and I could sense we were coming nearer to the store.

'Can I ask you something?' the Father said.

'Yes, of course.'

'I think Josie's still largely in the dark. But I don't know about you. How much you'd guessed before. How much you found out today. Perhaps you wouldn't mind telling me what you do know.'

'Before I visited Mr Capaldi today,' I said, 'I'd suspected some things, but had been ignorant of many others. Now, after this visit, I can understand Mr Paul's unease. And I can understand his initial coldness towards me.'

'I apologize again for that. So. They explained it all to you. How you fit into the picture.'

'Yes. I believe they told me everything.'

'And what do you think? Do you suppose you can pull it off? Perform this role?'

'It won't be easy. But I believe if I continue to observe Josie carefully, it will be within my abilities.'

'Then let me ask you something else. Let me ask you this. Do you believe in the human heart? I don't mean simply the organ, obviously. I'm speaking in the poetic sense. The human heart. Do you think there is such a thing? Something that makes each of us special and individual? And if we just suppose that there is. Then don't you think, in order to truly learn Josie, you'd have to learn not just her mannerisms but what's deeply inside her? Wouldn't you have to learn her heart?'

'Yes, certainly.'

'And that could be difficult, no? Something beyond even your wonderful capabilities. Because an impersonation wouldn't do, however skillful. You'd have to learn her heart, and learn it fully, or you'll never become Josie in any sense that matters.'

A public bus had stopped beside some abandoned fruit boxes. As the Father steered around it, the car behind us made angry horn noises. Then there were more angry horns, but these were further away and not aimed at us.

'The heart you speak of,' I said. 'It might indeed be the hardest part of Josie to learn. It might be like a house with many rooms. Even so, a devoted AF, given time, could walk through each of those rooms, studying them carefully in turn, until they became like her own home.'

The Father sounded our own horn at a car trying to enter the traffic line from a side street.

'But then suppose you stepped into one of those rooms,' he said, 'and discovered another room within it. And inside that room, another room still. Rooms within rooms within rooms. Isn't that how it might be, trying to learn Josie's heart? No matter how long you wandered through those rooms, wouldn't there always be others you'd not yet entered?'

I considered this for a moment, then said: 'Of course, a human heart is bound to be complex. But it must be limited. Even if Mr Paul is talking in the poetic sense, there'll be an end to what there is to learn. Josie's heart may well resemble a strange house with rooms inside rooms. But if this were the best way to save Josie, then I'd do my utmost. And I believe there's a good chance I'd be able to succeed.'

'Hmm.'

For the next few moments we drove without talking. Then as we passed a building saying 'Nail Boutique', and immediately after it, a row of peeling poster walls, he said: 'According to Josie, your old store is in this district.'

This might have been so, but the surroundings weren't yet familiar to me. I said to him: 'Mr Paul has spoken very frankly. Perhaps now he'd allow me, in turn, to speak frankly to him.'

'Feel free.'

'My old store wasn't the true reason I asked you to drive into this district.'

'No?'

'When we came this way earlier today, not far from the store, we passed a machine. It was being used by overhaul men and it was creating terrible Pollution.'

'Okay. Go on.'

'It's not easy to explain. But it's very important Mr Paul now believes what I'm about to say. This machine must be destroyed. That's the real reason I asked to be driven here. It must be somewhere nearby. It's easily identified because it has the name Cootings on its body. It has three funnels and each of them emits terrible Pollution.'

'And you want to find this machine now?'

'Yes. And to destroy it.'

'Because it causes Pollution.'

'It's a terrible machine.' I was leaning forward, already looking left and right.

'And how exactly do you intend to destroy it?'

'I'm not certain. This is why I wished to be frank with Mr Paul. I'm requesting his help. Mr Paul is an expert engineer, as well as an adult.'

'You're asking me how to vandalize a machine?'

'But first we must find it. For instance, please may we turn down this street?'

'I can't turn there. It's one-way. I don't like pollution any more than you do. But isn't this taking things a little far?'

220

'I'm unable to explain further. But Mr Paul must trust me. It's very important for Josie's sake. For her health.'

'How is this going to help Josie?'

'I'm sorry, I'm not able to explain. Mr Paul has to trust me. If we can only find the Cootings Machine and destroy it, I believe it will lead to Josie's full recovery. Then it won't matter about Mr Capaldi or about his portrait or how well I'm able to learn Josie.'

The Father considered this. 'All right,' he said eventually. 'Let's at least give this a try. You last saw this thing where, did you say?'

We continued to move and I spotted the RPO Building – the Fire Escapes Building beside it – rapidly approaching us. The Sun was falling behind them in the familiar way, and then we were passing the store itself. I saw again the colored bottles display and the Recessed Lighting notice, but I was so concerned I'd miss the Cootings Machine I hardly gave them attention. As we went over the pedestrian crossing, the Father said: 'I'm wondering if this street's taxis only. Look at them. Everywhere.'

'This turning perhaps. Please, if possible.'

The Cootings Machine hadn't been where I'd seen it earlier, and as the streets grew unfamiliar again, I gazed in every direction. The Sun sometimes shone brightly through the gaps between buildings, and I wondered if he was wishing to encourage me, or simply watching and monitoring my progress. When we turned into yet another street and there was again no sign of the Cootings Machine, my growing panic may have become obvious, because the Father said, in a kinder voice than any he'd so far used towards me:

'You really believe this, don't you? That this will help Josie.'

'Yes. Yes, I do.'

Something seemed to change within him. He sat forward – and then, like me, he was looking left and right with urgent eyes.

'Hope,' he said. 'Damn thing never leaves you alone.' He shook his head almost resentfully, but there was now a new strength about him. 'Okay. A vehicle, you say. One used by construction workers.'

'It has wheels, but I don't think it's a vehicle as such. It needs to be towed everywhere it goes. It has Cootings written on its body and is pale yellow.'

He glanced at his watch. 'The construction guys may have finished for the day. Let me try a few things.'

The Father began to drive more skillfully. We left behind the other vehicles, the passers-by, the storefronts, and entered the smaller streets shaded by windowless buildings, and large walls bright with cartoon writing. Sometimes the Father would stop, reverse, then steer slowly down narrow spaces beside wire-mesh fences, on the other side of which we could observe parked trucks and dirty cars.

'See anything?'

Whenever I shook my head, he'd make the car lurch forward again, in a way that made me anxious we'd strike a fire hydrant or the corner of a building as we turned sharply around it. We looked into more yards, and once, we entered between two crookedly open gates, even though there was a sign hanging from one saying 'Strictly No Admittance', and drove around a yard filled with vehicles, stacked crates and a construction crane at the far end. But there was still no Cootings Machine, and the Father then took us into a shadow neighborhood with broken sidewalks and lonely passers-by. He steered into another narrow lane beside a looming Floors For Lease building, and behind this building was yet another yard bound by wire-mesh fencing.

'There! Mr Paul, there it is!'

The Father jerk-stopped the car. The yard was on my side so I placed my head right against the window, and behind me the Father was adjusting in his seat to see better.

'That one there? With the funnels?'

'Yes. We've found it.'

I didn't take my gaze from the Cootings Machine while the Father reversed the car slowly. Then we stopped once more.

'That main entrance has a chain on it,' he said. 'But the side entrance there . . .'

'Yes, the small entrance is open. A passer-by could enter on foot.'

I released the safety belt and was about to get out, but then felt the Father's hand on my arm.

'I wouldn't go in there until you've decided exactly what you intend to do. It all looks ramshackle, but you never know. There may be alarms, there may be surveillance. You may not have time to stand around and think.'

'Yes, you're right.'

'Are you quite certain you have the correct machine?'

'Quite certain. I can see it clearly from here and there's no doubt.'

'And disabling it, you say, will help Josie?'

'Yes.'

'So how do you propose to go about doing that?'

I stared at the Cootings Machine sitting near the center of the yard, separated from the other parked vehicles. The Sun was falling between two silhouette buildings in the mid-distance overlooking the yard. His rays weren't for the moment blocked

223

by either building, and the edges of the parked vehicles were shining.

'I feel very foolish,' I said finally.

'No, it's not so easy,' the Father said. 'On top of which, what you're proposing would count as criminal damage.'

'Yes. However, if the people up in those high windows over there happened to see anything, I'm sure they'd be happy to see the Cootings Machine being destroyed. They'd know just what an awful machine it is.'

'That may be so. But how do you propose to do it?'

The Father was now leaning back in his seat, one arm quite relaxed on the wheel, and I had the impression he'd already arrived at a possible solution, but for some reason was holding back from revealing it.

'Mr Paul is an expert engineer,' I said, turning to face him directly. 'I was hoping he'd be able to think of something.'

But the Father kept gazing through the windshield at the yard. 'I couldn't explain it to Josie earlier in the cafe,' he said. 'I couldn't explain to her why I hate Capaldi so much. Why I can't bring myself to be civil towards him. But I'd like to try and explain it to *you*, Klara. If you don't mind.'

His switch of subject was highly unwelcome, but anxious not to lose his good will, I said nothing and waited.

'I think I hate Capaldi because deep down I suspect he may be right. That what he claims is true. That science has now proved beyond doubt there's nothing so unique about my daughter, nothing there our modern tools can't excavate, copy, transfer. That people have been living with one another all this time, centuries, loving and hating each other, and all on a mistaken premise. A kind of superstition we kept going while we didn't know better. That's how Capaldi sees it, and there's a part of

224

me that fears he's right. Chrissie, on the other hand, isn't like me. She may not know it yet, but she'll never let herself be persuaded. If the moment ever comes, never mind how well you play your part, Klara, never mind how much she wishes it to work, Chrissie just won't be able to accept it. She's too . . . old-fashioned. Even if she knows she's going against the science and the math, she still won't be able to do it. She just won't stretch that far. But I'm different. I have . . . a kind of coldness inside me she lacks. Perhaps it's because I'm an expert engineer, as you put it. This is why I find it so hard to be civil around people like Capaldi. When they do what they do, say what they say, it feels like they're taking from me what I hold most precious in this life. Am I making sense?'

'Yes. I understand Mr Paul's feelings.' I let a quiet few seconds go by, then continued: 'It seems then from everything Mr Paul says that it's even more important that what Mr Capaldi proposes is never put to the test. If we can make Josie healthy, then the portrait, my learning her, none of it will matter. So I ask you again. Please advise me how I might destroy the Cootings Machine. I have a feeling Mr Paul has an idea how we might do it.'

'Yes, a possibility has occurred to me. But I was hoping a better idea might come along. Unfortunately it's looking like that isn't going to happen.'

'Please tell me. Something may change at any moment and this opportunity will pass.'

'Okay. Well, here it is. That machine will contain inside it a Sylvester broad generation unit. Middle-market. Fuel-efficient and robust enough, but with no real protections. It means that machine can stand any amount of dust, smoke, rain. But if anything, let's say, with a high acrylamide content got inside its system, for example a P-E-G Nine solution, it wouldn't be able to handle it. It would be like putting gasoline into a diesel engine, except a lot worse. If you introduced P-E-G Nine in there, it would rapidly polymerize. The damage is likely to be terminal.'

'P-E-G Nine solution.'

'Yes.'

'Does Mr Paul know how we might now obtain P-E-G Nine solution at short notice?'

'As it happens, I do.' He went on looking at me for a second, then said: 'You'll be carrying a certain quantity of P-E-G Nine. There, inside your head.'

'I see.'

'I believe there's usually a small cavity. Just there, at the back of the head, where it meets the neck. This isn't my area of expertise. Capaldi would know much more. But my guess is that you could afford to lose a small amount of P-E-G Nine without it significantly affecting your well-being.'

'If . . . if we were able to extract the solution from me, would there be sufficient to destroy the Cootings Machine?'

'This really isn't my area. But my guess is that you might be carrying approximately five hundred milliliters. Even half of that should be sufficient to incapacitate a middle-market machine such as that one. Having said that, I have to emphasize. I'm not advocating we go down this road. Anything that jeopardizes your abilities would jeopardize Capaldi's plan. And Chrissie wouldn't want that.'

My mind was filling with great fear, but I said: 'But Mr Paul believes if we could extract the solution, we could destroy the Cootings Machine.'

'That's what I believe. Yes.'

'Is it possible Mr Paul has suggested this course not only to destroy the Cootings Machine, but also to damage Klara, and thus Mr Capaldi's plan?'

'That very thought did cross my mind too. But if I really wanted to damage you, Klara, I think there are far simpler ways. Truth is, you've started me hoping again. Hoping what you say might be for real.'

'How would we extract the solution?'

'Just a small incision. Below the ear. Either ear would do. We'd require a tool, something with a sharp point or edge. We need only to pierce the outer layer. Beyond that, well, there should be a small valve I can loosen, then tighten back again with my fingers.' He'd been searching through the Mother's car's glove compartment while saying this, and he now produced a plastic bottle of water. 'Okay, this will do to catch the solution. And here, it's not ideal, but here's a tiny screwdriver. If I sharpened the edge a little more . . .' He trailed off, holding the tool up to the light. 'After that, it's just a case of walking over there and carefully pouring the solution down one of those nozzles. We should use the central one. It's likely to connect directly to the Sylvester unit.'

'Will I lose my abilities?'

'As I said, your overall performance shouldn't be greatly impaired. But this isn't my area. There may be some effects on your cognitive abilities. But since your essential energy source is solar, you shouldn't be affected to any significant degree.'

He lowered the window on his side and holding out the plastic bottle, emptied the water out onto the ground outside.

'This is your call, Klara. If you want, we can just drive away from here. We have another, let me see, twenty minutes before our rendezvous with the rest of our party.'

I stared at the yard again through the wire-mesh fencing, trying to control my fear. My view of it from the car had remained

227

unpartitioned, and the Sun was still watching from between the two silhouette buildings.

'You know, Klara. I don't even know what this is about. But I want what's best for Josie. Exactly the same as you. So I'm willing to grasp at any chance that comes our way.'

I turned to him with a smile and nodded. 'Yes,' I said. 'Then let's try.'

■

Sitting beside the sushi cafe's window, looking out at the shadows growing longer outside the theater, I'd become excited by the possibility that the Sun might conceivably pour in his special nourishment straight away, through this very window, to Josie, now sitting across the table from me. But I realized how tired the Sun must be – that he'd all but finished for the day – and that it was both disrespectful and unreasonable to expect such an immediate response. A small hope continued to linger in my mind, and I watched Josie closely, but I soon accepted I'd have to wait until the following morning at the very earliest.

I'd also realized the reason I couldn't see so clearly through the sushi cafe's window was because it was dusty and smeared, and not so much to do with what had occurred in the yard. Indeed, despite its constant billowing in the breeze, I could still read the large cloth banner above the theater entrance saying 'Blissfully Brilliant!' And I had no difficulty deciphering the people arriving to join those already milling around outside the theater. Each time more people came, there would be greetings and humorous shouts. I couldn't hear their words clearly, but there was thick glass separating us, so this too was consistent with the prevailing conditions.

228

Our task in the yard hadn't delayed us unduly, but by the time the Father and I had finally located the correct sushi cafe, Josie, Rick, the Mother and Miss Helen had already been sitting for several minutes around the table beside the window. The Father had greeted everyone cheerfully, as though there hadn't been any tension at Mr Capaldi's, but soon afterwards, the Mother had risen and gone out to join the crowd outside, her oblong held to her ear.

Now, across the table, the Father was turning the pages of Rick's notebook and making appreciative sounds. But I was concerned at how uncharacteristically quiet Josie had become, and soon the Father noticed this too.

'You okay there, animal?'

'I'm fine, Dad.'

'We've been on the go for a long time now. Do you want to go back to the apartment?'

'I'm not tired. I'm not sick. I'm okay, Dad. Let me just sit here.'

Rick, sitting beside Josie, was also looking at her with concern. 'Hey, Josie, do you fancy finishing this for me?' He said this quietly, almost into her ear, as he slid the remainder of his carrot cake towards her. 'It might give you energy.'

'I don't need energy, Ricky. I'm fine. I just want to sit here, that's all.'

The Father looked carefully at Josie, then turned back to Rick's notebook.

'These are really interesting, Rick.'

'Ricky, darling,' Miss Helen said, 'it just occurs to me. It was an excellent idea to bring your diagrams along. But perhaps it's best you don't offer them to Vance unless he specifically asks you.'

'Mum, we've been over this.'

229

'It's just that it might look inappropriate. Too eager. This is supposed to be just a social meeting after all. A spontaneous encounter.'

'Mum, how can this be spontaneous when it's been so carefully set up and we've come in specially for it?'

'I just mean, darling, you must try and behave *as though* it's spontaneous. That's what will work best with Vance. Only if he asks specifically to see some of your work . . .'

'I understand, Mum. It's all under control.'

Rick looked tense, and I wished to do something to give him reassurance, but I was across the table from him and couldn't reach over to touch his arm or shoulder. The Father was again looking at Josie, but she didn't seem to me unwell so much as simply lost in her own thoughts.

'Drones were never my area,' the Father said after a while. 'But this, Rick, is truly impressive and exciting.' Then to Miss Helen: 'Lifted or not, genuine ability has to get noticed. Unless this world's *completely* crazy now.'

'You were always encouraging me, Mr Arthur,' Rick said. 'Right from when I first started getting into all this. So much of what you showed me back then forms the foundations of what you see there.'

'That's kind, Rick, but I'm sure it's entirely unwarranted. Drone technology was never my area, and I doubt if I was ever of much help to you. But I appreciate you saying that.'

Through the window I could now see the Sun's last patterns of the day falling across the black-suit women with bow ties, the theater's waistcoat officials handing out leaflets, the bright costume couples, and the musicians with small guitars moving amidst the crowd, snatches of their music coming through the glass.

'Hey, animal. Did your mother happen to say something to upset you? This isn't like you, sitting there so quiet.'

'I'm fine, Dad. I'm just not like a show, okay? I can't sparkle and entertain all day. Sometimes I just want to sit and chill out.'

'You know we do miss you, Paul,' Miss Helen said. 'Is it four years already? Oh look, even more people arriving. I wonder when they'll let them go inside. It's just as well there's no traffic allowed through here. Where's Chrissie now? Is she still out there?'

'I see her, Mum. She's still on her phone.'

'I'm so glad she's with us today. So reassuring. She's such a good friend to me. And I do appreciate all of you too, being here like this, extending your support to Rick and to me.' She looked around the table, appearing to make a special point of including me in her gaze. 'I won't pretend I'm not getting nervous. The hour being almost upon us. And not just on Rick's account, if I'm honest. Did I ever tell you, Paul? The man we're about to meet, he and I were once *passionate*. Not just for a weekend or a few months, but for years . . .'

'Mum, please . . .'

'Should you get a chance to talk with him, Paul, I think you'll find you have certain things in common. For instance, he too has fascistic leanings. He always has done though I always tried not to notice . . .'

'Mum, for God's sake . . .'

'Now, Helen, easy there,' the Father said. 'Are you implying that I . . .'

'It's only because of what you were saying a moment ago, Paul. About your community.'

'No, Helen, I can't have this. And in front of the kids too. What I was saying earlier has nothing to do with fascism. We have no aggressive agenda beyond defending ourselves should the need arise. Where you live, Helen, maybe you don't have to worry yet, and I sincerely hope it'll be that way for a long time. Where I am, it's different.'

'Then why, Dad, don't you move out of there? Why keep living in a place with gangs and guns?'

The Father seemed pleased Josie had finally participated. 'Because that's my community, Josie. It's not nearly as bad as this makes it sound. I like it there. I'm sharing my life with some very fine people, and most of them came down the same road I did. It's become clear to all of us now, there are many different ways to lead a decent and full life.'

'Are you saying, Dad, you're glad you lost your job?'

'In many ways, Josie, yes. And it's not like I really *lost* my job. It's all been part of the changes. Everyone's had to find new ways to live their lives.'

'I do apologize, Paul,' Miss Helen said, 'for suggesting you and your new friends were fascists. I shouldn't have done so. It's just that you did say you were all white people and all from the ranks of the former professional elites. You did say that. And that you were having to arm yourselves quite extensively against other *types*. Which does all sound a little on the fascistic side . . .'

'Helen, I won't have this. Josie knows it's not that way, but I don't like her even hearing you say it. I don't like Rick hearing it either. It just isn't true. There are different groups where we live, I'm not denying it. I didn't make the rules and it's just the way it naturally divided. And if another group won't respect us, and what we have, they need to know they'll have a fight on their hands.'

'Mum's way out of order,' Rick said. 'She's getting anxious, that's all. You'll have to excuse her.'

'Don't worry, Rick. I've known your mother a long time and I'm very fond of her.'

'His name is Vance,' Miss Helen said. 'The man we're waiting to meet. Rick and I are so grateful you're all here to lend moral support, but from here we're on our own. Let me tell you, Paul, there was a time when Vance was quite besotted with me. Rick, darling, please don't pull that face. Rick's never met him, this was all before his time. Oh, there was that one occasion, I suppose, but that hardly counts. When you see him, Paul, I dare say you'll wonder what on earth I saw in him. But I assure you, he was once even more handsome than you are. Oddly, the more success he had in life, the less handsome he became. Now he's rich and influential and looks appalling. Still, I'll try and see the handsome young man he once was within all those folds of flesh. I do wonder if he'll do as much for me.'

'What's happening out there, animal? Can you see your mother?'

'She's still on her phone.'

'I guess she's mad at me. She probably won't come back in so long as I'm sitting here.'

Perhaps the Father was hoping someone would contradict him, but no one did. Miss Helen even raised her eyebrows and made a short laughing sound. Then she said:

'Nearly time, Rick darling. I suppose we ought to go out there now.'

When I heard her say this, a fear filled my mind; I was no longer certain that the effects from what had occurred in the yard weren't growing more pronounced with the passing minutes, and that my new condition wouldn't become obvious to everyone if I attempted to negotiate the unfamiliar terrain outdoors.

233

'I do wonder,' Miss Helen was saying, 'when Vance suggested meeting outside a theater, if he realized there might be a show about to start and a crowd gathering. We should go out there. He might come early and the crowd will confuse him.'

Rick placed a hand on Josie's shoulder and asked quietly: 'Are you sure you're okay, Josie?'

'I swear I'm okay. So you go and do your best, Ricky boy. That's what I'm wanting more than anything.'

'That's right,' the Father said. 'And just remember. You've got talent. Well, maybe we should all leave now.'

He rose to his feet, and as he did so, his gaze fell on me, examining me more carefully than would have been normal. I immediately became worried the others would notice, even though the incision was well hidden under my hair. Then the Father's gaze moved once more to Josie.

'Animal, we need to get you back. Let's go and find your mother.'

■

As we came out of the sushi cafe, the Sun was making his final patterns for the day, and I let go of any small hope that he might send his special help in the short time remaining. I could now hear without hindrance the theater people's voices and music, and noticed how the streetlight outside the theater entrance was becoming their main light source. Indeed, for a moment, I thought the theater people were trying to circle around the streetlight in a previously agreed formation, but then their pattern dissolved and I saw that the crowd's shape was shifting randomly.

The Father and Miss Helen were a few paces in front of me, striding towards the crowd, while Rick and Josie were just behind, walking so close that had I been obliged to halt suddenly, they would have collided with me. I could hear Josie saying:

'No, Rick, later. I'll tell you about it then. Let's just say for now Mom's having one of her definitely weird days.'

'But what did she say? What's going on?'

'Look, Ricky, it's not what's important right now. What's important is this guy you're about to meet and what you're going to say to him.'

'But I can see you're upset . . .'

'I'm not upset, Ricky. But I *will* get upset, absolutely upset, if you don't focus and do your very best with this guy. This is important. Important for you and important for *us*.'

I'd thought that once I was no longer observing them through glass, the theater people would become more distinct. But now I was in their midst, their figures became more simplified, as if constructed out of cones and cylinders made from smooth card. Their clothes, for instance, were devoid of the usual creases and folds, and even their faces under the streetlight appeared to have been created by cleverly placing flat surfaces into complex arrangements to create a sense of contouring.

We kept walking until the noise was all around us. At one point I stopped and reached back for Josie's arm, but she was no longer behind me. And even though I could hear her voice saying to Rick, 'There's Mom over there,' when I turned to it, I saw neither Josie nor Rick, but a smooth forehead coming towards my own face. Someone pushed my back, though not unkindly, then I heard the Father's voice, and turning again, I saw him and Miss Helen standing beside a stranger's elbow. I could hear the Father saying:

'I didn't want to say this back there in front of the kids. But Helen, look. It's all very well calling me a fascist. Call me what you want. But where you're living now, it may not always remain so peaceful. You hear what happened in this very city last week? I'm not saying you're in danger right now, but you need to think ahead. When I speak to Chrissie about this, she just shrugs. But you need to think about this. Think ahead about Rick, as much as about yourself.'

'Oh, but I *am* thinking ahead, Paul. Why do you suppose we're here today? Why do you suppose I'm looking left and right for my long-lost lover? I'm thinking ahead, and I'm planning, and if I've done so correctly, Rick will soon be elsewhere. And not, I hope, in any community barricading itself with weapons. I mean for Rick to do well, and for that I need Vance's help. Oh where can he have got to? Perhaps he went to the wrong theater.'

'Rick's turned into a fine young man. I hope he's able to find a path through this mess we've bequeathed to his generation. But if things don't go so well, Helen, either for you or for him, then I want you to get in touch. I can find you both a place within our community.'

'That's very sweet of you, Paul. And I'm sorry if I was rude earlier. This might surprise you, but I'm not actually angry about the way we've become. If one child has more ability than another, then it's only right the brighter one gets the opportunities. The responsibilities too. I accept that. But what I won't accept is that Rick can't have a decent life. I refuse to accept this world has become so cruel. Rick wasn't lifted, but he can still go far, do very well.'

'I wish him the very best. All I'm saying is that there are all kinds of ways to lead a successful life.'

Many faces had been pushing in around me, but now a new one appeared in front of the others and kept moving closer till it was almost touching mine. Only then did I recognize Rick and let out a sound of surprise.

'Klara, do you know what's up with Josie?' he asked. 'Did something happen earlier?'

'I don't know what was said between Josie and the Mother,' I said. 'But I have very good news. The task that was given to me, that evening you helped me reach Mr McBain's barn. It's now been completed. It was a task I so wished to complete, but for a long time I couldn't see how to do so. Rick, it's really been done.'

'That's wonderful. But I'm not sure I know what you're talking about.'

'I can't explain yet. And I was obliged to give up something. But that doesn't matter at all, because now we can have hope again.'

Ever more cones and cylinders – or what appeared to be fragments of them – were squeezing into any spaces left around me. I then realized one of these fragments – a shape moving in to replace Rick – was in fact Josie. Once I'd recognized her, she became immediately more distinct, and I had no further difficulty holding her in my mind.

'Hey, Klara, this here's Cindy. She was waitressing our table earlier? She knows about your old store.'

There was a touch on my arm and I heard someone exclaim: 'Hey, I used to *love* your store!' When I turned towards the voice, I saw two tall funnels, one inserted into the other, the upper one tilting slightly forward towards me. When I smiled and said, 'How do you do?' the funnels went on:

'I was telling your owner here. I walked past it last weekend and it's become this furniture place? Hey, you know, I'm sure I saw you in that window once.'

237

'Klara wants to know where they moved to. Cindy, do you know?'

'Oh. I'm not sure if they *moved* . . .'

Someone was tugging my arm, but before me now were so many fragments they appeared like a solid wall. I'd also started to suspect that many of these shapes weren't really even three-dimensional, but had been sketched onto flat surfaces using clever shading techniques to give the illusion of round-ness and depth. I then realized that the figure now beside me, leading me away, was the Mother. She was saying, almost into my ear:

'Klara, I know we said a lot of things earlier. In the car, I mean. But you have to understand, I was thinking about three, four things at once. All I'm saying is don't take too seriously anything we said. You understand, right?'

'You mean, when we were in the car alone? When we were parked near the bridge?'

'Yes, that's what I mean. I'm not saying we're going back on anything. But I'm just saying so you know, okay? Oh, this whole thing's getting so confusing. And Paul doesn't help. Look at him. What's he telling her now?'

Not far from us, the Father was leaning forward so that his face was close to Josie's, saying something earnestly.

'He's so full of shit these days,' the Mother said, and began to go to them. But before she could do so, an arm came out of the crowd and grasped her wrist.

'Chrissie,' Miss Helen's voice said, 'leave them alone for another minute. They don't get to be together much these days.'

'Paul's distributed his brand of wisdom quite enough for one day, it seems to me,' the Mother said. 'And now look. They're quarreling.'

'They're not quarreling, Chrissie. I assure you they're not. So let them talk to each other.'

'Helen, I really don't need you to interpret for me. I can still read my own daughter and husband.'

'*Ex*-husband, Chrissie. And exes are unfathomable, as I'm having underlined this very moment. Vance swore he'd not keep us waiting, and now look. We weren't married, as you and Paul were, so the bitter aftertaste has a different flavor. But don't underestimate it, Chrissie. I haven't seen him in fourteen years, and then only fleetingly quite by chance. Is it possible we passed each other in this crowd and didn't recognize one another?'

'Do you regret it, Helen?' the Mother asked suddenly. 'You know what I mean. Do you regret it? Not going ahead with Rick?'

For a moment Miss Helen kept looking towards where the Father and Josie were talking to one another. Then she said: 'Yes. If I'm honest, Chrissie, the answer's yes. Even after seeing what it's brought you. I feel . . . I feel I didn't do my best for him. I feel I didn't even think it through, the way you and Paul did. I was somewhere else in my mind and I just let the moment go past. Perhaps that's what I regret more than anything else. That I never loved him enough to make a proper decision one way or the other.'

'It's okay.' The Mother placed a gentle hand on Miss Helen's upper arm. 'It's okay. It's difficult, I know that.'

'But I'm doing my best now. I'm doing my best for him this time round. I just need Former Lover to turn up. Oh! That's him there. Vance! Vance! Excuse me . . .'

'Would you care to sign our petition?' The man who had appeared in front of the Mother had a white-painted face and black hair. The Mother took a quick step back, as if the white-face material would come off on her, and said: 'What's it about?'

'We're protesting the proposal to clear the Oxford Building. There's currently four hundred and twenty-three post-employed people living inside it, eighty-six of them children. Neither Lexdell nor the city have offered any reasonable plan regarding their relocation.'

I didn't hear any more of what the black-and-white man was saying to the Mother because the Father moved in front of me and said to her:

'Jesus, Chrissie, what have you been saying to our daughter?' He was keeping his voice down, but he sounded annoyed. 'She's acting really strange. Did you by any chance *tell* her?'

'I didn't, Paul, no.' The Mother's voice was uncharacteristically uncertain. 'At least, not about . . . all of *that*.'

'So what exactly did you . . .'

'We just talked about the portrait, that was all. We can't keep everything hidden from her. She suspects so many things, and if we don't speak to her about any of it, we'll lose her trust.'

'You told her about the *portrait*?'

'I only told her it wasn't a painting. That it was a kind of sculpture. She remembers Sal's doll, of course . . .'

'Jesus Christ, I thought we agreed . . .'

'Josie isn't a small child, Paul. She can figure things out. And she's right to expect us to talk to her honestly . . .'

'Rick!' I recognized Miss Helen's voice behind me. 'Rick! Come on! Vance is here, I've found him. Come and say hello. Oh, Chrissie, I want you to meet Vance. A dear old friend. Here he is.'

Mr Vance was wearing a high-rank suit with a buttoned-up white shirt and blue tie. He was as bald as Mr Capaldi and less

240

in height than Miss Helen. He was looking all around himself as though puzzled.

'Hello, nice to meet you,' he said to the Mother. Then to Miss Helen: 'So what's happening here? Is everyone going to this show?'

'Rick and I were waiting here for you, Vance. Exactly as you told us to. How wonderful to see you again! You've hardly changed.'

'You're looking very good too, Helen. But what's going on here? Where's your son?'

'Ricky! Over here!'

I could now see Rick, standing a little way away, his hand raised in response. Then he started to move through the fragments towards us. I couldn't tell if Mr Vance, who was looking in the correct direction, had identified Rick or not. In any case, at that moment, one of the theater's waistcoat officials came and stood between Mr Vance and the approaching Rick.

'Do you already have a ticket for this show?' the waistcoat official asked. 'Or maybe you do, but you'd be interested in an upgrade?'

Mr Vance stared at him, saying nothing. Then Rick came past the waistcoat official and Mr Vance said: 'Hey! This is your boy? He looks terrific.'

'Thank you, Vance,' Miss Helen said quietly.

'Hello, sir,' Rick said, and his smile was like the one he'd had when first greeting the adults at Josie's interaction meeting.

'Hi, Rick. So I'm Vance. Old, old friend of your mother. Heard a lot about you.'

'It's kind of you to meet with us, sir.'

'So *here* you are!' Josie suddenly filled the space before me. Beside her was a girl of eighteen who I realized was Cindy, the

241

waitress, far less simplified now than when I'd last seen her.

'Yeah, I don't think your store actually *moved*,' Cindy said. 'But there's a new store opened inside Delancey's and maybe some of the AFs from your old store would have relocated there.'

'Excuse me.' A lady in a high-rank blue dress, who I estimated as forty-six years old, came in front of me, but facing Josie and Cindy. 'We were just wondering if you were intending to bring this machine into the theater.'

'Hey, what's it to do with you if we were?' Cindy said.

'These are sought-after seats,' the lady said. 'They shouldn't be taken by machines. If you take this machine into the theater, we'll have to raise an objection.'

'I don't see why it's any business of yours . . .'

'It's okay,' Josie said. 'Klara isn't going into the show and neither am I . . .'

'That's beside the point,' Cindy said. 'I'm angry about this.' Then to the lady she said: 'I don't know you! Who are you? Just coming up and speaking to us that way . . .'

'So this is your machine?' the lady asked Josie.

'Klara's my AF, if that's what you're asking.'

'First they take the jobs. Then they take the seats at the theater?'

'Klara?' The Father had brought his face close up to mine. 'Are you still feeling okay?'

'Yes, I'm fine.'

'Are you sure?'

'Perhaps I was a little disoriented earlier. But now I'm fine.'

'Good. Look, I have to be on my way very soon. So I'm wondering if you'd tell me now. Exactly what did we do back there? And what can we hope will happen as a result?'

'Mr Paul trusted me and that was wonderful. Unfortunately, as I said before, I can't tell you anything more without jeopardizing the very thing we achieved. But I believe there's real hope now. Please be patient and wait for good news.'

'As you please. I'll call in at the apartment in the morning to say goodbye to Josie. So I may see you then.'

The Mother's voice said somewhere behind me: 'We'll talk about this back at the apartment. We can't talk here.'

'But that's all I wanted to say,' Josie's voice said. 'I definitely don't want you sealing it up, the way you did with Sal's. I want it so Klara gets sole use of my room and she gets to come and go as she pleases.'

'But why are we even talking about this? You're going to get well, honey. We don't have to think about *any* of this . . .'

'Oh, Klara, here you are.' Miss Helen had appeared beside me. 'Klara, look, I've just been speaking with Chrissie. You're to come with us for now.'

'With you?'

'Chrissie wants to take Josie back to the apartment and have a quiet word with her, just the two of them. So you stay with us for now. Chrissie will come and collect you in half an hour.' Then leaning forward, she spoke quietly into my ear: 'Can you see? Rick and Vance are really hitting it off! All the same, dear, Rick will really appreciate having you beside him as he goes through this. It could still be something of an ordeal.'

'Yes, of course. But the Mother . . .'

'She'll come and collect you in very good time, don't worry. She just needs a few minutes alone with Josie.'

'What I want more than anything else,' Mr Vance said with a laugh, coming towards us, 'is for us to get out of this crush. Over there, that diner. That looks fine. Just somewhere we can sit down, look at one another and talk.'

There were arms encircling me, and I realized Josie was holding me in an embrace, not unlike the one she'd held me in that day at the store following the great decision. But this time, she spoke into my ear, so only I could hear:

'Don't worry. I'll never let anything bad happen to you. I'll talk to Mom. You go with Rick for now. Trust me.'

Then she released me, and Miss Helen was pulling me gently away.

'Come along, Klara, dear.'

We emerged from the theater crowd, Mr Vance leading the way towards the diner, Miss Helen hurrying to walk alongside him. Rick and I followed the adults a few steps behind, and as the emptiness and cool air moved in around us, I felt my orientation returning. When I looked back, I was surprised to see how dark and quiet the street actually was, aside from the single dense cluster of people around the streetlight. In fact, as we moved ever further away, this crowd – of which I'd so recently been a part – appeared like one of those insect clouds I'd seen in the evening field, hovering against the sky, each creature within it busily changing position, anxious to find a better one, but never straying beyond the boundary of the shape they made together. I saw Josie, waving with a puzzled expression from the crowd's edge, and the Mother, standing behind her, a hand on each of Josie's shoulders, watching us with empty eyes.

■

The darkness grew, and the noises of the theater crowd became more faint, but I knew my observational abilities hadn't been too badly impaired because I continued to see clearly before me the illuminated diner towards which we were walking. I could see how it was shaped like a pie segment, the sharp end pointed towards us; and how the street forked on either side of it, and how the diner's windows ran alongside both the diverging sidewalks, so that no matter which way passers-by went, they'd be able to look into its lit interior – at the shiny leather seats, the polished tabletops, and the bright see-through counter behind which the diner manager was waiting for customers in his white apron and white cap.

With no vehicles approaching and the surrounding buildings so dark, the diner was this area's only light source, throwing slanted shapes onto the paving stones. I wondered which side of the fork Mr Vance would choose, but as we came closer, I noticed a door just at the pointed corner itself. The only reason I hadn't spotted it earlier, I supposed, was because the door so resembled the diner's windows – it was made mostly of glass and had painted writing going across it. Mr Vance opened the door, then stood aside to allow Miss Helen to go in first.

When I came in behind Rick a moment later, I found the lighting so strong and yellow I couldn't immediately adjust to it. Only gradually did I make out the slices of fruit pie, each one shaped like the diner itself, displayed inside the see-through counter, and the Diner Manager – a large black-skinned man – standing very still behind it, his face fixed away from me. I then realized he was watching Mr Vance and Miss Helen as they chose their booth and settled themselves into it, facing one another.

I saw Rick's figure cross the shiny floor and sit down beside his mother. As I did so, Josie's parting words to me returned to my mind, and I wondered what important matter the Mother wished to discuss with her at the Friend's Apartment, and why my absence was necessary.

Miss Helen and Mr Vance continued to gaze at each other silently for the entire time it took me to go over to them. I didn't feel I knew Mr Vance well enough to sit beside him. Also, he was sitting midway across the seat intended for two, and I could see I wouldn't be able to take my seat without disturbing his comfort. So instead I sat down alone in the neighboring booth across the aisle.

Mr Vance finally stopped gazing at Miss Helen and, turning in his seat, called out instructions to the Diner Manager. Only then did it occur to me that though there were no customers but us, all the tables and seats had been carefully made ready in case others came in. I thought then that this Diner Manager might be lonely, or at least that he was lonely while he was in his diner, illuminated on both sides to anyone passing by in the night.

'Sir?' Rick said. 'I'm very grateful you're giving up time for me. And that you're even considering helping me.'

'You know, Rick,' Mr Vance said dreamily, 'I haven't seen this mother of yours for quite some time.'

'I appreciate that, sir. And you've never even met me before, except once fleetingly when I was two or something. So that makes this all the more generous of you, agreeing to see me like this. But then Mum's always saying how generous a person you are.'

'I'm relieved your mother's been speaking well of me. Maybe she's told you one or two negative things also?'

'Oh no. My mother's only ever spoken of you positively.'

'Is that so? And all these years I've thought . . . Well, never mind. Helen, I'm already impressed by this boy of yours.'

Miss Helen had been watching Mr Vance carefully. 'I need hardly tell you, Vance, how grateful I am also. I'd thank you at greater length, but this is Rick's chance and I'm not wishing to speak on his behalf.'

'That's well said, Helen. So Rick. Why don't you tell me what this is about?'

'Well, I'm not sure where to start, but here goes. I have a keen interest in drone technology. You could say it's a passion. I've been developing my own system, and I now have my own team of drone birds . . .'

'One second. When you say "own system", Rick, are you saying you've gone beyond what anyone else has done?'

Panic crossed Rick's face, and he glanced towards me. I smiled at him, trying to convey as I did so that the smile wasn't just mine, but on behalf of Josie. Whether he understood this or not, he appeared to take encouragement.

'No, sir, hardly,' he said with a quick laugh. 'I'm not claiming I'm a genius. But I'll say that my drone system *is* one I've worked out for myself, without help from any tutors. I've used various information sources that I found online. And my mother's been very supportive, ordering in some expensive books. Actually, I've brought with me some drawings, just in case you wanted a vague idea. Here they are. But no, I don't believe I'm doing anything so groundbreaking, and I know I'm not likely to without expert guidance.'

'I follow you. So now you aim to get to a good college. In order to do justice to your talent.'

'Well, something like that. My mother and I both thought that maybe Atlas Brookings, being a generous and liberal college . . .'

'Sufficiently generous and liberal to be open to all students of high caliber, even some who haven't benefited from genetic editing.'

'Exactly, sir.'

'And no doubt, Rick, you understand, because your mother will have told you, that I currently chair the college's Founders' Committee. That's to say, the body that controls the scholarships.'

'Yes, sir. That's what she told me.'

'Now, Rick. I'm hoping your mother hasn't been implying that the selection procedure at Atlas Brookings is subject to any favoritism.'

'Neither my mother nor I would ask you to help me out of favoritism, sir. I'm only asking you to help if you think I'm worth a place at Atlas Brookings.'

'That's well said. Okay, let's take a look at what you have here.'

Rick had already placed his notebook on the table, and Mr Vance now opened it. He stared at the diagram at which the notebook had fallen open, then, as he turned over the page and found another, he appeared to become absorbed. He continued to leaf slowly through the notebook, sometimes returning to an earlier page. At one point he murmured without looking up:

'These all refer to what you plan to create in the future?'

'Mostly, yes. Though some designs I've already realized. Like that one on the next page.'

Miss Helen was watching silently, a gentle smile on her face, her glance moving from Mr Vance to Rick's notebook. At that moment, I felt once more, fleetingly but vividly, the Father's hand holding my head at the required angle, and heard the trickling noise as the fluid entered the plastic bottle he was holding up close to my face with his other hand.

'Now, Rick,' Mr Vance said, 'I'm very ignorant about these matters. Even so, I'm getting the impression your drones have high surveillance capabilities.'

'The birds are data-gathering, that's right. But that doesn't necessarily mean they have to be used for privacy-invasive activity. They have many potential applications. Security, even babysitting. Then again, perhaps there are people out there we need to keep an eye on.'

'Like criminals, you mean.'

'Or paramilitaries. Or weird cults.'

'I follow you. Yes, these are all very interesting. You don't see any real ethical issues here?'

'I'm sure, sir, there are all kinds of ethical issues. But in the end, it's for legislators to decide how these things get regulated, not people like me. For now, I just want to learn as much as I can, so I can take my understanding to the next level.'

'That's well said.' Mr Vance nodded and continued looking through Rick's notebook.

The lonely Diner Manager had come over holding his tray, and he began to place drinks on the table in front of Miss Helen, Mr Vance and Rick. They each thanked him in hushed voices, then he walked away again.

'You appreciate, Rick,' Mr Vance said, 'I'm not trying to give you a hard time here. I'm merely, well, testing you a little, to see what you're made of.' Then to Miss Helen he said: 'And so far, he's coming out very impressively.'

'Vance, darling. Would you care for something to go with this coffee? Perhaps one of those donuts I see over there? You were always partial to donuts.'

'Thank you, Helen, but I'm meeting some people for dinner.' He glanced at his watch, then back at Rick. 'Now consider this, Rick. Atlas Brookings believes there are many talented kids out there, just like you, who for reasons economic or otherwise never received the benefits of AGE. The college also believes society is currently making a grave error in not allowing those talents to come to full fruition. Unfortunately most other institutions don't think this way. Which means we receive vastly more applications from people like yourself than we're able to accommodate. We can weed out no-hopers, but after that, frankly, it becomes a lottery. Now Rick. You said just now you're not seeking favoritism. Then let me ask you this. If that is really the case, *then why am I sitting here in front of you now?*'

With these words Mr Vance changed the mood so suddenly I almost let a surprised sound escape me. Rick too seemed startled. Only Miss Helen appeared not to be surprised, but as though something she'd feared all along had finally arrived. She smiled and said:

'I'm going to answer this one for him, Vance. Yes, we *are* asking you for a favor. We know you have it within your gift. So we're asking you to help us. I'll rephrase that. *I'm* asking you. I'm asking you to help my boy have a fighting chance in this world.'

'Mum . . .'

'No, Ricky darling, that's right. It's for me, not you, to ask Vance. And we *are* asking him to exercise favoritism. Of course we are.'

I'd been wrong in thinking we were Diner Manager's only customers. I now realized that in the booth three along from mine, there was a lady of forty-two sitting by herself. I hadn't seen her before because she was pressing herself right against the window, her forehead actually touching the glass, to gaze out into the darkness. I wondered if perhaps Diner Manager had also failed to notice her, and that she had become even more lonely, believing Diner Manager was deliberately ignoring her.

250

'You know, Helen,' Mr Vance said, 'this is a strange tactic you're adopting here. Favoritism, like any other form of corruption, works best when it remains unacknowledged. But leaving that to one side.' Mr Vance leaned forward. 'When I thought this was Rick asking, that was one thing. He's an impressive and charming kid. It was going well. But look what you've just done. You just told me this is about me doing you – you, Helen – a favor. After all these years. All these years of your not answering my messages. All these minutes and hours and days and months and years of my thinking about you.'

'Must you say this here? In front of Rick?' Miss Helen was still smiling gently, but her voice wobbled.

'Rick's an intelligent young man. He's the one who ultimately wins or loses. So why hide things from him? Let him see the whole picture. Let him see what this is about.'

Once again, Rick looked across the aisle to me, and once again I tried to send back encouragement with a smile that was from both me and Josie.

'But what is this about, Vance?' Miss Helen asked. 'Is it really so complicated? I'm simply asking you to help my son. If you're not willing to do so, then we can part politely and that will be that.'

'Who said I didn't wish to help Rick? I can see he's a talented young man. These drawings show true promise. I've every reason to believe he might do well at Atlas Brookings. The problem is that it's *you* asking me, Helen.'

'Then I shouldn't have spoken. Before I spoke, it was going well. I could see how you took to each other, and Rick spoke to you with genuine respect. But then I intervened, and now there's a problem.'

'Damn right there's a problem, Helen. Twenty-seven years'

251

worth of a problem. Twenty-seven years you refuse to have any communication with me. I wasn't harassing your mother during that time, Rick. I don't want you thinking that. At the start of it, I was, well, let's say I might have been emotional in tone. But I never harassed her, never threatened, never blamed. Just pleaded. Is that fair, Helen? A fair characterization?'

'Quite fair. You were persistent, but there was never any unpleasantness. But Vance, does this have to be said in front of Rick?'

'Okay. I respect that. Maybe I should stop doing the talking. Maybe it's time you did some talking instead, Helen.'

'Sir? I don't know what's gone on in the past. But if you feel there's something inappropriate about asking you to . . .'

'Just a minute, Rick,' Mr Vance said. 'I'm wanting to help you. But I think it's time we gave your mother a chance to explain herself.'

For several seconds none of them spoke. I looked towards Diner Manager, wondering if he had been listening, but he was staring out into the darkness beyond his windows, with no sign of having heard anything that interested him.

'I admit,' Miss Helen said, 'I behaved badly towards you, Vance. I accept that. But then I behaved badly towards myself, towards everybody. You mustn't feel singled out. My awfulness was universally distributed.'

'That may be so. But I wasn't just everybody. We'd been sharing a life for five years . . .'

'Yes. And I do so want to apologize. Sometimes, Vance – and Rick too, I don't mind saying this in front of you – I often wish I could line up all the people, everyone I've treated shabbily, have them all in a long line. Then I'd work my way along it, you know, the way a monarch might. One by one, shake each

252

person's hand, look each one in the eye and say, I'm so sorry, wasn't I awful.'

'Fantastic. So now I have to stand in line. For the honor of receiving her majesty's apology.'

'Oh dear, that came out badly. I'm just trying to express how . . . how I feel. I know it sounds dreadful when you put it like that. But when I look back on things, it's so overwhelming, and I think, if only there could be some sort of solution like that. If I was a queen, then yes, I could . . .'

'Mum, really, I know what you're trying to say. But maybe this isn't the best way . . .'

'Once you *were* a kind of queen, Helen. A beautiful queen. And you thought you could do whatever you wished with impunity. I'm kind of sad, but kind of glad too. To see you didn't get away with it. That it's caught up with you and you've had to pay a price after all.'

'And what price have I paid, Vance? Do you refer to my being poor? Because I don't mind that so much, you know.'

'You may not mind being poor, Helen. But you've become fragile. And I think you mind that a whole lot more.'

Miss Helen was silent for several further seconds while Mr Vance kept staring at her with big eyes. Finally she said: 'Yes. You're right. Since the days you knew me, I've become . . . fragile. So fragile that I'm liable to break into pieces in a puff of wind. I lost my beauty, not to the years but to this fragility. But Vance, dear Vance. Won't you forgive me now at least partially? Won't you help my son? Vance. I'd offer you everything, any-thing, but there's nothing I can think to offer you. Nothing at all, other than this pleading. So I'm begging you, Vance, to help him.'

'Mum, please. Stop this. There's no way . . .'

'You see my difficulty, Rick. I don't quite know what it is your mother's referring to here. She says she wants to apologize, but about what? It's all so broad. I think maybe this will work better, Helen, if we get down to specifics.'

'I'm just asking you to help my son, Vance. Isn't that specific enough?'

'Specifics, Helen. For example, that evening at Miles Martin's house. You know the evening I refer to.'

'Yes, yes. When I told them all that you'd not yet read the Jenkins Report . . .'

'You earned yourself a big laugh at my expense for that one, Helen. And you knew what you were doing . . .'

'Then Vance, I apologize about that evening. I was out of control, I was vindictive. I wish . . .'

'Another specific. No order, I'm working down the list randomly. That voicemail you left me in that hotel. In Portland, Oregon. You think that wasn't hurtful?'

'It was very hurtful. It was a despicable message and I haven't forgotten it. I . . . I hear it in my mind even now, it invades me when I least expect it. I have a quiet moment to myself, then there I am, in my mind, picking up the phone and leaving you that message all over again, except this time I change it. I edit it so that it's not quite so awful. Because I never actually heard it myself, only heard myself saying it, I feel sometimes it's not too late to amend it. I can't help it, it's a trick my mind plays and then I feel so dreadful all over again. Believe me, Vance, I've punished myself about that message so much. And you must appreciate, in those days, I didn't know how you technically erase a message once you've left one . . .'

'Mum, stop. Sir? I don't think this is doing my mother much good. She's been great recently, but . . .'

Miss Helen touched Rick's arm to silence him. 'Vance, I'm apologizing,' she went on. 'I'm pleading. I'm saying I behaved badly towards you and if you like, I'll vow to you that I'll punish myself and keep punishing myself until I've made it up to you.'

'Mum, let's go. This isn't good for you.'

'If you wish, Vance, we can arrange to meet again. Let's say in two years' time in this very place. Then you could check to see I've been keeping my promise. You could look me over and check that I've been punishing myself properly . . .'

'That's enough, Helen. If Rick wasn't here, I'd tell you what I think of that.'

'Sir? I don't wish you to do anything at all to assist me. I don't want any part of this now.'

'No, Rick, you don't know what you're saying,' Miss Helen said. 'Don't listen to him, Vance.'

Mr Vance rose to his feet and said: 'I have to go.'

'Mum, please calm down. None of this matters so much.'

'You don't know what you're saying, Rick! Vance, don't go just yet! Let's not part like this. You used to love donuts. Won't you have one now?'

'I agree with Rick. None of this is good for you, Helen. Best thing's for me to leave. Rick? I like those drawings and I like you. Take good care of yourself. Goodbye, Helen.'

Mr Vance walked off down the aisle between the booths, without looking back at any of us, then out through the glass door and into the darkness. Miss Helen and Rick went on sitting side by side, looking down at the space before them on the tabletop. Then Rick said: 'Klara. Come and sit over here with us.'

'I'm wondering,' Miss Helen said.

Rick moved closer to her, placing an arm around her shoulders. 'What are you wondering, Mum?'

'I'm wondering if that was enough. If that will satisfy him.'

'Honestly, Mum. If I'd known it was going to be even halfway like this, I'd have said never in a million years.'

I slipped into the seat vacated by Mr Vance, but neither Miss Helen nor Rick raised their glances to me. I looked at Miss Helen, and thought about how she and Mr Vance had once been besotted and in love. And I wondered if there had been a time when Miss Helen and Mr Vance had been as gentle to one another as Josie and Rick were now. And if it was possible that one day, Josie and Rick too might show such unkindness to each other. And I remembered the Father talking in the car about the human heart, and how complicated it was, and I saw him standing in the yard, directly in front of the low Sun, his figure and his evening shadow entwining into a single elongated shape as he reached up and unscrewed the protection cap from the nozzle of the Cootings Machine, and I stood anxiously behind him, holding the plastic mineral water bottle containing the precious solution.

'What happened just now?' Miss Helen asked. 'What's Vance going to do? Is he going to help? He could at least have told us one way or the other.'

'Excuse me,' I said. 'I don't wish to create unwarranted hope. But from what I observed I believe Mr Vance will decide to help Rick.'

'You really think so?' Miss Helen asked. 'Why?'

'I may be mistaken. But I believe Mr Vance is still very fond of Miss Helen and will decide to help Rick.'

'Oh you darling robot! I do so hope you're right. I don't know what else I might have done.'

'Mum, to hell with him. I'll be fine anyway.'

'He wasn't nearly as ugly as I'd been led to expect,' Miss Helen said, and looked out into the dark empty street. 'In fact, he wasn't so bad-looking at all. I just wish he'd told us. One way or the other.'

■

Our booth must have been clearly visible to the Mother as she pulled up by the curb on our side of the diner. But she dimmed the lights and remained in the car, perhaps wishing to give privacy, even though she could see Mr Vance had gone.

But when we came out and entered the car, and started to move through the night, I saw she was anxious about Josie being left alone in the Friend's Apartment – and keen to deliver me there as quickly as possible before she drove Rick and Miss Helen to their reasonable hotel. The Mother had asked, 'How did it go?' when we'd first got in, but after Miss Helen had replied, 'Not so good, we'll have to see,' there was little conversation in the car, each person becoming lost in their thoughts.

At night the Friend's Apartment was even harder to distinguish from its neighbors. The Mother led me up the correct steps, and from the top step I glanced back to the waiting car under the streetlight. I could then see the shapes of Miss Helen and Rick inside it, and wondered what they might be saying to each other now they were alone.

The Friend's Apartment was just as we'd left it when setting off for Mr Capaldi's, except of course it was now in darkness. From the entrance hall, I could see the Main Lounge, and the night patterns falling over the sofa on which Josie had waited for the Father's arrival. Her paperback was still on the rug where she'd let it fall, one corner palely illuminated.

The Mother indicated down the hall, saying softly: 'She should be fast asleep, so go in quietly. Anything concerns you, call me. I'll be twenty minutes.'

She was about to go out again, and I didn't wish to delay Rick and Miss Helen's return to the reasonable hotel, but I said quietly:

'It's possible now we can hope.'

'What do you mean?'

'In the morning when the Sun returns. It's possible for us to hope.'

'Okay. I guess that's helpful, the way you're always optimistic.' She reached for the door. 'Don't turn on any lights. They could disturb her, even inside there.' Then the Mother became oddly still, standing in the near-dark, her nose almost touching the surface of the door. Without turning, she said: 'Josie and I had a conversation earlier. It took some strange turns. I guess we were both tired. If she wakes up and says anything peculiar to you, don't pay it too much attention. Oh, and remember. Leave this chain off or I won't get back in. Goodnight.'

■

I entered the Second Bedroom carefully and found Josie sleeping soundly. The room was more narrow than the bedroom at home, but the ceiling was higher, and because Josie had left the blind halfway up, there were shapes falling across the wardrobe and the wall next to it. I went to the window and looked out into the night to establish the path the Sun might take in the morning, and how easy it would be for him to look in. Like the room itself, the window was tall and narrow. Surprisingly close

258

by were the backs of two large buildings, and I could decipher drainpipes marking vertical lines, and repeating windows, most of them empty or blanked out by blinds. Between the two buildings I could see the street beyond, and could tell that by the morning, it would be a busy one. Even now there was a steady flow of vehicles crossing the gap. Above the piece of street was a tall column of night sky, and I estimated the Sun would have no difficulty pouring in his special nourishment from it, narrow though it was. I realized too how important it was that I remain alert, ready at the first sign to raise the blind fully.

'Klara?' Josie stirred behind me. 'Is Mom back too?'

'She won't be long. She's just driving Rick and Miss Helen to their hotel.'

She appeared to return into sleep. But a few moments later I heard the bedclothes move again.

'I'd never let anything bad happen to you.' Her breaths became longer and I thought she'd fallen asleep again. Then she said in a clearer voice: 'Nothing's changing.'

She'd now become more awake, so I said: 'Did the Mother discuss with you some new idea?'

'Well, I don't think it was an *idea*. I told her nothing like that's ever going to happen.'

'I wonder what it was the Mother suggested.'

'Didn't she already talk to you about it? It was nothing. Some vague stuff traveling through her head.'

I wondered if she would say anything more. Then the duvet moved again.

'She was trying to . . . offer something, I guess. She said she could give up her job and stay with me the whole time. If I wanted that. She said she could become the one who was always with me. She'd do that if I really wanted it, she'd do it and let her job go, but I said, what would happen to Klara? And she was like, we wouldn't need Klara any more because *she* would be with me the whole time. You could tell it wasn't anything she'd thought through. But she kept asking, like I had to decide, so in the end I told her, look, Mom, this wouldn't work. You don't want to give up your job and I don't want to give up Klara. That was just about all of it. It's not going to happen and Mom agrees.'

We were quiet for some time after that, Josie hidden in the shadows while I continued to stand at the window.

'Perhaps,' I said eventually, 'the Mother thought if she stayed with Josie all the time, Josie would be less lonely.'

'Who says I'm lonely?'

'If that were true, if Josie really would be less lonely with the Mother, then I'd happily go away.'

'But who says I'm lonely? I'm not lonely.'

'Perhaps all humans are lonely. At least potentially.'

'Look, Klara, this was just a shitty idea Mom was having. I was asking her earlier about the portrait, and she got herself into a big knot and came up with this idea. Except it wasn't an idea, it wasn't anything. So please can we forget about it?'

She became quiet again, then she was asleep. I decided that if she woke up again, I should say something to prepare her for what might happen in the morning, at least to ensure she did nothing to impede his special help. But now, perhaps because I was in the room with her, her sleep continued to deepen, and eventually I left the window to stand by the wardrobe, from where I knew I'd see the first signs of the Sun's return.

■

260

We sat in the same positions as on the journey coming in. The height of the seat backs meant I could see the Mother only partially as she drove, and Miss Helen hardly at all except when she peered around her seat to emphasize what she was saying. Once – we were still in the city's slow morning traffic – Miss Helen turned to us in this way and said:

'No, Ricky, dear, I don't want you to say anything else unpleasant about him. You don't know him at all and you don't understand. How could you?' Then her face went away, but her voice continued: 'I suppose I said a lot of things myself last night. But this morning I realize how unfair that was. What right do I have to expect anything from him?'

Miss Helen had appeared to address this last question to the Mother, but the Mother seemed far away. As she drove us through another intersection, the Mother murmured: 'Paul isn't so bad. I think sometimes I'm too hard on him. He's not a bad guy. Today I feel sorry for him.'

'It's funny,' Miss Helen said, 'but this morning, I woke up with more hope. I feel it's quite possible Vance will still help. He rather worked himself up last night, but once he calms down and reflects, he may well decide he wants to be decent. He likes, you see, to nurture an image of himself as a very decent person.'

Rick stirred beside me. 'I've told you, Mum. I'm not having anything else to do with that man. And neither should you.'

'Helen,' the Mother said, 'is this really getting you anywhere? Going round and round this way? Why not just wait and see. Why torture yourself? You both did your best.'

Josie, on the other side of Rick from me, took Rick's hand and entwined her fingers with his. She smiled at him encouragingly, but also, I thought, a little sadly. Rick returned the smile, and

261

I wondered if they were exchanging secret messages just with their gazes.

I turned back to the window beside me, resting my forehead against the glass. I'd been watching and waiting since the earliest signs of dawn. But though the Sun's first rays had come straight into the Second Bedroom through the gap between the buildings, I hadn't for a second mistaken this for his special nourishment. I'd remembered of course that I should be grateful as always, but hadn't been able to keep the disappointment from my mind. Then all through the early breakfast, and the packing, and as the Mother moved through the Friend's Apartment checking security, I'd continued to watch and wait. And now, leaning forward and gazing past Rick and Josie, I could see the Sun, still on his morning ascent, flashing between the tall buildings as we moved past them. I thought then about the Father, closing the door of this very car, looking beyond me towards the yard and the Cootings Machine, saying, 'Don't worry, I heard it. The little fizzing sound. That's the telltale signal. That monster won't rise again.' And then a moment later, his face looming in front of mine, his voice asking: 'Are you okay? Can you see my fingers? How many do you see?' and I experienced again, as I'd done all morning, a wave of anxiety that the Sun wouldn't keep the promise he'd made in Mr McBain's barn.

'Listen, Rick,' the Mother said. 'Never mind what else happened last night, your work, your *portfolio*, got a thumbs up. You have to take heart from that. That's all the more reason to believe in yourself.'

'Mom, please,' Josie said. 'Rick doesn't need big lectures just now.' The adults couldn't see, but she tightened her grip on Rick's hand, and once again smiled at him. He gazed back at Josie, then said:

'I appreciate that, Mrs Arthur. You're always being kind to me. Thank you.'

'There's no telling,' Miss Helen said. 'No telling with Vance.'

I'd been aware for a few moments of the tall building now approaching on my side. It shared some characteristics with the RPO Building, but if anything was even taller, and because the traffic had slowed right down, I could study it carefully. The Sun was casting his rays onto its front, and one section of it had become like the Sun's mirror, throwing back an intense reflection of his morning light. The building's many windows had been organized into rows, vertical and horizontal, and yet the result was disorder, the rows often lining up crookedly, sometimes even running into each other. Within some of the windows, I saw office workers moving across, sometimes coming right up to the glass to gaze down at the street. But many of the windows were hard to see at all because of a gray mist drifting past them, and then in the next instant, as the Mother brought the car forward a little more, I saw through a gap between neighboring vehicles the Machine, sitting in its own space, protected from the oncoming traffic by the overhaul men's barriers. The Machine was pumping out Pollution from its three funnels, and the start of its name – the letters 'C-O-O' – was there on its body. And even as I felt disappointment flood my mind, I was able to observe that this was not the same machine the Father and I had destroyed in the yard. Its body was a different shade of yellow, its dimensions a little greater – and its ability to create Pollution more than a match for the first Cootings Machine.

'Just wait and see now, Helen,' the Mother said. 'Maybe there are other options for Rick anyway.' We moved beyond the New Cootings Machine and the gray pollution mist drifted past the windshield, so that the Mother, noticing, muttered under her breath: 'Look at this. How do they get away with it?'

'Even if there were, Mom,' Josie said, 'would those be colleges you'd let me go to?'

'I don't understand why you and Rick need to go to the same college,' the Mother said. 'What are you? Married already? Young people go to all kinds of places, they can still keep in touch.'

'Mom, do we have to talk about this right now? Rick really doesn't need this.'

I turned to look back through the rear windshield. The tall building was still visible but the New Cootings Machine had become hidden by other vehicles. I now knew why the Sun hadn't acted, and for a moment, I might have let my posture slump and my head hang down. Josie, leaning forward in her seat, looked at me.

'See, Mom,' she said, 'you've upset Klara too. And she was upset enough, what with her store moving away. We need happy talk right now.'

PART FIVE

Josie began to lose her strength eleven days after our return from the city. At first this phase seemed no worse than the ones she'd gone through before, but then came new signs, such as strange breathing, and her semi-waking in the morning, eyes open but empty. If during these spells I spoke to her, she wouldn't respond, and the Mother took to coming up to the bedroom early each morning. And if Josie was in her semi-waking condition, the Mother would stand over the bed, repeating under her breath, 'Josie, Josie, Josie,' as though this were part of a song she was memorizing.

There were better days when Josie sat up in bed and talked, even received tutorials on her oblong, but there were others when she just slept hour after hour. Dr Ryan began coming every day, his expression no longer smiling. The Mother went to her work later and later in the mornings, and she and Dr Ryan would have long conversations in the Open Plan with the sliding doors closed.

It had been agreed, during the better days immediately after our city visit, that I would assist Rick with his studies, so he came often to the house during this period. But as Josie grew worse, he lost interest in the lessons, and took to hovering in the hall, waiting for the Mother or Melania Housekeeper to call him up to the bedroom. Even if this occurred, he wasn't permitted any more than a few minutes standing just inside the doorway, looking at Josie's sleeping figure. Once, when he was watching in this way, Josie opened her eyes and smiled.

'Hey, Rick. Sorry. Too tired to draw pictures today.'

'That's okay. You just keep resting, you'll be fine.'

'How are your birds, Rick?'

'My birds are fine, Josie. They're coming on fine.'

That was all they were able to say before Josie's eyes closed again.

After that occasion, because Rick seemed so discouraged, I walked with him down the stairs and out the front door. We then stood on the loose stones together, looking at the gray sky. I could see he wanted to talk further, but perhaps aware we could be heard from the bedroom, he remained silent, prodding the stones with the toe of his sports shoe. So I asked, 'Would Rick perhaps walk with me a little?' and indicated towards the picture frame gate.

When we stepped into the first field, I saw that the grass was more yellow than it had been the evening we'd crossed to Mr McBain's barn. We walked slowly along the first part of the informal trail, the wind intermittently parting the grass to allow glimpses of Rick's house in the distance.

We reached a spot where the informal trail widened into a kind of outdoor room, and there Rick stopped and turned to face me, the grass rustling around us.

'Josie's never been this bad before,' he said, looking down at the ground. 'You kept saying there was reason to hope. You kept saying it like there was a *special* reason. So you had me hoping too.'

'I'm sorry. Perhaps Rick is angry. The truth is, I've been disappointed too. Even so, I believe there's still reason for hope.'

'Come on, Klara. She's just getting worse. The doctor, Mrs Arthur, you can see it. They've just about given up hoping.'

'Even so, I believe there's still hope. I believe help might come from a place the adults haven't yet considered. But we need to do something now quickly.'

'I don't know what you're talking about here, Klara. I guess it's to do with this big deal you can't share with anyone else.'

'To be truthful, ever since we returned from the city, I've been unsure. I was waiting and hesitating, hoping the special help would come regardless. But now I believe the only right course must be for me to go back and explain. If I made a special plea . . . But I shouldn't talk any more about this. I need Rick to trust me once more. I need again to go to Mr McBain's barn.'

'So you want me to carry you again?'

'I must go as soon as possible. If Rick isn't able to take me, I'll try on my own.'

'Whoa, hold on. Of course I'll help. I don't see how this helps Josie, but if you say it will, then of course I'll help.'

'Thank you! Then we must go without delay, this evening. And like the last time, we must get there just as the Sun is going down to his rest. Rick must meet me here, this same spot, at seven fifteen this evening. Will you please do that?'

'Hundred percent I will.'

'Thank you. There's one thing further. When I reach the barn, I'll of course offer my apologies. It was my error, I underestimated my task. But I must also have something else, something extra with which to plead. This is why I must ask Rick now, even though it might be stealing privacy. You must tell me if the love between Rick and Josie is genuine, if it's a true and lasting one. I must know this. Because if the answer is yes, then I'll have something to bargain with, regardless of what occurred in the city. So please think carefully, Rick, and tell me the truth.'

'I don't need to think. Josie and I grew up together and we're part of each other. And we've got our plan. So of course our love's genuine and forever. And it won't make any difference to us who's been lifted and who hasn't. That's your answer, Klara, and there won't be any other.'

'Thank you. Now I have something very special. So please, don't forget. Meet me here again at seven fifteen. This very place where we're standing.'

■

Now I was more accustomed to riding on Rick's back, I often reached out a free hand to help part the grass. Not only was the grass more yellow than on our previous journey, it was more soft and yielding, and even the clouds of evening insects broke kindly against my face as we passed through them. This time the fields never became partitioned, and once the third picture frame gate was behind us, I had a clear view ahead of Mr McBain's barn, the wide orange sky above it – and the Sun already close to the top of the roof's triangle.

As we came into the low-cut grass area, I asked Rick to stop and let me down. Then, as he and I stood watching the Sun sink lower and lower, the barn's shadow, as it had the last time, came stretching towards us across the weave-patterned grass. Once the Sun went behind the barn's roof structure, I remembered how important it was not to take any more privacy than necessary, and asked Rick to leave me.

'What goes on inside there?' he asked, but before I could give any sort of response, he touched my shoulder kindly and said: 'I'll be waiting. Same place I was last time.'

Then he was gone, and I was alone, waiting for the Sun to re-appear below the roof level and send his last rays to me through the barn. It occurred to me then not only that the Sun might be angry about my failure in the city, but also that this could well be my final chance to beg for his special help – and I thought about what it might mean for Josie if I failed. Fear entered my mind, but then I remembered his great kindness, and I walked without further hesitation towards Mr McBain's barn.

∎

As before, the barn was filled with orange light, and it was hard at first to see my surroundings. But I soon discerned the blocks of hay stacked up to my left, and I could see the low wall they formed had become even lower. There were the same particles of hay caught within the Sun's rays, but instead of drifting gently in the air, they were now moving agitatedly as if one of the hay blocks had recently crashed down onto the hard wood floor and disintegrated. When I reached up to touch these moving particles, I noticed how my fingers cast shadows stretching all the way back to the barn's entrance.

Beyond the hay blocks was the real wall of the barn, and I was pleased to see the Red Shelves from our old store still attached to it, though this evening they'd become crooked, slanting noticeably towards the rear of the building. The ceramic coffee cups had maintained their orderly line, but there were also signs of confusion: for instance, further on the same tier, I could see an object that was unmistakably Melania Housekeeper's food blender.

I remembered how the last time I'd waited for the Sun, I'd sat on a metal foldaway chair, and turned towards the other side of the barn, hoping to see again not only the chair, but also the front alcove of our store – and perhaps even an AF standing proudly within it. What I actually saw was the Sun's rays streaming by before me, following a near-horizontal trajectory, from the rear entrance to the front one. It was almost as if I were watching passing traffic in a busy street, and when I managed to throw my gaze over to the further side, I found it had been partitioned into numerous boxes of uneven dimensions. Only after a few seconds did I spot the metal foldaway chair – or rather, various parts of it within several of the boxes – and recalling how much comfort it had brought me the last time, I began to move towards it. But no sooner had I stepped into the Sun's rays, it occurred to me that if I wished to catch his attention before he moved on, I'd have to act without delay. So I began forming words inside my mind, even as I stood there caught in the intense light.

'You must be so tired, and I'm very sorry to disturb you. You'll remember, I came here once before in the summer, when you were so kind and gave me a few minutes of your time. I'm daring now to return this evening to discuss the same very important matter.'

These words had barely shaped themselves when the memory came into my mind of that day of Josie's interaction meeting, and the angry mother striding into the Open Plan shouting: 'Danny's right! You shouldn't be here at all!' Almost simultaneously I noticed, in one of the boxes to my right, angry cartoon writing like that I'd seen from the car on a building in the city. Regardless, I let more half-formed words rush through my mind.

'I know I've no right to come here like this. And I know the Sun must be angry with me. I let him down, failing completely to stop Pollution. In fact I see now how very foolish I was in not considering there'd be a second terrible machine to allow Pollution to continue without a pause. But the Sun was watching at the yard that day, so he will know how hard I tried, and how

272

I made my sacrifice, which I was only too pleased to do, even if now my abilities aren't perhaps what they were. And you must have seen how the Father too helped and did his utmost, even though he knew nothing about the Sun's kind agreement, because he saw my hope and placed his faith in it. I sincerely apologize for underestimating my task. It was my error and no one else's, and though the Sun is right to be angry with me, I'm asking he accept that Josie herself is completely innocent. Like the Father, she never knew about my agreement with the Sun, and still has no idea. And now she's becoming weaker and weaker each day. I've come here this evening like this because I've never forgotten how kind the Sun can be. If only he would show his great compassion to Josie, as he did that day to Beggar Man and his dog. If only he'd send Josie the special nourishment she so desperately requires.'

As these words swept through my mind, I thought of the terrible bull on the way up to Morgan's Falls, of its horns and its cold eyes, and of the feeling I'd had at that moment of some great error having been made to allow a creature so filled with anger to stand unconstrained up on the sunny grass. I heard the Mother's voice, somewhere behind me on the path, shout: 'No, Paul, not now and not in this goddam car!' and saw the lonely woman sitting by herself in Mr Vance's diner, unnoticed even by the Diner Manager, pressing her forehead against the window towards the dark street outside, and it occurred to me how very much the woman resembled Rosa. But I realized I couldn't afford to become distracted, that the Sun was likely to leave at any moment, and so I let more thoughts stream through my mind, no longer shaping them into formal words.

'I don't mind that I lost precious fluid. I'd willingly have given more, given it all, if it meant your providing special help to Josie. As you know, since I was last here, I've discovered about the other way to save Josie, and if that was all that was left, I'd do my very utmost. But I'm not yet certain the other way would work, however hard I tried, and so my deep wish now is that the Sun will show his great kindness once more.'

The hand I'd been holding out whilst crossing the Sun's rays made contact with something hard and I realized I was clutching the frame of the metal foldaway chair. I felt happiness to have found it again, but didn't sit down in case it appeared disrespectful. Instead, I steadied myself behind it, holding its back with both hands.

The Sun's rays coming from the back of the barn were too intense to face directly, so though it might seem rude, I turned my gaze once more to the drifting shapes to my right, perhaps hoping to glimpse Rosa sitting in the lonely diner booth. But now the Sun's pattern had fallen across the front alcove, momentarily illuminating it, and I saw there not an AF, but a large oval-shaped photograph fixed to the wall. It showed a green field on a sunny day, dotted with sheep, and in the foreground, I recognized the four special sheep I'd glimpsed from the Mother's car returning from Morgan's Falls. They seemed even more gentle than I'd remembered, lined up as they were in a neat row, their heads lowered to partake of the grass. These creatures had filled me with happiness that day, helping to erase the memory of the terrible bull, and I was pleased to see them again, if only in this oval photograph. But something was wrong: although the four sheep were positioned in a line in just the same formation I'd seen from the car, here they'd become oddly suspended, so they no longer appeared to stand on the surface of the ground. As a result, when they stretched down to eat, their mouths couldn't reach the grass, giving these creatures, so happy on the day, a mood of sadness.

'Please don't go away just yet,' I said. 'Please give me one more brief moment. I know I failed to perform the service I promised you in the city and I've no right to ask anything further of you. But I'm remembering how delighted you were that day Coffee Cup Lady and Raincoat Man found each other again. You were so delighted and couldn't help showing it. So I know just how much it matters to you that people who love one another are brought together, even after many years. I know the Sun always wishes them well, perhaps even helps them to find each other. Please then consider Josie and Rick. They're still very young. Should Josie pass away now, they'll be parted forever. If only you could give her special nourishment, as I saw you do for Beggar Man and his dog, then Josie and Rick could go together into their adult lives just as they wished for in their kind picture. I can myself vouch that their love is strong and lasting, just like that of Coffee Cup Lady and Raincoat Man.'

I now noticed, a few steps in front of the alcove, a small triangular object left on the floor. I thought for an instant that it was one of the pointed pie slices the Diner Manager had been displaying in his see-through counter. And I recalled Mr Vance's unkind voice, saying: 'If you're not seeking favoritism, then why am I sitting here in front of you now?' and Miss Helen saying quickly, 'We *are* asking him to exercise favoritism, of course we are.' Only then did I realize the triangle on the floor wasn't a piece of pie, but a corner of Josie's paperback, the one she'd let fall from the sofa in the Friend's Apartment while waiting for the Father. In fact, it wasn't triangular at all, but had merely appeared that way because only the one corner was protruding out of the shadows. To the left of the front alcove, boxes were drifting and overlapping as if in the evening wind. I saw in several of them the flash of bright colors, and noticed they contained, even if only in the background, the bottles display I'd glimpsed in the store's new window. The bottles were illuminated in contrasting colors, and in certain boxes I spotted also parts of the sign that said 'Recessed Lighting'. I knew then that my time was running out, and so continued quickly.

'I know favoritism isn't desirable. But if the Sun is making exceptions, surely the most deserving are young people who will love one another all their lives. Perhaps the Sun may ask, "How can we be sure? What can children know about genuine love?" But I've been observing them carefully, and I'm certain it's true. They grew up together, and they've each become a part of the other. Rick told me this himself only today. I know I failed in the city, but please show your kindness once more and give your special help to Josie. Tomorrow, or perhaps the next day, please look in on her and give her the kind of nourishment you gave Beggar Man. I ask you this, even though it may be favoritism, and I failed in my mission.'

The Sun's evening rays had started to fade, leaving the beginnings of darkness inside the barn. Although I'd been trying to remain facing the rear opening, through which his light had been coming, I'd been for a little while aware of some separate light source behind me over my right shoulder. I'd assumed at first it was some further manifestation of the colored bottles display, but as the Sun's own light in the barn continued to reduce, this new light source had become harder to ignore. I now turned around to look at it, and was surprised to see that the Sun himself, far from leaving, had come right within Mr McBain's barn and installed himself, almost at floor level, between the front alcove and the barn's front opening. This discovery was so unexpected – and the Sun's presence in the low corner so dazzling – that for a brief moment I was in danger of becoming disoriented. Then my vision readjusted, and ordering my mind, I realized the Sun wasn't really in the barn at all, but that something reflective had been left there by chance and was now catching his reflection during the last moments of his descent. In other words, something was behaving as the Sun's mirror in much the way the windows of the RPO and other buildings sometimes did. As I walked towards the reflective surface, the light became less fierce, though it remained glowing and orange amidst the surrounding shadows.

Only when I was standing over it did the nature of the reflective object become clear. Mr McBain – or one of his friends – had left leaning against the wall at this spot several rectangular sheets of glass, stacked one upon the other. Perhaps Mr McBain was finally planning to do something about his missing walls, and perhaps hoping to create windows. In any case, I could see reflected inside the glass rectangles – I estimated seven in all, propped up almost vertically – the Sun's evening face. I stepped closer still, almost speaking the words out loud.

'Please show your special kindness to Josie.'

I stared at the glass sheets. The Sun's reflection, though still an intense orange, was no longer blinding and as I studied more carefully the Sun's face framed within the outermost rectangle, I began to appreciate that I wasn't looking at a single picture; that in fact there existed a different version of the Sun's face on each of the glass surfaces, and what I might at first have taken for a unified image was in fact seven separate ones superimposed one over the other as my gaze penetrated from the first sheet through to the last. Although his face on the outermost glass was forbidding and aloof, and the one immediately behind it was, if anything, even more unfriendly, the two beyond that were softer and kinder. There were three further sheets, and though it was hard to see much of them on account of their being further back, I couldn't help estimating that these faces would have humorous and kind expressions. In any case, whatever the nature of the images on each glass sheet, as I looked at them collectively, the effect was of a single face, but with a variety of outlines and emotions.

I continued to stare intently, and then all the Sun's faces began to fade together, and the light inside Mr McBain's barn grew dim, and I could no longer see even the triangle of Josie's paperback, or the sheep stretching down their mouths towards the out-of-reach grass. I said, 'Thank you for receiving me again. I'm so sorry I wasn't able to perform the service I promised to you. Please consider my request.' But even within my mind, I spoke these words softly because I knew the Sun had departed.

■

In the days that followed, Dr Ryan and the Mother often argued in the Open Plan about whether or not Josie should go to a hospital, and although their voices collided – I could hear them through the sliding doors – they seemed always in the end to agree that such a place would only contribute to her misery. Despite this agreement, each time Dr Ryan came, they would go into the Open Plan and go through the discussion all over again.

Rick came each day, and took his turn sitting in the bedroom, watching over Josie, while the Mother and Melania Housekeeper rested. Both adults by this point had ceased to keep traditional hours, sleeping only when they became overwhelmed by tiredness. My own presence, though appreciated, was for some reason considered insufficient by itself, even though the Mother knew I was likely to spot danger signals before anyone else. In any case, as the days passed, the Mother and Melania Housekeeper became so tired it showed in their every movement.

Then six days after my second visit to Mr McBain's barn, the sky grew unusually dark after breakfast. I say 'after breakfast', though by then all household routines had become so disrupted there were no breakfasts, or any other meals, being taken at their usual times. That particular morning the sense of disorientation was made worse by the sky's darkness, and Rick's arrival was one of the few things to remind us it wasn't still night.

As the morning continued, the sky became ever darker, the clouds more dense, then the wind grew very powerful. A loose section of building started to bang at the rear of the house, and when I looked from the bedroom front window, the trees at the rise of the road were bending and waving.

But Josie slept on, oblivious, her breathing shallow and rapid. Midway through that dark morning, while Rick and I were together watching Josie, Melania Housekeeper appeared, her eyes half closed with tiredness, and said it was her turn to take over. I then watched Rick descend the staircase in front of me, shoulders heavy with sadness, and sit down on the lowest step. Deciding it best to give him privacy for a few moments, I'd gone past him and into the hall, when the Mother came out of the Open Plan. She was in the thin black dressing gown she'd been wearing throughout the night, which displayed the fragility of her neck, and strode past quickly as though in need of her coffee. But at the kitchen doorway, she turned and, noticing Rick sitting on the bottom step, stared at him. It took Rick a moment to realize the Mother was looking at him, but when he did he smiled with courage.

'Mrs Arthur, how are you?'

The Mother went on staring at him. Then she said, 'Come on in here,' and disappeared into the kitchen. Rick gave me a puzzled glance as he rose to his feet. Although the Mother hadn't invited me, I thought it best to follow behind him.

The kitchen appeared different because of the darkened sky outside. The Mother hadn't switched on any lights and, by the time we came in, she was gazing out of the large windows towards the road she normally took to her work. Rick stopped uncertainly near the Island, and I myself paused at the refrigerator to give privacy. From that position, I was able to see the large windows, and beyond the Mother's figure, the highway rising into the distance, and the waving trees.

'I wanted to ask you something,' the Mother said. 'You don't mind, do you, Rick?'

'Please go right ahead, Mrs Arthur.'

'I was wondering if right now you might be feeling like you're the winner. Like maybe you've won.'

'I don't understand, Mrs Arthur.'

'I've always treated you okay, haven't I, Rick? I hope I have.'

'You certainly have. You've always been very kind. And a great friend to my mother.'

'So I'm now asking you. I'm asking you, Rick, if you feel like you've come out the winner. Josie took the gamble. Okay, I shook the dice for her, but it was always going to be her, not me, who won or lost. She bet high, and if Dr Ryan's right, she might soon be about to lose. But you, Rick, you played it safe. So that's why I'm asking you. How does this feel to you just now? Do you really feel like a winner?'

The Mother had said all this while staring at the dark sky, but she now turned to face Rick.

'Because if you're feeling like the winner, Rick, I'd like you to reflect on this. First. What exactly do you believe you've won here? I ask because everything about Josie, from the moment I first held her, everything about her told me she was hungry for life. The whole world excited her. That's how I knew from the start I couldn't deny her the chance. She was demanding a future worthy of her spirit. That's what I mean when I say she played for high stakes. Now what about you, Rick? Do you really think you were so smart? Do you believe of the two of you, you've come out the winner? Because if that's so, then please ask yourself this. What is it you've won? Take a look. Take a look at your future.' She waved a hand at the window. 'You played for low stakes and what you've won is small and mean. You may feel pretty smug just now. But I'm here to tell you, you've got no reason to be feeling that way. No reason at all.'

While the Mother had been speaking, something had ignited in Rick's face, something dangerous, till he was looking very much as he'd done during the interaction meeting when he'd challenged the boys wanting to throw me across the room. He now took a step towards the Mother, and suddenly she too seemed to feel alarm.

'Mrs Arthur,' Rick said. 'Most times I've come here lately, Josie hasn't been well enough to talk. But last Thursday she had a good day, and I was sitting close by the bed so I wouldn't miss anything. And what she said was that she wanted to give me a message. A message for you, Mrs Arthur, but one she wasn't ready for you to hear. What I mean is, she was asking me to hold this message for her till the correct time. Well, I'm thinking perhaps now's the correct time.'

The Mother's eyes became large and filled with fear, but she said nothing.

'Josie's message,' Rick went on, 'was something like this. She says that no matter what happens now, never mind how it plays out, she loves you and will always love you. She's very grateful you're her mother and she never even once wished for any other. That's what she said. And there was more. On this question of being lifted. She wants you to know she wouldn't wish it any other way. If she had the power to do it again, and this time it was up to her, she says she'd do exactly what you did and you'll always be the best mother she could have. That's about it. As I say, she didn't want me to pass it on until the correct time. So I'm hoping I've judged this right, Mrs Arthur, telling you now.'

The Mother stared expressionlessly at Rick, but while he'd been speaking, I'd spotted something – something possibly very important – through the large windows behind her, and now, taking advantage of Rick's pause, I raised my hand. The Mother ignored me and went on staring at Rick.

'That's some message,' she said finally.

'Excuse me,' I said.

'Jesus,' the Mother said, and sighed quietly. 'That's some message.'

'Excuse me!' This time I'd almost shouted, and both the Mother and Rick turned my way. 'I'm sorry to interrupt. But there's something occurring outside. The Sun's coming out!'

The Mother glanced at the large windows, then back at me. 'Sure. So what? What's the matter with you, honey?'

'We must go upstairs. We must go up to Josie straight away!'

The Mother and Rick had been looking at me with puzzled expressions, but when I said this, they looked fearful, and even as I turned towards the hall, they both rushed past me, so that I found myself hurrying up the staircase behind them.

They may not have understood why I'd called out as I had,

and perhaps believed Josie was in sudden danger. So when they burst into the bedroom, they must have been relieved to find her asleep as before, breathing steadily. She was lying on her side as she often did, her face mostly hidden by the hair falling over it. There was nothing unexpected about Josie herself, but the room was another matter. The Sun's patterns were falling over various sections of wall, floor and ceiling with unusual intensity – a deep orange triangle above the dresser, a bright curved line crossing the Button Couch, brilliant bars across the carpet. But Josie herself, in her bed, was in shadow, as were many other parts of the room. Then the shadows started to move and I realized – my vision adjusting – that they were being created by Melania Housekeeper, standing at the front window, tugging at the blind and the curtains. The blind was already fully lowered, and she was pulling the curtains over it to form a double layer, and yet the piercing light was somehow coming past the edges to create the shapes around the room.

'Damn Sun!' Melania Housekeeper called out. 'Go away, damn Sun!'

'No, no!' I went quickly to Melania Housekeeper. 'We must open them, open everything! We must let the Sun do his best!'

I tried to take the curtain material from her, and though she at first didn't let go, she did so eventually with a look of surprise. By then, Rick had appeared at my side and, seemingly coming to some intuitive conclusion, also reached forward to raise the blind and pull back the curtains.

The Sun's nourishment then came into the room so abundantly Rick and I reeled back, almost losing balance. Melania Housekeeper, her hands covering her face, said again: 'Damn Sun!' But she made no further attempt to block his nourishment.

I'd stepped back from the window, but not before noticing that outside the wind was as powerful as ever, and that not only were the trees still waving, there were many tiny funnels and pyramids – each looking as though drawn in sharp pencil lines – blowing swiftly across the sky. But the Sun had broken through the dark clouds, and all at once – as if each of us in the room had received a secret message – we turned to look at Josie.

The Sun was illuminating her, and the entire bed, in a ferocious half-disc of orange, and the Mother, standing closest to the bed, was having to raise her hands to her face. Rick seemed now somehow to have guessed what was occurring, but I was interested to observe how both the Mother and Melania Housekeeper seemed also to have grasped its essence. So, for the next few moments, we all remained in our fixed positions as the Sun focused ever more brightly on Josie. We watched and waited, and even when at one point the orange half-disc looked as if it might catch alight, none of us did anything. Then Josie stirred, and with squinting eyes, held a hand up in the air.

'Hey. What's with this light anyway?' she said.

The Sun continued relentlessly to shine on her, and she shifted till she was on her back, propped up by the pillows and headboard.

'What's going on?'

'How are you feeling, honey?' the Mother asked in a whisper, staring at Josie as if in fear.

Josie slumped back against her pillows till she was almost looking up at the ceiling. But there was an obvious new strength to the way she'd maneuvered herself.

'Hey,' she said. 'Is the blind stuck or something?'

The loose piece of house structure was still banging somewhere, and when I next glanced out of the window, the darkness was once more spreading across the sky. Then even as we watched, the Sun's patterns faded over Josie, till she was lying there in the gray of an overcast morning.

'Josie?' the Mother said. 'How do you feel?'

Josie looked at her with a tired expression, shifting herself to face us better. The Mother, seeing this, moved forward, perhaps with the intention of making Josie lie down again. But even as she reached Josie, she appeared to change her mind, and began to assist Josie in finding a more comfortable sitting posture.

'You look better, honey,' the Mother said.

'Look, what's going on?' Josie asked. 'Why's everyone here? What are you all staring at?'

'Hey, Josie,' Rick said suddenly, his voice filled with excitement. 'You look a complete mess.'

'Thanks. You're looking pretty good yourself.' Then she said: 'But you know, I do feel better. Kind of dizzy though.'

'That's enough,' the Mother said. 'Just take it easy. Do you want to drink something?'

'Water maybe?'

'Okay, let's assume nothing,' the Mother said. 'We have to take this one step at a time.'

PART SIX

The Sun's special nourishment proved as effective for Josie as it had for Beggar Man, and after the dark sky morning, she grew not only stronger, but from a child into an adult.

As the seasons – and the years – went by, Mr McBain's vehicles cut down the tall grass in all three fields, leaving them a pale brown color. The barn now looked taller and more sharply outlined, but Mr McBain still didn't build additional walls for it, and on cloudless evenings, as the Sun went towards his resting place, I was still able to see him sinking to the far side of the barn before fading into the ground.

Josie worked hard on her tutorials, and there were many arguments about which college she might go to. Josie and the Mother each held strong views on the matter, but Atlas Brookings – now Rick no longer wished to go there – was rarely mentioned. The Father seemed to agree with neither Josie's nor the Mother's ideas, and once turned up at the house to make his points more strongly. It was the only time I saw him come to the house, and although I was myself happy to see him again, we all understood he'd infringed a rule in doing so.

Josie herself went away from the house much more over this period, sometimes for several days at a time, to visit other young adults, or to attend retreats. These trips, I knew, were an important part of her preparations for college, but she preferred not to talk much about them to me, so they remained largely outside of my knowledge.

Rick had continued to come regularly in the early days after

Josie's recovery, but as the time passed, and certainly by when Mr McBain cut the grass, he was coming far less. This was partly because of Josie being away so often, but Rick too had become busy with his projects. He'd bought a car, which he'd named 'the Wreck', and would regularly drive to the city to meet his new friends. Rick preferred to leave the Wreck in the loose stones area because, he said, it was easier for him to start his journey from there than to negotiate the narrow and circuitous route out from his own house. So it was increasingly the presence of the Wreck, rather than Josie, that brought Rick to us, and it was there on the loose stones that I had my last conversation with him.

Both Josie and the Mother were away that morning, and so when I heard his tread outside, I saw no reason not to go out and exchange greetings. He wasn't in his usual hurry to drive away, so we talked for several minutes, a light breeze moving over us, Rick leaning against the body of the Wreck, while I stood just a little way away. The sky was overcast that morning, and that was perhaps why Rick was reminded of that day.

'Do you remember, Klara,' he asked, 'that morning the weather went really strange, and the Sun came right into Josie's room?'

'Of course. I'll never forget that morning.'

'I often think about it now. It almost seems like that was when Josie first started to get better. Maybe I've got this all wrong. But when I look back, it almost feels that way.'

'Yes. I agree.'

'You remember that day? We were all so exhausted. And in despair. Then everything turned around. I always wanted to ask you, except you seemed so closed up about it. I always wanted to ask if what happened that morning, all that strange weather, everything else, if it had to do with the other stuff. You know.

Me carrying you over the fields, you making some secret deal. At the time, I thought it was all, well, AF superstition. Something just to bring us good luck. But these days, I keep wondering if there was more to it.'

He was watching me carefully, but I said nothing for quite a long time.

'Unfortunately,' I said, eventually, 'I don't dare speak about this matter, even today. It was such a special favor, and if I speak about it to anyone, even just to Rick, my fear is that the help Josie received will be taken back.'

'Then stop there. Don't say anything. I don't want to open up even a tiny chance of her getting ill again. But the doctors always say once you get through the stage she did, you're safe.'

'All the same, we must be cautious, because Josie's was such a special case. But since Rick is now talking about this matter, perhaps I might mention something related to it that's been worrying me.'

'And what's that, Klara?'

'Rick and Josie still show kindness to each other. And yet, they're now preparing such different futures.'

He turned towards the rise in the road, his hand playing with the Wreck's wing mirror. 'I think I follow you,' he said. 'I'm remembering that day, the second time we went over to the barn. How before we went, you became very serious and asked if our love was genuine. The love between me and Josie. And I think I told you it *was* real. Real and everlasting. So I'm guessing that's what you're now worrying about.'

'Rick is correct. It brings me anxiety to see Rick and Josie with such separate plans.'

He gently prodded the loose stones before him with his foot. Then he said: 'Look. I don't want you to say anything to put

Josie's health at risk again. But let me say this much. When you passed it on that Josie and I really loved each other, that was the truth at the time. No one can claim you misled or tricked them. But now we're no longer kids, we have to wish each other the best and go our different ways. It couldn't have worked out, me going to college, trying to compete with all those lifted kids. I've got my own plans now, and that's how it should be. But that was no lie, Klara. And in a funny way, it still isn't a lie now.'

'I wonder what Rick can mean by that?'

'I suppose I'm saying Josie and I will always be together at some level, some deeper one, even if we go out there and don't see each other any more. I can't speak for her. But once I'm out there, I know I'll always keep searching for someone just like her. At least like the Josie I once knew. So it wasn't ever a deception, Klara. Whoever that was you were dealing with back then, if they could see right into my heart, and right into Josie's, they'd know you weren't trying to pull some fast one.'

After that we stood there on the loose stones, not talking for a little while. I thought at any moment he would straighten and get into the Wreck. But he asked, in a lighter voice:

'Do you ever hear from Melania? Someone said she went to Indiana.'

'We believe she's now in California. When we last heard from her, she was hoping to be accepted by a community there.'

'I used to be so afraid of that lady. But I got kind of used to her. I hope she's okay. And that she finds somewhere safe. And what about you, Klara? Are you going to be okay? I mean, once Josie leaves for college.'

'The Mother is always very kind to me.'

'Look, if you ever need my help, you just say, okay?'

'Yes. Thank you.'

As I sit here on this hard ground, I have been thinking again about Rick's words that morning and I'm sure he is correct. I no longer fear that the Sun will feel cheated or misled, or that he will consider retribution. In fact, it could be that even as I was making my plea to him, he already knew Josie and Rick were bound to go their separate ways, and yet understood that, despite everything, their love would last. When he'd posed his question – about children really understanding what it meant to love – I believe he was already sure of the answer and was simply raising the question for my benefit. I even think, at that moment, he may have been thinking about the Coffee Cup Lady and Raincoat Man – after all, we'd been talking about them the previous moment. Perhaps the Sun was supposing that after many years, and after many changes, Josie and Rick might once again meet as the Coffee Cup Lady and Raincoat Man had done.

■

As Josie's college days drew closer, there were frequent visits to the house from other young adults. They were female, and mostly came one at a time, though occasionally in pairs. A hire driver might bring them, or sometimes they would come driving their own car, but the young adults were now never accompanied by parents. Two nights, sometimes three, was the average length of visit, and I would know when such a visit was expected because, a day or two beforehand, the New Housekeeper would move a futon or camping cot into Josie's bedroom.

It was because of the young adult visitors that I discovered the Utility Room. Naturally there was not enough space during such visits for me to remain in the bedroom myself, and in any case, I understood that my presence wasn't appropriate as it once had been. If Melania Housekeeper had still been with us, I believe she would have made a plan for where I might go, but as it was, I found the room myself, up on the top landing. 'No one's saying you have to hide,' Josie had said, but she didn't come up with any alternative plan, and so that's how I came to occupy the Utility Room.

These were busy weeks, and even when Josie didn't have a visitor, I would hear her moving hurriedly around the house, shouting at the Mother or the New Housekeeper. Then one afternoon, the door of the Utility Room opened and Josie was looking in with a smile.

'So,' she said. 'This is where you've been hanging out. How are things?'

'Everything is fine, thank you.'

Josie stretched out her arms, a hand resting on each vertical of the doorframe. She was looking into the room with a stoop, as if she feared she might accidentally hit her head on the sloping ceilings. Her gaze went quickly around the various stored items, then settled on the room's one high small window.

'Do you ever get to look out of that there?' she asked.

'Unfortunately it's too high. Its purpose is to provide ventilation, not a view.'

'We'll see about that.'

Josie stepped further into the room, her head still stooped, her glance moving everywhere. Then she began to work, lifting one item, pushing another, creating new piles where none had existed. Once, failing to anticipate her rapid movements, I nearly collided with her, and she laughed loudly.

'Klara! Just stay over there. Right over there. I'm trying to do something.'

Before long she'd cleared a space immediately beneath the

high small window, then pushed a wooden trunk into the space. She next picked up and carried over a plastic crate with a tight-fitting lid and lowered it carefully on top of the trunk.

'There you go.' She stood back, pleased with what she'd done, though the rest of the room had become very untidy. 'Give that a go, Klara. Just be careful. The second step's quite high. Come on, I want you to try it.'

I came out of the corner and without difficulty negotiated the two steps she'd created, till I was standing on the lid of the plastic crate.

'Don't worry, those things are really strong,' she said. 'Just treat it like a floor. Trust me, it's safe.'

She laughed again, and kept watching me, so I smiled, then looked out of the high small window. The view was similar to the old one from Josie's rear window two floors below. Of course, the trajectory had altered, and a part of the roof was intruding into the right of my picture. But I could see the gray sky stretching over the cut fields all the way to Mr McBain's barn.

'You should have told me before,' Josie said. 'I know how much you love looking out.'

'Thank you. Thank you so much.'

For a moment we looked at each other with gentle smiles. Then she glanced around at the items strewn over the floor.

'Boy, what a mess! Okay, I promise to tidy everything. But just now I've got to go attend to something. Don't try doing any of this yourself. I'll do it later, okay?'

■

The Mother, like Josie, had less to do with me during this period, sometimes not looking my way even when she encountered me

295

around the house. I understood that this was a busy time for her, and also that possibly my presence brought back difficult memories. But there was one occasion when she gave me special attention.

Josie herself was away that day, but it being the weekend, the Mother was at home. I'd been up in the Utility Room for most of the morning, but when I'd heard the voices below, I'd gone out onto the top landing. I then quickly realized the man speaking with the Mother down in the hallway was Mr Capaldi.

I was surprised because there hadn't been any mention of Mr Capaldi for a long time. He and the Mother were talking in easy tones, but as they continued, I could hear tension enter the Mother's voice. Then her footsteps sounded, and I saw her looking up at me from three floors below.

'Klara,' she called up. 'Mr Capaldi's here. You'll remember him, of course. Come on down and say hello.'

Then as I was descending carefully, I heard the Mother say: 'That wasn't the agreement, Henry. That wasn't what you said.'

To which Mr Capaldi said: 'I just want to put it to her. That's all.'

Mr Capaldi was heavier than when I'd last seen him that day in his building, and the hair around his ears had become a lighter gray. He greeted me warmly, then led the way into the Open Plan, saying: 'Just wanted to run a few things past you, Klara. You could be of great help to us.'

The Mother said nothing as she followed us in. Mr Capaldi sat down on the modular sofa, leaning back into the cushions, and this relaxed posture reminded me of the boy Danny, at the interaction meeting, sitting on the same sofa with a leg extended across it. In contrast to Mr Capaldi's manner, the Mother remained standing very straight in the center of the room, and when Mr Capaldi invited me to sit, she said:

'I think Klara's happier standing. Let's get on with this, Henry.'

'Come on, Chrissie. This is nothing we have to stress about.'

Then he came out of his relaxed posture, leaning forward towards me.

'You'll remember, Klara, how much I've always been fascinated by AFs. I've always regarded you as our friends. A vital source of education and enlightenment. But as you know, there are people out there who worry about you. People who are scared and resentful.'

'Henry,' the Mother said. 'Please get to the point.'

'Okay. Here it is. Klara, the fact is, there's growing and widespread concern about AFs right now. People saying how you've become too clever. They're afraid because they can't follow what's going on inside any more. They can see what you do. They accept that your decisions, your recommendations, are sound and dependable, almost always correct. But they don't like not knowing how you arrive at them. That's where it comes from, this backlash, this prejudice. So we have to fight back. We have to say to them, okay, you're worried because you don't understand how AFs think. Fine, then let's go take a look under the hood. Let's reverse-engineer. What you don't like are sealed black boxes. Okay, let's open them. Once we see inside, not only do things get a lot less scary, we'll learn. Learn amazing new things. So this is where you come in, Klara. Those of us on your side, we're looking for help, for volunteers. We've already succeeded in opening a number of black boxes, but we really need to open up a whole lot more. You AFs, you're magnificent. We're discovering things we'd never have believed possible.

That's why I'm here today. I've never forgotten you, Klara. I know you'll be uniquely useful to us. Please, will you help?'

He was staring at me so I said: 'I'd like to assist. So long as it doesn't inconvenience Josie or her mother . . .'

'Wait a minute.' The Mother moved swiftly around the coffee table until she was standing beside me. 'This isn't at all what we talked about over the phone, Henry.'

'I just wanted to ask Klara, that's all. This is a chance for her to make a lasting contribution . . .'

'Klara deserves better than that.'

'You may be right there, Chrissie. And I may have badly misjudged this. Even so, now I'm here, and Klara's standing in front of me, do I have your permission just to ask her?'

'No, Henry, you don't. Klara deserves better. She deserves her slow fade.'

'But we have work to do here. We have to resist this backlash . . .'

'Then go resist it elsewhere. Find some other black boxes to prize open. Leave our Klara be. Let her have her slow fade.'

The Mother had stepped in front of me, as though to shield me from Mr Capaldi, and because in her anger she'd taken her position hurriedly, the rear of her shoulder was almost touching my face. As a result, I not only became very conscious of the smooth woven fabric of her dark sweater, but was reminded of the moment she'd reached forward and embraced me, in the front of her car, the time we'd parked beside the Grind Our Own Beef cafe. Peering around the Mother, I saw Mr Capaldi shake his head and lean back again into the cushions.

'I can't help feeling,' he said, 'that you're still mad at me, Chrissie. That you've been mad at me for a long time. And that's unfair. Back then, it was *you* who came to *me*. Remember? And

I just did my best to help you. I'm glad it worked out well with Josie in the end. I truly am. But that's no reason for you to be so mad at me all the time.'

■

The last days before Josie's departure were filled with both tension and excitement. Had Melania Housekeeper still been with us, things might have been calmer. But the New Housekeeper often left tasks undone until the last moment, then tried to do several all at once, and this added to the nervous atmosphere. I felt it important not to get in the way, and remained in the Utility Room for long periods, standing on the platform Josie had made for me, looking out of the high small window across the fields, listening to the noises around the house. Then one afternoon, two days before the departure, I heard Josie's step on the top landing, and she appeared in the doorway.

'Hey, Klara. Why don't you come down for a while to the bedroom. I mean, if you're not busy, that is.'

So I descended with her and found myself once more in the old room. Many details had changed. Aside from Josie's own bed, there was now a permanent second cot for her visitors, while the Button Couch had been removed altogether. Many smaller details had also changed – for instance, Josie was now sitting in a new desk chair with castors on its feet, so that if she wished, she could move about while still sitting. But the Sun's patterns on the wall were just as I'd remembered them from the many afternoons we'd spent there together. I sat down on the edge of her bed, and for a while we talked happily.

'Everyone you speak to says they're not scared of college,' Josie said at one point. 'But you wouldn't believe, Klara, just how scared some of them really are. I'm kind of scared too, I'm not going to pretend I'm not. But you know what? I'm not going to let fear get in my way. I've made myself a solemn promise about that. Hey, did I tell you this before? We're all supposed to set these official targets. Two targets in each of five categories. I had to fill in a form about it, but I cheated, because I figured out my own secret targets, nothing to do with the ones on the form. Boy, would they not like my *real* list! And no way is Mom ever hearing about it either!' She laughed cheerfully. 'Even you, Klara. I'm *not* sharing my secret targets with you. But if you're still here when I get back at Christmas, I'll tell you how many I've got through.'

This was one of few allusions Josie made during this period to my own possible departure. And she referred to it again on the morning she finally drove away with the Mother.

She'd hoped, I knew, that Rick would come to wave her off. But as it turned out, he was many miles away that day, meeting his new friends to talk about his hard-to-detect data-gathering devices. So it was just myself and the New Housekeeper who stood in the loose stones area, watching Josie and the Mother place the last of her luggage in the Mother's car.

Then, once the Mother was ready behind the wheel, Josie came back towards me, the caution that had never left her walk making her feet sink noisily into the pebbles with each step. She looked excited and strong, and before she'd reached me, held up her arms as though trying to form the largest Y she could. Then she held me in an embrace that lasted many moments. She'd become taller than me, so she had to crouch a little, resting her chin on my left shoulder, and her long, rich hair fell across a section of my vision. When she pulled away, she was smiling, but I could see also some sadness. That was when she said:

'I guess you may not be here when I get back. You've been just great, Klara. You really have.'

'Thank you,' I said. 'Thank you for choosing me.'

'No-brainer.' Then she gave me a second hug, this one more brief, and stood back again. 'Bye, Klara. You be good now.'

'Goodbye, Josie.'

She waved cheerfully once more as she was getting into the car – the wave aimed at me rather than the New Housekeeper. Then the car moved away up the road, past the windy trees and over the hill, in just the way Josie and I had watched it do many times before.

■

Over the last few days, some of my memories have started to overlap in curious ways. For instance, the dark sky morning when the Sun saved Josie, the trip to Morgan's Falls and the illuminated diner Mr Vance chose will come into my mind, merged together into a single setting. The Mother will be standing with her back to me, watching the mist from the waterfall. Yet I am not watching her from the wooden picnic bench, but instead from my booth in Mr Vance's diner. And although Mr Vance isn't visible, I can hear his unkind words coming from across the aisle. Meanwhile, above the Mother and the waterfall, the dark clouds have gathered, the same dark clouds that gathered the morning the Sun saved Josie, small cylinders and pyramids flying by in the wind.

I know this isn't disorientation, because if I wish to, I can always distinguish one memory from another, and place each one back in its true context. Besides, even when such composite memories come into my mind, I remain conscious of their rough

301

borders – such as might have been created by an impatient child tearing with her fingers instead of cutting with scissors – separating, say, the Mother at the waterfall and my diner booth. And if I looked closely at the dark clouds, I would notice they were not, in fact, quite in scale in relation to the Mother or the waterfall. Even so, such composite memories have sometimes filled my mind so vividly, I've forgotten for long moments that I am, in reality, sitting here in the Yard, on this hard ground.

The Yard is large, and from my special place here, the only tall object I can see is the construction crane in the far distance. The sky is very wide and open, and if Rick and I were once more crossing Mr McBain's fields – especially now the grass has been cut – the sky might appear to us just like this. The wide sky means I'm able to watch the Sun's journeys unimpeded, and even on cloudy days, I'm always aware of where he is above me.

I thought when I first came here that the Yard was untidy, but I've now come to appreciate its good order. The initial impression, I realized, was due to many of the objects here having in themselves an untidy identity – with the remains of severed cables protruding or with dented grille panels. On closer observation it becomes clear how hard the yardmen have worked to place each piece of machinery, crate or bundle into orderly rows, so that a visitor walking down the long passages that have been created in this way – even if that visitor must be careful not to trip on a rod or wire – will be able to take in the objects one by one.

Because of the wide sky and lack of tall objects, I become quickly aware of any visitors in the Yard. I spot their figures even if they are far in the distance and only small shapes moving among the rows. But visitors aren't frequent, and when I hear human voices, they most often belong to the yardmen calling to each other.

Sometimes birds will come down from the sky, but they soon discover there is little in the Yard to interest them. Not long ago a group of dark birds descended in elegant formation to perch on some machinery not far in front of me, and I thought for a moment they might be Rick's birds sent to observe me. Of course they weren't Rick's birds, but natural ones, and they remained calmly perched on the machinery for some time, not moving at all, even as the wind ruffled their coats. Then they flew off all at once.

Around the same time, a kind yardman stopped in front of me and told me there were three AFs on the South Side, and two in the Ring. If I wished, he said, he could transport me to one or the other of these areas. But I told him I was content with my special spot, and he nodded and went on his way.

Several days ago, there was a very special incident.

Although I'm not able to move from place to place, I can turn my head easily to see everything around me. So I'd been aware for some time of the long-coated visitor moving behind me. Once, when I turned, the figure was in the mid-distance, and I saw it was that of a woman, and that she was wearing at the end of a strap a pouch-like bag. Whenever she leaned forward to examine an item on the ground, the bag would swing before her. Because she was behind me, I couldn't keep close watch on her, and then for a while – perhaps another memory had presented itself – I stopped thinking about her altogether. Then I heard a sound and the long-coated visitor was standing there before me. And even before she crouched down to look at my face, I recognized Manager, and happiness filled my mind.

'Klara. It *is* Klara, isn't it?'

'Yes, of course,' I said, smiling up at her.

'Klara. How wonderful. Just a moment. Let me bring something to sit on.'

She returned, dragging a small metal crate that made an unpleasant noise along the rough ground. When she placed it in front of me and sat down, despite the wide sky behind her, I was able to observe her face clearly.

'I've been hoping I'd find you here. Once, oh, almost a year ago now, I found something here in this yard, and I thought for a moment it was you, Klara. But it wasn't. But this time it's definitely you. I'm so glad.'

'I'm happy to see Manager again.'

She went on smiling at me. Then she said: 'I wonder what you can be thinking just now. To see me again after all this time. It must be so confusing.'

'I feel only happiness to see Manager again.'

'Then tell me, Klara. Have you all this time – until you came here, I mean – have you all this time been with the people you went to from the store? Forgive my asking, but I no longer have easy access to such information.'

'Yes, of course. I was with Josie all the time. Until she went to college.'

'So it was successful. A successful home.'

'Yes. I believe I gave good service and prevented Josie from becoming lonely.'

'I'm sure you did. I'm sure she barely knew the meaning of loneliness with you there.'

'I hope not.'

'You know, Klara. Of all the AFs I looked after, you were certainly one of the most remarkable. You had such unusual insight. And observational abilities. I noticed it right away. I'm so glad to hear it all went well. Because you never know, even with abilities as remarkable as yours.'

'Does Manager still look after AFs?'

'No. Oh, no. That finished some time ago.' She glanced around the Yard, then smiled at me again. 'That's why I like to come here from time to time. I sometimes go to the yard at Memorial Bridge. But I like this place the best.'

'Does Manager come . . . just to look for AFs from her store?'

'Not just that. I like to collect little souvenirs.' She indicated her pouch bag. 'They don't allow us to take anything substantial. But smaller things, they don't mind. The workers here know me. But you're right. Whenever I come here I'm hoping to come upon one of my old AFs.'

'Did you ever come across Rosa?'

'Rosa? Yes, actually I did. I found her here, oh, it must be at least two years ago. Things didn't go as well for Rosa as they did for you.'

'So she didn't like her teenager?'

'It wasn't so much that. But you mustn't worry. Never mind Rosa. Tell me about you. You had such a special ability. I hope your child came to appreciate it.'

'I think she did. Everyone in the house was very kind to me. I was able to learn so many things.'

'I remember the day they came in and chose you. The lady testing you first, asking you to walk like the daughter. It made me worry. After you left, I kept thinking about it.'

'There was no need for Manager to worry. It was the best home for me. And Josie was the best teenager.'

Manager, for a moment, remained silent, gazing at me and smiling. So I continued:

'I did all I could to do what was best for Josie. I've thought

305

about it many times now. And if it had become necessary, I'm sure I could have continued Josie. But it's much better the way it turned out, even though Rick and Josie aren't together.'

'I'm sure you're right, Klara. But what do you mean, "continue Josie"? What's that mean?'

'Manager, I did all I could to learn Josie and had it become necessary, I would have done my utmost. But I don't think it would have worked out so well. Not because I wouldn't have achieved accuracy. But however hard I tried, I believe now there would have remained something beyond my reach. The Mother, Rick, Melania Housekeeper, the Father. I'd never have reached what they felt for Josie in their hearts. I'm now sure of this, Manager.'

'Well, Klara, I'm glad you feel things worked out for the best.'

'Mr Capaldi believed there was nothing special inside Josie that couldn't be continued. He told the Mother he'd searched and searched and found nothing like that. But I believe now he was searching in the wrong place. There *was* something very special, but it wasn't inside Josie. It was inside those who loved her. That's why I think now Mr Capaldi was wrong and I wouldn't have succeeded. So I'm glad I decided as I did.'

'I'm sure that's right, Klara. It's what I always want to hear when I come across my AFs again. That you're glad about how it all went. That you have no regrets. Did you know, there are some B3s over there, over on that far side? They're not from our store, but if you'd like some company, I could ask the men to move you.'

'No, thank you, Manager. You're as kind as ever. But I like this spot. And I have my memories to go through and place in the right order.'

'That's probably wise. I wouldn't have said this in the store, but I was never able to feel towards B3s as I did towards your

306

generation. I often think the customers felt something similar. They never really took to them, for all the B3s' technical advances. I'm so glad I came across you today, Klara. I've thought about you so often. You were one of the finest I ever had.'

She rose to her feet, her bag swaying again in front of her.

'Before you go, Manager. I must report to you one more thing. The Sun was very kind to me. He was always kind to me from the start. But when I was with Josie, once, he was particularly kind. I wanted Manager to know.'

'Yes. I'm sure the Sun has always been good to you, Klara.'

As she said this, Manager turned to the wide sky behind her, raising a hand to her eyes, and for a moment we looked at the Sun together. Then she turned back to me and said: 'I have to get on. Well, Klara. Goodbye.'

'Goodbye, Manager. Thank you.'

She reached down to the metal crate she'd been sitting on, and dragged it back to its original position, making the same unpleasant noise. She then walked away down the long passage between the rows, and it was noticeable how she walked differently to the way she had in the store. With each second step, she would lean to her left in a way that made me worry her long coat on that side might touch the dirty ground. When she was mid-distance, she stopped and turned, and I thought she might look back one last time at me. But she was gazing at the far distance, in the direction of the construction crane on the horizon. Then she continued to walk away.